TAHOE
ICE GRAVE

*High on a mountain,
hidden in a cave,
is something
to kill for ...*

TODD BORG

An Owen McKenna Mystery Thriller

PRAISE FOR TAHOE BLUE FIRE

"A GRIPPING NARRATIVE...A HERO WHO WALKS CONFIDENTLY IN THE FOOTSTEPS OF SAM SPADE, PHILIP MARLOWE, AND LEW ARCHER"   *- Kirkus Reviews*

"A THRILLING MYSTERY THAT IS DIFFICULT TO PUT DOWN... EDGE OF YOUR SEAT ACTION"   *- Elizabeth, Silver's Reviews*

PRAISE FOR TAHOE GHOST BOAT

"THE OLD PULP SAVVY OF (ROSS) MACDONALD...REAL SURPRISE AT THE END"   *- Kirkus Reviews*

"NAIL-BITING THRILLER...BOILING POT OF DRAMA"
                           - Gloria Sinibaldi, Tahoe Daily Tribune

"A THRILL RIDE"   *- Mary Beth Magee, Examiner.com*

"BORG'S WRITING IS THE STUFF OF A HOLLYWOOD ACTION BLOCKBUSTER"   *- Taylor Flynn, Tahoe Mountain News*

"ACTION-PACKED IS PUTTING IT MILDLY. PREPARE FOR FIRE-WORKS"   *- Sunny Solomon, Bookin' With Sunny*

"I LOVED EVERY ROLLER COASTER RIDE IN THIS THRILLER 5+ OUT OF 5"   *- Harvee Lau, Book Dilettante*

PRAISE FOR TAHOE CHASE

"EXCITING, EXPLOSIVE, THOUGHTFUL, SOMETIMES FUNNY"
                           - Ann Ronald, Bookin' With Sunny

"THE LANDSCAPE IS BEAUTIFULLY CRAFTED... PACE BUILDS NICELY AND DOESN'T LET UP"

                                        - Kirkus Reviews

"BE WARNED. IT MIGHT BE ADDICTING"
                           - Gloria Sinibaldi, Tahoe Daily Tribune

"OWEN McKENNA HAS HIS HANDS FULL IN ANOTHER THRILL-ING ADVENTURE"

                                   - Harvee Lau, Book Dilettante

PRAISE FOR TAHOE TRAP

"AN OPEN-THROTTLE RIDE"
> - Wendy Schultz, Placerville Mountain Democrat

"A CONSTANTLY SURPRISING SERIES OF EVENTS INVOLVING MURDER...and the final motivation of the killer comes as a major surprise. (I love when that happens.)"
> - Yvette, In So Many Words

"I LOVE TODD BORG'S BOOKS... There is the usual great twist ending in Tahoe Trap that I never would have guessed"
> - JBronder Book Reviews

"THE PLOTS ARE HIGH OCTANE AND THE ACTION IS FASTER THAN A CHEETAH ON SPEED"
> - Cathy Cole, Kittling: Books

"A FASCINATING STORY WITH FIRST CLASS WRITING and, of course, my favorite character, Spot, a Great Dane that steals most of the scenes."
> - Mary Lignor, Feathered Quill Book Reviews

"SUPER CLEVER... More twists in the plot toward the end of the book turn the mystery into an even more suspenseful thriller."
> -Harvee Lau, Book Dilettante

"AN EXCITING MURDER MYSTERY... I watch for the ongoing developments of Jack Reacher, Joanna Brady, Dismas Hardy, Peter and Rina Decker, and Alex Cross to name a few. But these days I look forward most to the next installment of Owen McKenna."
> - China Gorman blog

PRAISE FOR TAHOE HIJACK

"BEGINNING TO READ TAHOE HIJACK IS LIKE FLOOR-BOARDING A RACE CAR... RATING: A+"
> - Cathy Cole, Kittling Books

"A THRILLING READ... any reader will find the pages of his thrillers impossible to stop turning"
> - Caleb Cage, The Nevada Review

"THE BOOK CLIMAXES WITH A TWIST THE READER DOESN'T SEE COMING, WORTHY OF MICHAEL CONNELLY"
> - Heather Gould, Tahoe Mountain News

TAHOE
ICE GRAVE

by

TODD BORG

THRILLER PRESS

Thriller Press Revised First Edition, August 2002

TAHOE ICE GRAVE
Copyright © 2002 by Todd Borg

Library of Congress Control Number: 2002100524

ISBN: 978-1-931296-13-7

Cover design and map by Keith Carlson.

Manufactured in the United States of America

For Kit

ACKNOWLEDGMENTS

I owe heartfelt thanks to several people for editing and critique.

Kate Nolan is a rare judge of how fictional characters work, and her observations about my characters made this a better story.

Liz Johnston provided much thoughtful comment along with thorough copy editing. She is more perceptive than she knows and she helped a great deal.

Jenny Ross explained how Tahoe-area law enforcement works. She deserves credit for whatever I got right, while any mistakes I made are all mine. In addition, she had many helpful suggestions for which I'm very grateful. This is a much better book as a result.

I'd like to thank Keith Carlson for another great cover and interior map. He made helpful comments on the story as well.

Thanks also to my agent Barbara Braun. As always, her observations helped me write a better novel.

Further thanks are due to Amber Bradford and Abby Gallup who keep the world turning while I write.

Last, special thanks go to my sweetheart Kit whose ear for story, character and dialogue has much better pitch than mine. She takes the roughness out of my rough drafts, smooths out my rewrites and puts the polish on the final edit.

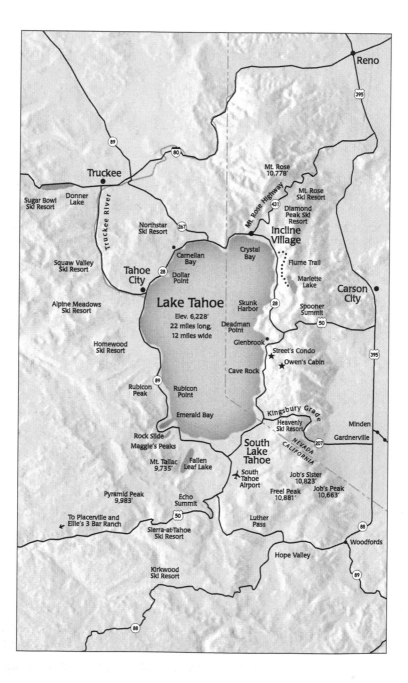

PROLOGUE

Thos Kahale stood naked in the snow near Rubicon Point on the west side of Lake Tahoe. It was six in the morning the second Sunday in January. The sun would not rise for over an hour. A cold gale blew from the northeast and the dark, white-capped waves were pushed into five-foot breakers by an angry wind.

Although the ice-cold lake and its perimeter of snow-covered mountains were nothing like Kauai, the Hawaiian island where Thos was born and raised, the waves strangely reminded him of home.

He shut his eyes and went there in his mind.

He was on a tiny crescent of beach down below the cliffs of Princeville where wealthy tourists played golf and spoke of their helicopter rides into the cloud-shrouded caldera of Mt. Waiale'ale, the volcano that is the rainiest spot on earth.

The breakers crashing onto the beach were the legendary waves of Hawaii, traveling across three thousand miles of open ocean. They hit the undersea volcanic uprising and were thrust twenty-five feet up into the sky before they curled over and made the turquoise tunnels that put surfing champions to the ultimate test.

Thos Kahale was one of those champions until a freak accident on a huge wave. The board twisted, Thos went up, and the monster wave pounded him down onto the bottom so hard that he broke his femur. It took Thos's enormous reserve of will and strength to fight the rip currents and drag himself back up onto the beach.

What he was about to do now would require even more willpower. But it was the only recourse his honor left him.

Dawn was just beginning to color the cloudy sky a rose gray as Thos walked into Lake Tahoe.

He knew the water's temperature was 36 degrees and he had prepared himself for the shock. Even still, it seemed to rip his breath out of him. The waves hit him hard and splashed ice water onto his abdomen, then his chest. He pushed on, toes digging into the sand. Soon, he was swimming.

Thos knew about hypothermia. He understood how the water sucked heat out of the body rendering the muscles impotent. He knew he had about two minutes before he would succumb to the cold and be unable to move. His only desire was to get far enough out. He'd studied the map that showed the bottom of the lake. If he swam hard, he'd make it to the correct spot before two minutes were up. Whatever happened, the outcome of his swim was certain.

Thos thrust into the water with strong arms and legs. At first, he made good speed heading out into the savage waves. But as the seconds ticked by his movements slowed. Despite his thick, well-muscled body, the cold sapped his strength. His limbs grew lethargic.

Thos turned and took a sighting on two points of land. They were dimly lit by the dawn. From his study of the map, he knew he had to swim until they lined up. He had 40 yards to go. He turned back toward the dark open lake and redoubled his effort. Once he made it, he could die in peace.

His swimming slowed to a crawl. His arms and legs were barely moving. 30 yards. A shiver went through his trunk but never made it out into his frozen limbs. 20 yards. He commanded his muscles to move, but they didn't respond. Thos focused his will with the same intensity that had won him three surfing championships. His arms no longer moved, but his legs still made a feeble motion. 10 yards.

Thos never felt the rifle shot.

The bullet entered the back of his skull, mushrooming on impact. Hot, deformed lead created a shock wave that destroyed Thos Kahale's brain before blowing a large exit hole out of his forehead.

ONE

I was cross-country skiing a quarter mile up above my cabin, to the side of last fall's forest fire burn, when I saw Street Casey pull her VW Beetle into my drive. As she got out I whistled.

Street looked up and scanned the mountain for several seconds before she saw me waving. She waved back. Spot, my Harlequin Great Dane, saw her and bounded down the mountain ahead of me. He kicked up white clouds of snow that sparkled against the deep blue backdrop of Lake Tahoe.

I watched for a moment and then concentrated on what I was doing as I came to a steep pitch. Although my wide backcountry skis have the full mountaineering boot and binding setup, they are designed for touring and offer little control on the steeps compared to standard downhill equipment. As my speed picked up I got down into a tuck, not because of aerodynamics, but because Street was watching.

The trail steepens further and then makes a turn to the right. If you miss the turn, you hit trees head on. If you make the turn, you still might hit trees, just different ones. In the back country, as in developed ski areas, the first rule is never to hit trees because they always win.

I made the turn carrying more speed than I should have. But the woman of my dreams was watching, so I had little choice what with my Y chromosomes being in control and mandating a plethora of flawed behaviors.

Compared to the bright sun on the snow, it was dark in the

trees and hard to see. I hit a little lip and went airborne. When I reconnected with the snow, only my left ski was in the groove of the track while my right ski had suddenly decided to secede from the union. The resulting somersault was impressive.

Street and Spot were running across the road as I came sliding down the snow bank on my back. Spot made it to me first and, wagging furiously, jumped his 170 pounds directly on top of me.

"My God, Owen! Are you all right?" Street called out.

I fended Spot off, stood up and shook myself off. "Never better," I replied. I bent and kissed her. "A move I've been practicing. What do you think?"

"I think they should make you get a learner's permit until you can steer better."

"But I missed the trees."

She reached up and pulled a small branch and a bundle of pine needles from the fold in my knit cap. "You mean you missed their trunks."

"Critical part," I said.

Street looked up at me, shook her head and smiled. The sun glinted off her cheekbones and added highlights to her hair which had recently been black but was now a more natural auburn. Street had never used much makeup, preferring to let the little acne scars show. But now it seemed that whatever she used to do that made her cheekbones look severe was gone. Her eyes were softer as well. She looked ravishing. There was a new lightness to her movements, a playfulness in her smile, as if it were May instead of mid-January.

Street had been on the mend – two parts physical, eight parts psychological – since her kidnapping last fall, and today for the first time I saw that the tension was gone from her shoulders. It had been a long climb back from the hell of the mine shaft with the forest fire raging above.

For months, every lock was checked five times. She never answered the door unless it was someone she knew and even then she held a can of pepper spray behind her back. The pepper spray stayed under her pillow when she slept and went with her during late-night trips to the bathroom. Spot never left her side even when she was at work at her insect lab. And I'd virtually moved into her condo. We only came up to my cabin when she found time to take a day off.

Today was one of those days. She had told me earlier that she had a morning appointment in Reno and wanted to go alone. Not even Spot was invited along for the ride.

"How did it go?" I asked.

"My little road trip? Fine. No abductions. Not even one forest fire." She walked across the mountain drive that I share with my five ritzy neighbors, reached into the open window of her VW Bug and pulled out a bag. "It's so warm and sunny, I thought we could have a picnic out on your deck." She handed me the bag. "Look inside. I brought you a surprise."

I opened the bag and saw a baguette, a block of cheddar cheese, an apple, an orange and a bottle of wine. The silver label gave it away before I could pull the bottle out. "Silver Oak Cab! What's the occasion?"

Street grinned. "We're celebrating my independence. In fact, I'm going to try to sleep alone again."

"Not even Spot is staying with you?"

Street gave me that universal steely grin of determination and confidence, like that of a pilot who, after a long recuperation from a crash, has finally decided to get back into the cockpit and take off into the sky. "I'm going to go solo again."

"At least the wine will keep me warm now that I'm being banished to my own bed."

"Spot can keep you warm," she said. At the sound of his name, he stuck his snout into her palm and pushed her hand around.

I shook my head. "The first paragraph in the Great Dane Handbook says never to let your Dane on your bed. If you do, he'll take it over and you'll end up sleeping on the couch."

"But your little cabin doesn't have a couch."

"That's why it is so important." We were talking around her decision instead of discussing it directly, but it made sense to keep things light.

"Here, I brought you something else." She reached into the back of the VW and pulled out a flimsy cardboard box. "I saw this in the window of a little boutique in Reno and thought you had to have it." She handed it to me.

I opened the box and lifted out a contraption made of black wire curved into graceful arcs, and small flat pieces of metal cut into rounded, abstract shapes. The flat pieces were all painted black except for one which was fire-engine red. Each curved wire had a flat piece attached to one end like an abstract leaf at the end of a branch. Some of the pieces were tangled with one another. I freed them and set the device on the roof of Street's car.

"It's a Calder mobile!" The various components hung from each other, and they bobbed and danced and turned back and forth in a complex motion.

"It doesn't even say which of his mobiles it's supposed to be," Street said. "So it could be one of those illegal knockoffs. In which case, maybe I shouldn't have bought it."

"Thanks so much." I bent down and kissed Street on her temple, one of those sacred spots on her body with delicate skin and a soft caress of hair. "I love it." I picked it up, the wires and pancakes bouncing and gyrating.

I picked up the wine with my other hand. Spot ignored the mobile, but his eyes followed the wine as if it might be a treat for him. "Shall I fetch the corkscrew or just have his largeness bite the neck off the bottle?"

"Corkscrew," she said. "And a knife." She took the bag from me and walked out onto my deck.

I joined her a few minutes later.

The January air was cool, but the 7200-foot altitude of my deck made for a hot sun. In minutes, I'd stripped down to my T-shirt while Street, ever warm with her high-speed metabolism, took off her jacket and snow boots. She had on pale yellow anklets that showed her perfect ankles and three inches of skin below her tight black pants. My heartbeat immediately went up into the workout range. I'd read about the medicinal effects of red wine on strained hearts, so I busied myself with the corkscrew.

"To flying solo," I toasted after I poured the wine. My throat constricted at the thought of Street and me separating and going back to our own abodes after living together these last few months, but I didn't show it.

While I drank the amazing vintage, Street moistened her lips and maybe even her tongue with the precious elixir. It wasn't that she didn't like fine wine. But Street's rough childhood had made her an adult who was all about control when it came to appetites, both the good ones and the bad ones. Maybe I was an appetite as well.

Street started slicing the cheese.

Ever the opportunist, Spot nosed over next to her. I lowered my glass and gave him a dirty look. He took the hint and lay down on the edge of the deck. From where I sat it looked like his nose was directly over the lake, a thousand feet below.

"Did you hear about the murder Sunday over on Rubicon Point?" Street asked as she tore off a miniature piece of bread, broke a corner off a cheese slice and set them delicately into her mouth. "It was on the radio again this morning."

I nodded as I ate. "I stopped at the office this morning and had a message on my machine. It was the victim's mother from what I could understand, but she was very stressed and her words were hard to hear. I called back but got her machine. So I left my home number."

"She wanted to hire you?" Street asked. She picked up the knife and began cutting up the apple into small boats.

"Not sure. She wanted to meet with me. Apparently she got my name from Diamond Martinez. What did the radio say about the murder? It seems that each day I only catch the tail end of the reports."

"Just that the victim was male and was shot in the head. What I didn't understand was something about the body being naked and found in the lake."

I raised my eyebrows.

Street stood up and stretched her arms up above her head in that way that made her shirt rise up and reveal her flat midriff. I got a flash of her navel and thought that I should stop studying about art and learn how to make art. Street would be a spectacular subject. Manet's Olympia was trailer trash by comparison.

"I'm going to get a glass of water," Street said. "Want some?"

Just then the phone chirped from inside the cabin.

"I can get it," Street said. She went inside and was gone for what seemed like a long while.

Her face was distressed when she came back. "It's the murder victim's mother. She wants to talk to you."

"Why such a concerned look?" I said. "Was she rude to you?"

"No. But she sort of blurted out something disturbing. She's obviously very distraught."

"What did she say?"

"She said that before her son was murdered he'd written a suicide note."

TWO

I went inside and picked up the phone. "Hello, Owen McKenna speaking."

"Mr. McKenna, my name is Janeen Kahale, Th...Thos Kahale's mother." She pronounced the last name 'Ka-ha-lay.' Her voice shook. "I would like your help. Will you please come and see me?"

"Certainly."

"Would it be too soon to meet at four o'clock today?" she asked.

"That would be fine," I said. "Where do you live?"

"Do you know Spring Creek Road under Mt. Tallac?"

"Yes."

"Near the end, Cornice Road angles off to the right. Take that about two hundred yards. We're the middle of the three driveways."

Later, when our picnic was over, Street kissed me goodbye and left. I picked up the Calder mobile from the kitchen counter and set it on the shelf next to Rodin's Eternal Spring, a copy of the original bronze. Street had given me the work a couple of years earlier. It was a realistic sculpture of a young nude couple reaching to embrace each other. The woman was kneeling, her head and body arched backward. The man sat slightly above her, leaning toward her, about to take her in his arms.

When Street first presented me with such a lavish and expensive gift, I'd been profoundly appreciative of the thought behind it, yet inside I was judgmental about what I thought was a clichéd rendition of two perfect young bodies. But in time, I'd grown very attached to the emotion that permeated the work. My earlier reaction to the Rodin, private as it was, embarrassed me now.

The Calder swayed and danced next to the quiet, powerful Rodin bronze. They seemed like antipodes. The Calder was all about movement and harmony and balance. The Rodin was all about emotion and passion.

Balance and passion. A yin and yang of art.

Spot and I got in the new used Jeep I'd gotten to replace the one that burned in last fall's forest fire blowup. It was essentially a duplicate of the other one except for its green color. The better to blend into the forest when someone decides to shoot at me, I'd thought when I wrote out the check.

I dialed Captain Mallory of the South Lake Tahoe Police on my cell as I drove. I got his voice mail. So I tried the Douglas County Sheriff's number and asked to be put through to Diamond.

"Deputy Martinez," he answered. Judging from the background sounds, he was driving in heavy traffic.

"What's happening to Douglas County?" I said, visualizing the beautiful valley down below the mountains east of Tahoe. "All that noise in the background sounds like the L.A. freeway."

"Our bucolic little hamlet is emulating the big city," Diamond said, his Mexican accent very faint.

"Both bucolic and emulating in the same sentence?"

"I could throw in homogenization. Golden arches, Taco Bells."

"Is that on the citizenship exam?"

"Should be," Diamond said.

"The murder off Rubicon Point," I said. "You put the victim's mother on to me and I'm on my way out to see her. How familiar are you with the crime?"

"A little. Word gets around, something like that happens."

"I thought if you knew anything, you could fill me in."

"Not much to say," Diamond said. A truck horn blasted in the background. Diamond didn't speak until it quieted down. "Man was shot in the head while swimming. No murder weapon found. No shell casings. No slugs."

"Awful cold water to go swimming in this time of year," I said.

"Sí. The medical examiner said the victim would have died of hypothermia in a couple minutes even if he hadn't been shot."

"Any chance you saw the suicide note?"

"A copy. Not much there. I expect the victim's mother will show you."

"How'd that come about?" I asked.

"What? A Nevada sheriff's deputy being consulted in a California homicide? They found a little totem thing floating in the water. Mallory wanted me to come around just in case I could shed some light on it."

"What's a totem thing?"

"I don't know what to call it. Gringo like you would probably call it a talisman or mojo or something. It's a little figure carved of wood, two inches tall. Big head, no arms, three legs. Painted shiny blue except for two red eyes. Big red circles with black dots for centers. Creepy looking."

"Three legs?"

"Yeah. Or maybe two legs and a tail. Or a big-time phallus. Who knows?"

"It was floating in the water?"

"A couple yards from the body from what Mallory said. The waves were throwing it and the body against the rocks."

"Why you?"

"That's what I said. Mallory has been hearing something on the streets about a black wind. Some kind of Native American spirit going around one of the local gangs."

"Black wind means...?"

"I have no idea," Diamond said. "But Mallory used it like it was some seriously bad shit."

"There's a Native American gang in South Lake Tahoe?"

"No, no. There's barely any Indians in Tahoe at all. He thinks it's a Latino gang."

"So he called you because you're a Mex?"

"Partly," Diamond said. "And partly because the totem thing looks Native American and the only significant numbers of Native Americans near Tahoe are in my territory. Douglas County."

"The Washoe who live down in the Carson Valley," I said.

"Right. Mallory wanted me to show the totem around Minden and Gardnerville, see what I could find out."

"And shake your Latino finger at the gang kiddies while you're at it?"

"Something like that. Besides, I got mestizo ancestry."

"Then you should know all about black wind and spirit stuff," I said.

"I know about busting your ass in the fields. Not a lot of spirits help you pick lettuce."

"What did you find out when you showed the totem around?"

"Nothing. Talked to some Washoe elders, but they'd never seen the totem. I asked about a black wind and they just shook their heads like I was some no-brain white guy. Imagine that."

"You gonna show it to the Latino gang kids?"

"Sure. I'll let you know."

I thanked Diamond and hung up.

THREE

Spot and I drove across South Lake Tahoe. The traffic was heavy with tourists up from Sacramento and the Bay Area and, for that matter, in from all over the world to play in the snow. Tahoe has a higher concentration of ski resorts in a small area than any place outside of the Alps, thus the traffic in the middle of January. Skiers and boarders were streaming back into town from the dozen-plus resorts around the lake. There was still a five-foot tall snow berm in the center lane left by the plows after the last storm. It hadn't yet been trucked away, and the lack of openings and turn lanes had a thousand vacationers frustrated as they tried to get back to their condos and hot tubs.

I eventually got to the "Y" intersection at the far end of South Lake Tahoe, turned north on 89 and headed out toward Emerald Bay. Spring Creek Road winds into a forested neighborhood below 9700-foot Mt. Tallac, the most distinctive mountain on Lake Tahoe.

The west side of the Tahoe Basin lies just under the Sierra crest and as a result gets three times as much snow as the eastern sunbelt side where I live. The snow along Spring Creek Road was so deep that no ordinary snowplow could push it clear. So they'd brought in the giant rotary plows, strange-looking snowblowers with rotating blades six feet high and eight feet wide. They roar like 737s at takeoff as they chew up the snow and shoot it a hundred feet into the forest. The cuts they'd made into the snow left the roads with vertical walls taller than my Jeep. Navigating the walled neighborhood was difficult with most of the street signs buried.

I eventually found Cornice Road twenty minutes before the appointed time, and as I drove around its twisting curves I could see how it got its name. It had a grand view of the cornice of snow that grew off of one of Mt. Tallac's cliffs 3000 feet above.

At the end of Cornice Road stood two houses, one with a steep roof and a dramatic prow front of glass. The other was a Frank Lloyd Wright imitation with a flat roof and cantilevered decks that looked out of place in Tahoe. While the snow had mostly slid off the house with the steep roof, it was piled so high on the flat surfaces of the Wright look-alike that I wondered if the structure was strong enough to hold up under the heavy load.

As if in answer to my question, I saw movement on its roof. A man was shoveling snow. He chucked small scoops of the white stuff over the edge and into the air. Against the mounds of snow he confronted on the various roofs, the job looked like the equivalent of clearing the Echo Summit highway with a nine-horse snowblower. To top it off, he had a crutch propped under one shoulder as he worked.

I stopped next to a snow bank that loomed above the Jeep, got out and walked toward his house.

"Excuse me," I called out. "I'm looking for Mrs. Kahale. She said she was the middle of three houses." I gestured in question at the two houses before me. "Am I in the wrong place?"

The man stopped shoveling, held up a finger as if to say 'give me one minute,' and, leaning on his crutch, made his way across the roof onto an adjacent deck and down wide stairs that had already been cleared of snow. As he drew close I could see that he was younger than me, in his middle thirties. His left leg was cocked at an angle, the foot held six inches above the ground. He sported a tightly-trimmed moustache and black hair that was thick and short enough it would make a good scrub brush.

"May I ask your name?" he said in a British accent that had a hint of Cockney flavoring.

"Owen McKenna. I have a four o'clock appointment with

Mrs. Kahale." At six-six, I was a good eight inches taller than he was, and he raised a hand to shade his eyes as he looked up at me.

"That's what the last man said and it turned out he was just another reporter lying through his bloody teeth." His dark brown eyes were narrowed by suspicion.

I handed him one of my McKenna Investigations cards. "She wants to talk to me about her son's death. Can you tell me where she lives?"

The man glanced at my card, then seemed to burn through me with his intense stare. He pulled a yellow cellphone out of his pocket and dialed a number from memory. "Hi, Phillip, it's Jerry," he said into the phone. "Is your grandmother there? May I speak to her?" After a moment, he continued. "Hello, Janeen. I've a fellow here who claims to have an appointment with you." He looked again at my card. "His name is Owen McKenna. Oh, he's okay? Right away, then. I'll send him up." He folded his phone and slipped it back into his pocket. "Seems you're expected," his expression softening. "Can't be too careful, you know. Dreadful business with her son. As if dealing with the loss isn't enough, the poor woman has been besieged by the coppers and reporters and those sicko onlookers who seem to come off the moor whenever anything ghastly happens. Sorry to put you through the inquisition. But neighbors must watch out for one another." He pointed at the house with the prow front. "The Weintraubs are only here during holiday, so that leaves it to me. At least when I'm around, that is." He hobbled a step forward and held out his hand. "Name's Jerome Roth."

We shook.

"Janeen and I share the first part of our driveways. Just past that large Jeffrey pine, hers splits off from mine. Do you see where the land rises up to the right? Her house is up there in the trees."

Looking where he pointed, I could see where the other drive was hidden between giant berms of snow.

"Thank you," I said.

"Great Dane, eh?" he said, pointing at Spot who, despite the cool winter weather, was hanging his head out the rear window and panting, his monstrous tongue flapping with each breath.

"Yes. Name's Spot."

"Reminds me of a time I was on a wild boar hunt on an island in the Marquesas chain. This chap from South Africa kept going on about Great Danes. Apparently, they were originally bred to hunt wild boar in Germany in the middle ages. Long legs, big strong neck and all that. They would chase down the boar and hold it from above so that the squirmy devil couldn't get at the dogs with those big boar teeth. The Danes would keep holding the boar until the hunters could get there and club it to death. Charming, eh? But I suppose you know all that. Anyway, there we were, on this little jungle island in the middle of the South Pacific, and every time we'd glimpse a boar this Afrikaaner would start jabbering about how if only we had a Great Dane we could send it after the bloody boar. I guess he'd rather go back to the lodge and sip gin and tonics instead of being stuck out in the jungle slapping mosquitoes. I'll never forget that week, let me tell you. Still think of it every time I see a Great Dane."

Jerome Roth gestured with his crutch toward Spot. "Awfully big fellow. Friendly, is he?"

"Yes," I said. "Anything for a pet."

Jerome took a step forward and held out his hand. Spot did the requisite sniffing and then turned his head in happy bliss as Jerome scratched behind his ears. "Well," Jerome said, looking at his watch. "Janeen will be looking for you. Don't want to cause you to be late."

"Thanks, Jerome," I said as I turned toward the Jeep.

"Call me Jerry," he said. "And let me know if I can do anything for Janeen and Phillip. When I'm in Tahoe, I'm around the house most of the time. I like to be helpful."

It was still a couple of minutes before my appointment. "What kind of business are you in, Jerry?" I asked.

"Was. Maritime financial services. Mostly, I'm retired. But I try to stay busy."

"Been in Tahoe long?"

"Let's see, coming up on two years. I've skied here a few times in the past. That's before I tore out my ankle playing polo." He looked with disgust down at his bad leg. "Anyway, I always thought Tahoe would make a beautiful home base. Odd, really, considering I think of myself as an ocean man. But then again, I suppose that's the appeal of Tahoe. The land is so evident here. Everywhere you look, you see mountains. So much the opposite of the ocean, don't you think? Opposites attract, as they say."

"You are a yachtsman."

"Of late, yes. I keep a boat down in Long Beach."

"What's involved in maritime financial services?"

Jerry Roth gave a sheepish smile. "Ah, yes, anything for money. That's really just fancy talk for selling sailboat timeshares to the English middle class. You know. Chaps from my background who dream of the life of Greek shipping tycoons. I discovered that if you show them a picture of a beautiful boat with girls in bikinis on the afterdeck and Cypress on the horizon, they'll sign anything. After a few years of that, I've been able to sample the good life myself. Anyway, sorry if I've talked your ear off, old man. Good to meet you. Please be kind to Janeen. Phillip, too. He's shy, but he's special. Cheers." He turned and hobbled on his crutch back toward his snow-covered roofs.

FOUR

I followed Janeen Kahale's driveway up a rise, through a thicket of Lodgepole pine to a small and rundown clapboard cabin. Next to the cabin was an old carport that appeared to list under the massive weight of snow on the roof. The car inside was an early '80s Olds with a peeling vinyl roof.

I walked up a narrow path with snow piled so high on either side that the walkway felt like a tunnel. The door opened as I approached. A small, pleasant-looking woman in her late fifties stepped out so tentatively it was as if she were afraid the front step would burn her feet. The worry on her face was intense.

"Mrs. Kahale? I'm Owen McKenna."

"Thank you for coming." She gave me a nervous handshake. Her hand had the thickening of arthritis and her skin, though soft, showed the wear of decades of physical labor.

"Please come in," she said. She had a round face and looked as if she had Native American ancestry. Her skin was a mix of reddish sienna and olive umber tones. Thick black hair with a few strands of gray swept back into a long, heavy ponytail. The lines on her face were few but deep. Her eyes were as black and moist as a seal's. Under her eyes were dark smudges.

She led me through a doorway so short I had to duck my head. We entered a simple room with a low ceiling that made me feel taller than I am. The ceiling and walls were knotty pine and the floor was plain fir planks worn into a relief that left the harder grain raised above the softer. Thick, handwoven rugs in reds and oranges made the room cozy and warm.

Janeen Kahale gestured toward the couch. I took a seat. She sat on the only other seat in the room, a bench in front of a large floor loom. She gave me a weak smile, started to speak and then stopped as if gathering her thoughts to rephrase what she was about to say. I looked around to give her time.

The worn-out couch was draped with woven blankets. Like the rugs, the blankets were heavy with a dramatic weave in a harmonious blend of reds and browns and triangles of yellow. On the arms of the couch were beautiful lap blankets. The designs were reminiscent of Navajo but more serene. A gentle aroma of cinnamon came from a pot of potpourri on a wood stove.

Stacked in piles on one end of the couch were a dozen or more handwoven baskets. I recognized the designs as those of the Washoe Indians, a small group of Native Americans who summered in Tahoe and wintered in the Carson Valley for centuries before Fremont claimed to discover Tahoe and heralded the arrival of white men. The baskets represented a unique and spectacular art that was being lost forever to the pull of the modern world. In just one more generation, it was likely that no one would know the special techniques that made the baskets so beautiful that museums collected them and yet so tough and practical that they held water like ceramic bowls.

"Your weaving and basketry are wonderful," I said.

"Thank you, Mr. McKenna. Would you like a cup of coffee?"

"No thanks. I've already had too much. I'm very sorry to hear about your son, Mrs. Kahale."

"Please call me Janeen."

"Owen is good for me as well."

After a long moment she spoke. "I'd like you to look into my son's death." The tiniest modulation in her voice belied her effort to stay calm.

"I understand he was found in the lake," I said.

"Yes. The coroner's report said he was in the water at the time of his death."

"Yet he left a suicide note," I said.

"Yes." She looked down. Although her eyes were moist, there were no tears. The silence that followed was significant though not uncomfortable. I had the sense that while Janeen Kahale was a taciturn woman, she was not shy. It wasn't discomfort that kept her quiet, but reserve. She would speak when ready.

"The policeman who took the note made me a copy." She stood up and walked through a door into the kitchen, then returned with a piece of paper. She handed it to me.

The copy was clear, the writing distinct. The murdered son's handwriting was small and dark and carefully formed.

"Dear Mom,

I'm very sorry to do this to you and Shelcie and Phillip. I know it is the worst thing a person can do to those they love. But because of me, three people are dead. If I'd gone to the police immediately, they would still be alive. But I used very bad judgment. I didn't intend for my actions to cause their deaths, but as you always said, intentions don't count, actions and results do. You also taught me about honor and character. Dad did, too, although you may not believe that. Now, because of what I've done, I have no honor and my character is worthless. This leaves me no choice. You will say that I must not be thinking clearly. But if I don't do this, the killer will kill me anyway. Worse, if he thinks I told you who he is, he will kill you. Even Phillip. I can't go to the police now, because they will charge me in at least one of the deaths. I will do anything to avoid prison. I'm doing this in a way that should stop the killings. I'm sorry. I love you.

Thos"

"How did you receive the note?"

"Thos left it in my baking cupboard. He knew that Phillip never opened that cupboard."

"Do you know who these people are that Thos refers to? The ones that died?"

"No. I have no idea."

I set the copy of the note on the couch's end table. "Janeen, it is unlikely that I could add anything helpful to what the police will learn in their investigation."

"But you could concentrate on it in a way the police could not. They have so many distractions. Even if you discovered nothing, at least I would know I had tried. I've heard about you. You saved that woman from the maniac who lit the forest fires." She was referring to Street and obviously didn't know of my relationship with her.

Janeen looked at me, her dark eyes enormously sad. "I've saved a decent amount of money over the years. I'm sure I can pay whatever your rate is."

After a moment I said, "Before I take this on I need to explain something. I've learned that when I work for the family of a murder victim, things can get awkward. The family often ends up resenting my investigation. They are sometimes outraged at me for bringing to light certain facts that explain why someone was murdered." I paused and looked at her to see how she was taking it. She seemed level and steady.

I continued, "If I look into your son's death, I'll have to ask many questions. Some of them will be uncomfortable. It is likely you will regret learning what may come out."

"I've thought about that," Janeen said. "If Thos had been a victim of a random murder, like a holdup in a parking lot, then it would be cleaner in some ways. But it seems likely that the things he refers to in his note are very distasteful. I am prepared."

"It sounds like you are," I said. "This note," I said, holding it up, "Can you tell if it is in your son's handwriting?"

"Yes. Thos always wrote in that meticulous style. Everything he did was like that, careful and perfect. Even so..." she trailed off.

"You think it is not truthful?" I asked.

She clenched her teeth. "I think Thos was telling the truth as he knew it. But I don't think he knew the truth. I don't think he caused anyone to die, directly or indirectly."

"Is this a hunch, or do you have some specific information

about what he is referring to?"

"I know nothing of what he is referring to. But I know he wouldn't kill anyone."

I'd heard such statements from mothers before. They usually thought, Not my son. My son was a sweet boy. He wouldn't hurt a fly.

Janeen looked at me, her eyes anxious. It was clear that her son's murder was chewing away at her.

I leaned forward, elbows on knees. "Janeen, you question the truth of your son's note as regards whether or not he caused the death of three people. What about the truth of the note regarding killing himself? He doesn't actually state it. He only implies it. Do you think your son actually meant to commit suicide?"

Janeen thought a moment. "Yes."

"But he was murdered before he could kill himself," I said. "Can you think of why anyone would want to murder him?"

"The only thing that makes sense is that it must have something to do with the people he refers to in the note. Someone blames Thos for their deaths and shot him in revenge."

"What about him being in the lake when he was shot?" I asked. "Can you think of a reason for that?"

"I suppose the killer forced him to strip and swim out into the lake. Maybe he thought that Thos's body would never be found."

I nodded. It was one possibility. "Janeen, I'm sorry to ask difficult questions, but please bear with me. Had Thos not been murdered, do you think he would have actually followed through on killing himself?"

She seemed to withdraw inward, her eyes losing their focus. She cleared her throat. "Mr. McKenna, do you have children?"

"No."

"Then perhaps you'll find it hard to think in these terms. But the only thing a parent can imagine that is worse than the death of a child is the death of a child by his own hand. So it is nearly impossible for me to contemplate Thos committing suicide." She pointed toward the note. "But there is the suicide note in his own handwriting. "I've thought about the phrasing," she continued, "and wondered if he could have been forced to write it. But if the note had been dictated to him it wouldn't have sounded like Thos. This note does.

"Or maybe the killer made Thos put it in his own words. But Thos was a smart boy. If he'd been told to write it in his own words, he would have used different phrasing as a tip-off."

I picked the note up and read it again.

Janeen said. "So, in answer to your question, hard as it is to contemplate, yes, I think Thos did intend to kill himself." She stared down at her cup, conjuring up images no parent should ever have to face.

She refocused on me and spoke. "Thos was a strong-willed child. He always did anything he set his mind to. When he took up surfing as a boy he announced that one day he would be the world champion. To his father and me it didn't sound unreasonable. We knew his determination, so we just figured that if he decided to be the champion, he would probably succeed. We never signed Thos up for any lessons. The boy taught himself. Sure enough, he won three international competitions by the age of twenty-two.

"I never knew anyone with more courage," she continued, "so if he said he would kill himself, then I suppose..." she broke off, her lower lip shaking.

"I'm sorry, Janeen."

"It's okay," she said. "Go on."

"If, in fact, he was going to kill himself, do you think he intended to do it by swimming into the ice-cold water? Would that be like him?"

"You mean, to die of hypothermia? I don't know. Maybe. It would be a non-violent death. Thos was never violent."

"Then he wouldn't hire someone to shoot him?"

Janeen's eyes seemed to flash at me. She looked horrified. "No! I can't imagine him doing such a thing."

Just then came the sound of a door opening into the kitchen. It shut with a loud bang. A blast of cool air blew into the small living room followed by a small boy, maybe 10 years old. His arms were up, a baseball cap in his hand, as he pulled an anorak over his head. Bits of snow flew and struck the wood stove, sizzling into steam. He stuck the baseball cap on backward and spoke in an excited voice.

"Nana, I found the place where..." he stopped as he saw her distress. He turned and saw me sitting to his side. His face went from joy to fear in an instant. He ran to Janeen's side and sat next to her.

"Hello, sweetie," she said and put an arm around the boy's shoulders.

The boy whispered in her ear. He looked at me with more suspicion than Jerry Roth had back at the entrance to their driveway.

"This man is Owen McKenna," Janeen said. "He's a detective. He's going to help us find out what happened to Thos. Owen, please meet Phillip. Phillip is Thos's nephew."

I smiled. "Hi, Phillip." I raised my arm in a greeting and started to rise out of the couch but stopped when I saw that my movement made the boy shrink back and clutch at Janeen.

The boy whispered again into Janeen's ear. His agitation at my presence was so pronounced that I thought I should leave.

"Maybe we should do this another time," I said.

"No, please stay," Janeen said.

I gave them a weak smile. "I don't want to..."

"It's okay," Janeen said. "Phillip just doesn't want me to be upset, that is all." She turned to the boy. "I'm okay, Phillip. I'm just sad about Thos. Mr. McKenna and I were talking about Thos when you came in. I'm better now. Honest." She touched his cheek. "Phillip, why don't you go play and let me talk to Mr. McKenna."

He resisted and wouldn't let go of her dress. She asked him again and he slowly released her, stood up and, keeping the maximum distance between himself and me, went through a door and down a hall where the bedrooms must have been.

As he walked away from me I saw two things I hadn't noticed before. One was that his right hand was malformed, with a strangely-shaped thumb and only two fingers opposing it. The other was in his back pocket.

Stuffed into his jeans the way other kids might carry a pocket video game was a narrow object, about two inches wide and six inches long. The part that projected out revealed rows of little wheels.

After Phillip had gone into a bedroom and shut the door, Janeen spoke in a soft voice that Phillip wouldn't hear. "I see you noticed his abacus."

"Yes. I couldn't remember what it was called. It's an ancient calculating device, isn't it?"

Janeen nodded. "Phillip says some Chinese still use them."

"Interesting to see one in an age of electronic calculators."

Janeen lowered her voice even further. "I think he likes it because of his hand. You know how children can be cruel. Well, Phillip uses his funny hand – his words, not mine – to manipulate the abacus. He can do it so fast that he can come up with answers in math class even quicker than the kids with electronic calculators. It's his way of showing everyone that he isn't really handicapped."

"Smart kid," I said.

"Very. What else do you need for your investigation, Owen?"

"I'll need you to give me a complete background on Thos. It will take some time." I glanced toward the hall where Phillip had disappeared. "It's getting late. Why don't I come back tomorrow?"

"Okay," Janeen said. She looked at her watch. "I volunteer at the hospital in the morning while Phillip is at school. Would two o'clock be okay?"

"Certainly."

FIVE

I got Street on my cellphone as I drove back around the lake. "I know you're flying solo tonight, but my understanding of the rules still allows for dinner together. Am I wrong?"

"Not if you like barbecued shish-kebabs."

"I'll be there in a flash."

"Can you stop for more charcoal? I'm out. Or should we go up the mountain to your cabin? You have the better view, anyway."

"I'm already past the store, so I'll pick you up and we'll go for the view."

Spot and I knocked at the door to Street's condo a few minutes later.

Street came to the door wearing a Pink Panther apron over black jeans and a white cotton shirt. She looked glamorous and sleek in spite of the goofy apron. Maybe it was her perfect bare feet. Or the tiny, black obsidian earrings set in gold that I'd given her after her kidnapping last fall. She reached up on tiptoes and gave me a kiss. "I'm almost done skewering. Let me throw some foil around them. Do you have some rice?"

"Yes, I think."

"Great."

Street came out of her kitchen a couple minutes later carrying a foil package, an open bottle of Sierra Nevada Pale Ale and slipped her feet into some running shoes without bending over. "Would you grab my jacket, please?"

I picked the black ski jacket off the rack and shut the door behind us.

Once we were in the Jeep, Spot leaned over the seat, his huge head filling the space between me and Street. He knew better than to stick his nose down by Street's beer and shish-kebabs, so he just sniffed the air from a foot away. He quivered with self-restraint. His nostrils flexed and twitched and the whites of his eyes glimmered in the dark as he strained to look down at our dinner.

I reached up and coaxed him back into the rear seat by tapping on his nose with the back of my hand. "Remember, your largeness, resisting temptation is easier in proportion to the distance the temptation is from you." I wondered if that applied to me and Street.

Judging by his sigh as he lay down on the seat, Spot thought I was clueless.

We climbed up the two-mile drive and were in my little cabin a few minutes later.

"What can I do to help?" I said after Street took her food into the kitchen nook.

Because only one person at a time can fit into my kitchen, she reached into my icebox, pulled out a beer and handed it to me. "You can get the charcoal going and put on some music. Maybe light a fire, too, if you want."

"I want."

I found a Bonnie Raitt CD and put it on, then went out on the deck to pile up the charcoal. While the lighter fluid was still burning I came back in and lit a fire in the woodstove. It was roaring by the time Street came out of the kitchen.

"A little cold to go barefoot, isn't it?" I said when I noticed that she'd kicked her shoes off by the front door.

"That's why I asked for the flames." She dialed down my dimmer switch to very low, sat down in my big leather chair and propped her feet up in front of the fire. I pulled the rocker up next to her, sat down and gulped half of my beer. She picked hers up, tipped it back and drained it.

"Finishing a beer? I'm impressed."

Street glanced at her watch. "I thought what with sleeping alone again I should get started early on some chemical sleep enhancement." She set the bottle down. "Only took me two hours to get all the way through it. At that rate, I'll blow away my two-beer record before bedtime."

Street was a woman who needed to stay disciplined and productive, the result of a childhood without discipline or productivity. She would no sooner get intoxicated than she would watch sitcoms on TV. Although she enjoyed alcohol, she used it judiciously and infrequently. Fortunately for me, she didn't mind that my approach to beer and wine was more like they were one of the basic food groups, part of a balanced diet.

"How did your appointment go? I forget her name, the murder victim's mother?"

"Janeen Kahale. We only started to get acquainted."

"Any reason at all for the man's murder?"

"No. Unless his method of suicide was hiring someone to shoot him. But to the extent his mother can even think about it, she says he would not commit suicide in a violent way. He was a non-violent person. I see her again tomorrow. Maybe I'll learn something revealing then." I glanced out the slider toward the charcoal. A quarter moon floated high in the western sky. Although I'd just shoveled the deck in the morning, some of the day's clouds had dropped an inch of snow. The white deck glowed in the moonlight.

I stood up. "Time to spread the coals." I stepped out through the slider into the crisp, cold air of a January night. The snow on the mountains made them look like white fangs above the black water.

I arranged the charcoal, then took another look at the scenery, a view I never tire of. I was turning to go back inside when something stopped me.

It was not a clear thought or sound or movement that caught my attention. More like a nagging sense that something was not right.

I turned back toward the charcoal as if tending to the grill. My senses were suddenly hyper alert, my muscles ready to spring, but I gave no outward indication. I fussed with the grill, casually shifting my stance just like any other barbecue chef.

Thirty seconds passed before my senses picked anything up. Movement in my peripheral vision, in the distance off to the north.

The slider opened. "How's it coming, hon?" Street asked, leaning her head out of the opening.

"Great," I said, struggling to sound normal. I turned and gave her a smile. "We'll be ready to put them on in twenty minutes."

"Okay." Street pulled her head back inside and shut the door.

I maneuvered around to the side of the grill and dropped my charcoal mitt. I bent down to pick it up. My head was behind the charcoal cook pot. I leaned a couple inches to the side to peek out toward the north.

At first, I saw nothing. Then a faint movement a long distance away. I couldn't tell what I was looking at. Another movement. It was a person. He was in a clearing, out on a rise to the north of my cabin. 200 yards distant. Impossible to see at night but for the moon.

I'd been squatting too long. I stood up, picked up the lid to the grill and made like I was wiping out the inside. My hand movements were circular, nowhere near convincing up close, but it would look like I had purpose from a distance.

I used the lid to shield my face from the glow of the charcoal. I kept my head bent and looked up and out at the spot where I'd seen the person.

I saw nothing. No movement. No human shape. I kept up the scrubbing movements with my hand.

Normally, a person out on the snow in the mountains at night, especially at some distance, was no cause for alarm. Tahoe is a recreation paradise and people come from all over the world to play in the snow. But this was different.

The clearing where I'd seen him was a deserted area of deep snow. It was not near any trail that I knew of. The closest house was my cabin. The closest road was the drive I share with my neighbors, and the closest point the drive came to the clearing would be a hundred yards away and a couple hundred feet below. It would be a hard climb to get there from the drive.

So, while nothing about the person's presence was overtly threatening, everything about it was wrong. I put the lid over the charcoal, then picked up the snow shovel that leaned against the deck railing.

The light snow allowed me to walk in long passes, accumulating the snow in front of the shovel until I reached the edge of the deck and pushed the snow off to the ground below. I oriented my direction so I could watch the distant clearing as I walked.

On my sixth pass I saw another movement. A dark figure, tiny at such a long distance, moved from one tree, across a patch of moonlit snow, to another tree.

It made no sense. Unless he was watching.

The sight lines were clear to my cabin. At night with a moon you could hike in without a light. Hide behind a tree and look out with binoculars.

I finished shoveling and walked back inside.

"It's probably nothing, Street, so don't worry. But there is a person in the woods to the north watching us."

She turned slowly and stared at me with frightened eyes.

"So when you stand up, stay away from the area where he could see in through the window." I gestured at the part of the room that could be on view.

I walked to the kitchen and pulled out the kitchen stool. "You should come and sit here while I go check."

"Bring Spot," she said, fear in her voice. He lifted his head at the sound of his name.

"No, thanks, sweetheart. We learned that lesson last fall.

Now, please stay calm and don't say his name again. We don't want him agitated. I want him to stay lying right where he is. Anyone looking at this cabin will see domestic tranquillity. Don't draw the blinds, or change the lights. If nothing changes, the person won't be alarmed and I can find out what he's doing. Like I said, it is probably nothing, but keep inside the cabin and don't open the door for anyone but me."

Not hearing his name again, Spot put his head back down onto his paws. I eased Street back until she hit the stool and sat down.

"Be careful, Owen." Her voice shook. Her beautiful eyes had terror in them.

"I will. I'm going out the front door, in the shadows. I'll slip on my cross-country skis and come up through the woods. The truth is that I saw nothing scary out there. I just want to check it out. And I don't want you to take any chances. Everything will be fine." I kissed her forehead and turned toward the door. There was no point in elaborating on what we both knew, which was that last fall someone had kidnapped her, taken her from her own front doorstep and tried to burn her to death in a forest fire.

I kicked off my shoes and pulled on my cross-country ski boots. I grabbed my dark wool jacket because the fabric is silent, and pulled on my black leather gloves. While my back was turned from Street I carefully lifted my telescoping baton off its hook and slipped it into my pocket. I turned off the switch that sent power to the motion-detector floodlight, opened the door a crack and slipped out into the dark, locking the door behind me.

Outside my front door is a small space with a roof over it, providing shadow from the moon. I stood there letting my eyes adjust once again to the night. I gave my baton a twist and pulled it out to its full length. It has an auto-lock feature, a custom grip and is weighted such that it is a formidable weapon. Of course it was nothing against a gun, but I'd given them up ever since I left the force in San Francisco.

I grabbed my skis and poles from the corner by the front door and left, keeping to the tree shadows. The air was cold enough to sear my lungs, but my tension kept me warm.

At the other side of the drive, I moved under a large Jeffrey pine, set my skis down in the snow and snapped my boots into the bindings. I put the ski pole straps over my gloves, holding both the baton and a ski pole in my right hand.

The snow was deep and fluffy, allowing me to ski in silence. I traversed across the mountain, following its contours while climbing up at a slight angle. I stayed under the trees for their shadows, but was careful to pick a course through the biggest trees where there weren't low branches. I didn't want to bump a branch and send a mini-avalanche of snow down the back of my neck.

Not far away was the burned area from last fall's forest fire. It was now an open snowfield dotted with the blackened stumps that were all that remained of the forest. There were no moon shadows in the burn, so I wanted to gain enough elevation to cross it well above where the forest intruder might notice.

As I got closer, I realized I hadn't gotten high enough. I stopped, did a kick turn and switch-backed up behind where I'd been, edging hard into the steep slope, still hidden in the tree shadows. After a couple hundred feet I about-faced one more time and approached the burn again.

This time I was high enough that the undulating contours of the mountain kept me out of sight from the place where I'd seen the person. I hurried across the open, moon-bright burn, feeling like I was on a white stage under an intense spotlight. In a minute I entered the deep forest and its cover of shadows on the other side.

Despite a persistent weather pattern that had given us a constant stream of storms, the sky tonight was crystal clear with stars and moon that were dazzling. The result of no clouds was a very cold night. My breath left huge mist clouds in the moonlight. I worried that they could be seen long after I disappeared into the trees.

I charted a course that took me around and behind the clearing where I'd seen the moving figure. I came down from above and stopped when I got close.

I watched for a long time. Nothing moved. I willed myself to study the dark, shadowed sides of the trees and make them into human shapes. No luck.

Minutes passed. Street would be starting to worry. I thought about moving sideways to get a different view of the clearing below, but I couldn't see a spot where the view would be any better.

After ten minutes of long, cold wait, a person stepped out from a tree shadow and walked into the full moonlight of the clearing. He seemed a slight but tall figure at that distance. For a moment I thought it might have been a woman.

From the nature of the steps I could tell the person was not on skis. That meant he was wearing snowshoes. Otherwise, he'd sink in deep.

The person turned again and moved away from me.

I pushed off with my poles and skied straight down the mountain. The deep snow piled up around my skis and boots. The amount of resistance kept me from building up too much speed as I descended. I came in fast and quiet, my baton held tight in my hand. When I got to the clearing I had just enough momentum to carry me across the small flat area. I was fifty feet behind him when my left ski binding caught on a branch that was hidden in the deep snow.

My inertia spun me sideways and I crashed into the snow with a soft, deep thump.

Snow slammed into my eyes and ears as my head and body were buried. I concentrated on holding onto my baton as I tried to right myself. For a moment I couldn't tell what was up and what was down.

I jerked and thrashed in an effort to gain purchase on the snow. But every time I pushed against it, I sunk in farther. I managed to get my head up enough to look around, but saw no one.

I finally got both of my poles together and pushed them down into the snow. They went straight in, my arms following them up to my armpits. I changed position and tried again until finally they hit what must have been a boulder hidden beneath the snow. I pushed up and leveraged myself into a standing position.

Wiping snow from my eyes, I looked around again for the man, but saw nothing. He had stayed in the moon shadows where it was difficult to see his tracks.

I struggled to follow, wishing I had a flashlight. Every time I came around a tree the tracks went off in a new direction. I heard the starter of a car. I looked through the trees, moved sideways and looked again.

A hundred feet down was a vehicle in the moonlight. It shot down the drive toward the highway, lights off, brake lights briefly flashing.

I went back to the clearing where the man had stood for half an hour or more. His snowshoe tracks meandered back and forth, but seemed to concentrate at one spot. I stood on that spot and looked around.

There was nothing special about the place except that it had the best view of my cabin. I looked at my cabin through the trees and across the little valley where the drive went down. It was far enough away that even with ordinary binoculars you couldn't see any great detail.

I brushed the remaining snow off my jacket and skied back toward home.

Street was very upset when I came in the door, covered in snow, scratches on my cheeks from my headfirst dive into the snow.

"Owen, please don't do that again," she said, hugging me. Her fear was palpable and I understood her tone. "Next time we leave together and drive away. Or you take me and Spot with you. But don't leave me alone like that." She held me away from her and looked up at me. "Do you understand? I can't go through that again. I thought you were..." she broke off, tears filling her eyes.

"I'm sorry," I said and held her tight. Spot had gotten up and was sniffing me all over, trying to discern where I'd been and what I'd been doing.

Street pushed away again and looked up at me. "So what was it? Was it nothing?"

"No. There was a person. I fell in the snow and he got away before I could question him." I wondered how much I should tell her. I had no concrete threat, but it wasn't fair to tell her anything but the truth. "I looked around from the place where he'd been. There was nothing there."

"So what was his purpose?"

"I don't know. But it was clear from the position that he was there to watch us."

"I want to go," Street said suddenly.

"But he left. I saw him drive away."

"I don't care. I want to go. We'll stay at my place. You and Spot. I'll sleep alone some other time."

I nodded and kissed her.

Street put the food in the fridge while I shut the vents on the charcoal to starve it of oxygen. We turned off the lights and left.

SIX

The next day, Street went to her lab and Spot and I drove across to the west side of the lake. I knocked on Janeen Kahale's door at two o'clock.

She let me in with a warm smile. I ducked my head going through the short doorway.

"Let's sit in the kitchen," she said. "Can I get you a cup of coffee?"

"No thanks, I've had my limit for the day."

I followed the woman through another low doorway into the kitchen and stopped at a sight that gave me a curious shiver as if someone had puffed air across the back of my neck.

Across the small kitchen, in a narrow space behind the kitchen sink's back splash, in a place where no one shorter than me would ever see, stood a small figurine. It had large red, surreal eyes on a shiny blue body, no arms and three legs.

"Mr. McKenna, what is wrong? What are you staring at?"

The little figure seemed to stare back at me, its eyes intense. I gestured toward it. "May I?"

"I don't know what you're referring to," Janeen said, obviously unable to see it from her perspective.

I stepped across the kitchen to the sink, reached into the narrow space behind the counter edge and picked up the figurine. It was light in weight, its blue paint glossy. It had been carved of wood and sanded to a polish before being painted. I handed it to Janeen who pulled away. She put her arms behind her back.

"How did that get there?" she said, her voice tense.

"You've seen this before?"

She nodded. "Captain Mallory showed it to me. He said the El Dorado deputies found it near Thos's body. But I thought he took it with him."

"Let me check," I said. I pulled my cellphone out of my pocket and got Diamond back on the line. "The little carved totem you told me about. You still have it, right?"

"Of course," he said, sounding irritated. "You think I'm going to throw away evidence? It's right here in my cup holder."

"Then it has a twin that's been hiding behind Janeen Kahale's kitchen sink."

"You've seen it?"

"Holding it in my hand," I said.

"Well, hang onto it for Mallory."

We said goodbye and hung up.

I turned back to Janeen. "Had you ever seen one of these before Mallory brought one around?"

She shook her head.

"Any idea what it is?" I asked.

"Like I told Captain Mallory, I have no idea. It looks like some kind of satanic doll. I don't like it. Maybe Phillip has seen one. He was at school when Captain Mallory showed me the other one."

"Can we ask him about it?"

Janeen went into the living room and called out. "Phillip, would you please come to the kitchen? I have a question." Janeen returned and stared at the figurine in my hand. I handed it to her. She took it gingerly between the tip of her thumb and forefinger. She held it away from herself for a moment, then set it down on the kitchen table. It looked precariously balanced, yet it stood on its three legs without falling over.

Phillip appeared at the doorway, peeking in, unwilling to come any closer to me.

"Phillip, do you know about this...this little doll?" She pointed to it. He looked from Janeen to the figurine and back twice. He moved his head slightly.

"Are you certain?" Janeen asked.

Another slight shake.

"Did Thos or one of your friends give this to you?"

Again, the barely perceptible negative movement.

"Okay, Phillip. Thank you."

"What do you think?" I said when Phillip was gone.

"I'm not sure," she said softly so that Phillip wouldn't hear. "With Phillip you can't tell sometimes. From his reaction, he may have been the one to put it behind the sink."

"Janeen, have you ever heard of a black wind?"

"No. Why?"

"Apparently, Mallory has heard the phrase in connection with a gang in South Lake Tahoe. He thought it was a Native American concept and that this figurine may be some kind of Indian representation of a black wind."

Janeen was shaking her head. "He's confusing it with dark wind which comes from some tribes but not the Washoe as far as I've ever heard. Mind you, even though I'm Washoe, I'm no expert on Washoe culture. Which, I guess, is why our customs are dying out."

"What about the figurine?" I gestured at the little wooden doll which still balanced near the edge of the kitchen table. "Does it look like anything the Washoe ever carved?"

"No. Not to my knowledge."

"What about the idea that Native American concepts have been adopted by a gang in Tahoe?"

"I can't speak for other tribes. Some of them were capable of violence. But not the Washoe. The Washoe were, and still are, the most peaceful and loving people there could be." Janeen looked at me solidly. There was no imploring in her eyes. She didn't think she needed to try to convince me of a simple fact.

I reached for the totem. "May I?"

Janeen nodded. I slipped it into my pocket. "I guess I'll have that cup of coffee, now," I said.

SEVEN

Janeen Kahale gave me a steaming mug of black coffee and poured a generous dollop of milk into her own.

"Where shall I start?" she asked.

"At the beginning. Where and when was Thos born?"

"Thirty-one years ago next month. In Lihue, the main town on the Hawaiian island of Kauai."

"The Garden Isle."

Janeen nodded. "You've been there?"

"Once, years ago. The thing I most remember is those amazing cliffs, but I forget their name."

"The Na Pali cliffs," Janeen said. "My ex-husband took me hiking there several times. They are amazing, indeed. They are the tallest cliffs in the world that rise directly from the ocean."

"You lived in Hawaii. But you said you were Washoe." I gestured toward the woven baskets. "These are Washoe designs, right?"

"Yes. My parents were both Washoe Indian. I was born in Gardnerville, Nevada. Just down in the Carson Valley, one of the ancient wintering grounds for my people. But of course you know that. My father is still alive and lives there.

"By contrast, my ex-husband Jasper is one hundred percent Hawaiian, born in Poipu, Kauai. Jasper's father died only a month ago from lung cancer. Both of Thos's grandmothers died when he was young. My mother died from diabetes. My ex's mother was on a ferry that sunk."

"Where did you and Jasper meet?"

"Here in Tahoe. I was working as a maid in one of the casino hotels. Jasper Kahale came to town on a company sponsored vacation. Kauai Sugarcane Company. Twice I was cleaning his room when he walked in. I still remember how I was struck by his magnificent smile. He gave me a piece of raw sugarcane he'd brought with him. I was fascinated by its sweetness. Everything about him was sweet. He even spoke sweetly. Still does, I must admit. After I met him in the hotel room he asked me to have coffee with him after my shift. We spoke for hours in the hotel café, and I was late getting home.

"My parents were frightened and very upset. They called me names for loose women and said I had dirtied the honor of the family and the tribe. We had a major argument. I ended up running out and sleeping at a girlfriend's house.

"By the end of the week, Jasper asked me to come back to Hawaii with him and get married." She stared at the far wall, remembering.

I said, "Your parents had already decided you were an impetuous young woman, so you decided to go."

"Yes. In retrospect, it was not the best way to begin a marriage."

"What went wrong with you and Jasper?"

"It wasn't what went wrong so much as what didn't go right. We never found a closeness and we never shared intimacies beyond a perfunctory physical kind. All of his interests were social. Whether Jasper was out on the golf course or having a backyard barbecue or hosting a sales meeting, he was always with a crowd. And yet now I think he is, sadly, very much alone.

"But I've always been an introvert. My interests were weaving and reading and, of course, my children. Never did Jasper and I ever sit together quietly and have a conversation of any substance. A marriage like that was enough for him, but not for me. I still don't think he understands why I divorced him. He thinks everyone would naturally want as many people around them as possible and he simply cannot understand that a person could be different from him that way."

Janeen sipped her coffee. "I spoke to him about Thos just yesterday. He said he still loves me and it made me very sad. He is quite a bit older than I am, and I think his mind is just beginning to go. I now realize that he will go to his grave without understanding our basic differences."

Janeen looked at me, her soft face frowning. "Have you ever met another person like me, Owen? A person who divorced a perfectly sweet spouse? A spouse who was never abusive or rude or adulterous, a spouse who gave nice presents and made breakfast every morning? A spouse whose only crime was to be happy and gregarious when I wanted peace and quiet and a meaningful conversation now and then?" Janeen Kahale didn't wait for an answer, perhaps afraid of what it might be. "It makes me feel worthless," she said. "Look at all the intervening years. It's not like I've been able to replace him with anything better."

I thought it best to change the subject. "You said that your grandson Phillip was Thos's nephew. Who are your other children?"

"My daughter Shelcie. She is Thos's little sister. She was addicted to methamphetamines and almost died of an overdose six years ago. Since then, she has been in a rehab program in L.A. I've been raising Phillip."

"I'm sorry," I said.

"Yes," she said. "But I'm grateful for having Phillip in my life. He is the best grandson a person could have. Of course, he should have a mother in his life, but Shelcie..." she stopped talking.

"Why do you think your daughter got hooked on drugs?"

"When Jasper and I got divorced, Thos was ten, Shelcie six. Thos stayed with his father in Kauai while I moved with Shelcie back to Gardnerville. My mother had died and my father had softened considerably in his stance toward me. He was a good grandfather to Shelcie. But Shelcie never adjusted to the move. She had no respect for Washoe customs. She said they were dumb.

"I suppose it was too much to expect her to assimilate. She seemed to hate everything about her new life and cried endlessly. She hated me for divorcing her father. She got in with some bad kids and ran away the first time when she was twelve. It nearly broke my heart. She was in and out of my life after that. When Phillip was born she claimed not to even know who the father was." Janeen's face reddened at the thought.

She continued, "When Shelcie finally entered a drug rehab program, I thought that maybe our lives were back on track. Phillip has adjusted very well to living with me. But now with Thos..." Janeen bowed her head and cried. Her sobs were silent, her head nodding with each spasm, her hands motionless on the kitchen table.

I pulled my chair over next to her and put my hand over hers. "Do you have anyone else who can help you? Another relative?"

"No," she said, keeping her head bowed. "My father is too old now. I don't get along well with my other relatives, a hangover from the problems with Shelcie." Tears dropped to her lap.

"A neighbor?"

She shook her head. "My neighbor Jerry is nice enough. He wants to be helpful, but he doesn't really understand us and our situation. And he's gone a lot."

"What about your friends?"

"I don't really have any close friends. Lyla Purdue lives nearby, but I don't think I'd burden her with these problems. Most of my tribe live down in the valleys to the east of Tahoe." She lifted her head and looked at me. "I don't mean to be rude, Mr. McKenna, but your people do not mingle much with the Washoe. Many whites are nice to us, but it is often with a kind of sympathy. It's hard to be friends with someone who feels sorry for you. Native people need to feel pride about their heritage. Instead, we often feel that others look at our ethnicity as a handicap. I suppose I should have stayed down in the valley with my people. But there are less than two thousand people in the tribe and it seems that everybody knows all about Shelcie's problems. I thought It would be better for Phillip to join me in Tahoe."

"Could Shelcie come up from L.A. to be with you?"

"I asked her," Janeen said. "But she is so upset over Thos's death that she says she can't face it all just yet. She's going to stay in L.A. for the time being. She's never really matured emotionally. I love Phillip more than I can say, but Shelcie never should have had that child. Is that bad of me to say?"

"No, Janeen, I don't think so."

"Of course, look at me and Jasper. We got married without really being in love. Then we had children without thinking about the long term. Now we've been divorced for twenty years and we split Thos and Shelcie up all that time. What kind of terrible thing is that? I have to wonder if Jasper and I don't deserve the blame for Shelcie's problems and Thos's death." Janeen let go of my hand, pulled some Kleenex out of a nearby box, dabbed at her eyes and blew her nose. "Let's go sit in the living room." We both stood up, picked up our coffee mugs and sat side by side on the living room couch.

"Tell me about Thos," I said. "What kind of a boy was he?"

"As I've said, he was a very determined child. Quite stubborn, actually. But not willful like his sister. Much less self-focused. Better behaved. He was a medium student, not because he didn't have the intellect to get better grades, but because he was always thinking about surfing.

"He was a strong child and grew into a strapping young man. Lots of muscles. I think that must be his Polynesian ancestry. Jasper is certainly a good-sized man. Not tall. But wide.

"Anyway, when Thos started attending the community college in Honolulu, he talked about possibly transferring someday to U.C. Davis to study winemaking. But then he became a surfing champion and he focused on that for years until he broke his leg. The break was bad enough that it put him out of competition."

"It must have been hard to have a successful surfing career evaporate just like that," I said.

"Worse than hard. It was devastating. For years he'd been

world-famous in surfing circles. He was on the covers of magazines, and kids were always wanting his autograph wherever he went. The next minute it was all gone and someone else was the champion."

"What did he do then?"

"He tried doing some coaching and instruction, but it didn't work out. A TV station in Honolulu even tried him as a sports commentator, but he didn't have the style they were looking for. So he took a variety of jobs. Nothing clicked for him until recently when he went back to the idea of wine, something he's always had a taste for. He felt he was too old to go back to college, so he set up a little company that would bring California wines to Hawaii."

"A wine distributorship. Sounds like something I'd enjoy."

"You like wine?"

"Yes."

"Oh, that's nice," Janeen said. She seemed inordinately pleased. I liked something that Thos liked.

"Thos did some research," she said, "and found all the small wineries in Sonoma and Napa that weren't being distributed in Hawaii. He approached them and managed to set up accounts with several of them. Then he called on outlets all over Hawaii, especially restaurants. Last I spoke to him about it, it was quite a growing business. He had several employees and was always flying between California and Hawaii."

"What was he doing in Tahoe?"

"Just a family visit. He hadn't seen me in awhile, and of course he adored Phillip."

"How long was he going to be here for?"

"Just the weekend. He came up last Friday night and said he was going to be leaving Monday morning." Janeen's face suddenly darkened. "But then he wrote the suicide note. So maybe he'd already planned this whole thing when he told me his schedule. Oh, Lord." Janeen started shaking. Her lip quivered, but no tears fell this time.

"Janeen, do you have any idea why someone would want to kill him?"

"No. He may not have been the chummiest young man, but he didn't make enemies. Not even as a child."

"What about other businessmen? A wine competitor?"

"I wondered that, too," she said. "But just this last visit he was saying that the beauty of his business was that he had no competitors to speak of. Every account he set up was a winery or a restaurant that hadn't been approached by a Hawaiian distributor. It doesn't seem that he took business away from anyone, he just created business where there wasn't any before."

"What about his friends?"

"He didn't have many. He was always something of a loner. I think it went back to his surfing days. His intense focus on the competitions precluded any time for friends. He would mention going fishing with someone now and then, but I don't remember who."

"I take it he wasn't married."

"No. He dated, but I never heard that he got serious about any girl. He seemed content to be a bachelor."

"Where did he live?"

"A couple of years ago he bought a townhouse in Princeville, a resort area on the north shore of Kauai. Princeville has several championship golf courses that Thos liked to play on. He also sold a lot of wine to the Princeville restaurants."

"Any roommates?"

"No. As I've said, Thos liked to be alone. I guess he got that from me."

We sat in silence for awhile. Without asking, Janeen got up and refilled my coffee cup and I said thanks.

"Janeen," I said. "You've given me the picture of a typical young man who was bright and ambitious. But nowhere do I see a place to start looking for a murderer. I need something else. A problem. A fight he had. A dilemma that he was desperate to get out of. Someone who hated him or saw him as the obstacle to everything they wanted. Is there anything you can think of?"

Janeen looked inward and thought. "No. I'm sorry, but I don't know of anything like that."

"Did Shelcie's drug problem ever touch Thos? Or did he get involved in it in any way?"

Janeen shook her head.

"Did he ever owe any money to anyone?"

"Not to my knowledge."

"There must be something. Some incident that caused someone else pain. Some ongoing struggle between Thos and an acquaintance."

Janeen shook her head.

I continued, "A disagreement with one of his business accounts. An argument over a traffic accident."

Janeen kept shaking her head.

"Some trouble with the law. A family secret. A..." I saw that she stopped shaking her head. "What is it, Janeen?"

"I'm sure it's nothing."

"Tell me anyway."

"It's not even a secret in the sense of something that would get Thos in trouble. It has nothing to do with anybody doing something wrong."

"Tell me, Janeen."

"I feel silly talking about it," she said. "It's just that in my ex-husband's family there is a tradition dating back many generations. It has to do with where they put a person's most precious possessions when they die. Sort of an offering to the gods."

"Who decides what possessions?"

"The person dying does. Usually when they are younger and healthier. You know, like when I've told Shelcie I want her to have my loom. And Phillip gets all my baskets. Only, in this situation, the person designates what goes to the family shrine. It's a cave in a cliff."

"The place is secret?"

"Yes."

EIGHT

"Is this family shrine a Hawaiian tradition or just a Kahale family tradition?"

"I've always thought it was a family tradition. But then, the Washoe Tribe has always had our own sacred cliffs. Like Cave Rock. So maybe some other Hawaiians do, too."

"Do you know where the Kahale place is?"

"No. Only that it is somewhere up on the Na Pali cliffs in Kauai."

"Who knows the location?" I asked.

"Only two people ever know at any one time. The grandfather and his eldest son. When the grandfather dies, then the son tells *his* eldest son. And so on."

"You said that your ex-husband Jasper is still alive."

"Yes."

"But his father died a month ago from lung cancer?"

"Right."

"So Jasper recently passed on the location to Thos."

"Correct."

I pondered that for a moment. "How is Jasper's health?"

"Fine, as far as I know. Do you think this could have something to do with Thos's death?"

"I have no idea. You say that this place has been used by the Kahale family for generations?"

"Yes. Always, as far as anyone knows."

"And the most valuable possessions of family members have been placed there? Valuables from dozens or even hundreds of family members over the years?"

"That's right." Janeen's eyes grew intense. "I've never thought of it like that before. But I don't think it would be any kind of a treasure trove. Most people just designate sentimental objects. Gifts from loved ones and such."

"But there could be valuables that anyone would treasure, correct?"

"You mean, like gold jewelry or something? Yes, I suppose so. Even so, nothing there could possibly be worth killing someone over."

"That's probably true. But that wouldn't matter."

"What do you mean?" Janeen asked.

"Because it is secret, what is actually there might not count. What may matter is what someone imagines is hidden in this cliff cave."

Janeen Kahale was scowling at what I said when Phillip appeared from the hallway. He stopped at the entrance to the living room. He carried a small pair of snowshoes made of aluminum frames with nylon webbing.

"Are you going to go snowshoeing, Phillip?" Janeen said with as much enthusiasm as possible. "It is a perfect day for it!"

Phillip whispered something in Janeen's ear and went into the kitchen. I heard the rustle of his anorak as he pulled it on.

"Remember, Phillip," Janeen called out. "Stay in the level woods and away from the open slope."

There was the sound of the door opening along with a blast of cool air. In a moment we saw Phillip going by the window, a baseball cap facing backward on his head. His pace was brisk as he headed over the deep snow toward the woods. Phillip's snowshoes sunk only eight or ten inches into snow that would otherwise engulf him up to his shoulders. Janeen and I watched him through the window. I saw that he'd put on gators over his boots and calves so that the snow would not get into the top of his boots.

Phillip strode on by, then stopped abruptly when he saw

Spot. They stared at each other, Spot's head hanging out the car window, Phillip just standing still. Spot gave a woof. I couldn't see it behind the Jeep's windows, but I knew that his tail was wagging.

"Oh, Lord," Janeen said as she watched out the window.

"What's wrong?" I asked.

"Nothing. He's smiling. That's the first time he's smiled since..." she broke off.

"Do you think he'd like to play with my dog? Spot is good with kids."

"I don't know. Maybe."

"I'll go ask him." I stood up.

"I'm not sure if..." Janeen's words trailed off again.

She seemed a sweet but overly protective grandmother. She'd be happy to see the boy romp with Spot. I opened the door and stepped outside. Phillip was still standing on the snow bank at the side of the drive looking out and down at Spot in the Jeep. Spot swung his head around toward me for a second, then back toward Phillip. He knew who would be more fun.

"Hey, Phillip," I called out. "Would you like to play with my dog? His name is Spot and he likes to run in the snow."

"Phillip jerked around to face me across the drive. His eyes were wide with alarm.

"Spot won't hurt you," I said. "He loves kids."

Phillip turned toward the forest and ran, his snowshoes kicking up puffs of powder snow behind him as he disappeared into the woods.

I stepped back inside the little house where Janeen stood with a worried face. "I'm sorry," I said. "I seemed to succeed only in frightening Phillip."

"He'll be okay," she said, sounding more like she was trying to convince herself than me.

"Janeen, you told Phillip to stay in the woods and away from the open slope?" I said. "Is that because of the avalanches?"

"Yes. Trees aren't able to grow where there are frequent

avalanches. So I've taught Phillip that mature woods are a decent indication of avalanche-free zones. Of course, every year there are exceptions which is why I always remind him to stay off the steep areas. When you live backed up to a steep mountain that gets forty feet of snow every winter, you have to be careful. With mountains so beautiful it's hard to remember that they can kill you."

"I'm glad you're teaching Phillip to be respectful of them." I drank more coffee.

"He's out there so often that it's essential. Like Thos and me, Phillip likes to spend time by himself. I think he feels his own company is better than that of most other kids. Or adults, for that matter." She smiled at me.

"These days, it's nice to see a kid spend any time out of doors."

Janeen nodded. "Maybe you and I should. Would you like to walk a bit?"

"Certainly. Do you have snowshoes? I have a pair in my Jeep."

"I was thinking we could stroll down the drive."

"Of course."

In a minute we were walking toward Jerry's house.

"In the winter," Janeen said, "Phillip lives in his snowshoes. Every year, when the school has all the kids do a long distance run, Phillip wins the race. His fitness is partly why I am so strict about staying off the slopes. Where most kids stay off the mountains because they get so pooped climbing up them, Phillip would just run up them. Thos took him climbing last summer and said he did just that."

"Run up the mountain?"

"Yes. Thos was always in great shape, but he said Phillip ran non-stop. He'd be waiting for Thos at each lookout."

We passed Jerry's house. It was dark. We headed on out Cornice Road.

"Tell me more about this tradition of the Kahale shrine," I

said.

"I asked my ex-husband Jasper about it once. He said it had been going on for hundreds of years."

"Exactly how does it work?"

"Whenever someone dies, the family assembles the person's three most sacred possessions. There are no rules as to what they must be. The Kahales refer to the sacredness of the items and the place where they will be entombed, but it isn't in a strict religious sense. It's a personal sacredness. If the person didn't designate their three items before they died, then the family chooses what they think was especially important to the individual."

"So the chosen things could be trinkets or a Bible."

"Right. I remember when one of Jasper's aunts died suddenly of a heart attack. Everyone in the family knew that the three items most sacred to her were the photographs of the parrots she used to have. So Jasper took them up to the shrine."

"But sometimes an individual will designate their own items before they die?"

"Yes. More often than not, I think."

"Can you think of anyone in the family who designated valuable items? Items someone might want to steal?"

Janeen frowned. "I imagine there were valuable items now and then, but nothing comes to mind. One of Jasper's uncles designated three little fish sculptures that he carved out of soapstone. Jasper's other uncle said that the only thing he wanted put in the sacred cliff was his sketchbook. He didn't sketch often, but over the years he'd nearly filled a thick hardbound volume with exquisite pencil sketches. Landscapes mostly, from what I saw. Before Jasper put it in the sacred cliff, he wrapped the book in several layers of thick plastic to protect it from moisture."

"Just one item?" I asked.

"Right. As far as I know, the family didn't add any items against his wishes."

"Who is in the inner circle, the people who are allowed to put items in the shrine? Family descendents expand to vast numbers after a few generations."

"They solved that problem by designating only direct descendents of the eldest son. Jasper was the eldest son, so both Shelcie and Thos are included. If Thos had had children then they would have been part of the group. But Shelcie's children would not."

"Not very fair from Shelcie's point of view," I said. "That is, if she would want Phillip included."

"True. But doesn't the eldest son always come before the other sons? Or the daughters, for that matter? These things weren't designed for fairness. They were designed for efficiency in passing on kingdoms and such."

"And sacred cliff shrines," I said. "What about spouses?"

"Only the wife of the eldest son was in the inner circle. Presumably because her children were in line for inclusion."

"So you are included?"

"I would have been. But I am the exception because I broke the covenant by getting divorced." We came to a side road. Janeen turned down it. The walls of snow were so high it was like walking down a large white hallway.

"Had Thos designated his sacred items?"

Janeen's face darkened.

I wondered if she was finally resenting my questions.

"No," she said. "I can't imagine that he'd even thought about it. I think he was still young enough that he didn't sense his mortality. But then he wrote the note..."

"This tradition," I said, breaking an uncomfortable silence. "Is it spoken of freely among the Kahale relatives?"

"I suppose it varies from generation to generation. I always had the sense that people didn't find it that interesting. I imagine that everyone knows about it, even the cousins who don't participate. But it isn't an intense focus of interest. For example, my own kids always knew about it. But they never thought it interesting. For them it is just another strange thing about old people."

"What about when the grandfather dies?" I asked. "When the

eldest son tells his eldest son the location? I picture that moment as an important rite of passage."

"Yes, I think it is a great honor to learn the location."

"Can the father just tell the son the location, or do they have to go there?"

"They have to go there. We were just married when Jasper was told. He disappeared for two days and came back quite scratched as if he'd been climbing in the jungle."

"Did you get an idea of where the shrine might be?"

"Not at all. The Na Pali cliffs are four thousand feet high and run for fourteen miles. There are no roads to them because they drop straight into the ocean."

"I remember," I said. "There's a foot trail along the base of them. Otherwise, the only access is by boat, right?"

"Yes. Even boat access is cut off in the winter because the waves are too ferocious. So the Kahale shrine could be anywhere. I imagine you could search for centuries and never find it."

"Do you know for certain if Jasper told Thos about the location of the sacred place?"

"Yes. It was after Jasper's father died a month ago. Jasper needed to bring his father's sacred items up to the shrine as well as show Thos where it is. I remember that I had tried calling Thos and got his machine several times. He didn't call back for three days. When I told him I was worried, he said that his father had taken him to the Na Pali cliffs.

"It was just in time," she continued, "because when Jasper's brother died shortly after, Jasper had a blood clot in his leg and couldn't go to the shrine. So the honor went to Thos."

"Jasper's brother died just recently?"

"Yes. John senior."

"How?"

"A car accident. He drove off a cliff on the Waimea Canyon road."

"How did it happen?"

"It was at night. They think he had too much to drink and

missed a turn."

"Janeen, Thos's note says he was responsible for the deaths of three people. Jasper's father and brother have died in the last few weeks. Could they be two of the people Thos referred to?"

"Of course not. Jasper's father died of lung cancer. His brother in a car accident. Obviously, Thos could not have had anything to do with either death."

Our walk brought us to a dead end. We turned around and started back.

"Was John senior a heavy drinker?"

"Not that I know of. More like Jasper. He liked to party, to have a good time. They tested his body for alcohol. I understand he wasn't drunk, but apparently he'd had enough to misjudge a turn."

"Any idea why he was out driving on that particular road?"

"Jasper thought that his brother had simply gone up there with some friends to watch the sunset and drink a few beers. But they never found any friends who would admit to drinking with him that night. Perhaps they felt some responsibility for his death and were afraid to come forward."

"Where does the road go?"

"It climbs up the backbone of the island, right along the edge of Waimea Canyon. At the top, the road comes to a dead end."

"I remember, now," I said. "There's a lookout with a fantastic view of the Pacific and the Na Pali cliffs."

"Right. It's really spectacular during the day. But there's nothing to see at night unless there's a full moon. And it was at night that Jasper's brother died. So the only thing that makes sense is that he went up there to drink some beer and watch the sunset."

I wondered if the death of Jasper's brother could have had anything to do with the shrine. "Is there any possibility that Jasper's brother knew the shrine's location?"

"I don't think so. Jasper seemed respectful of the tradition."

"Did Thos give you any idea of where the shrine is?"

"I asked him about it and he would only speak about it in the vaguest terms."

"Now that Jasper once again is the only one who knows the location, who does the secret get passed onto?"

"The system always favors the son next in line. If we had another son, then he would be given the information. Because we don't, Jasper would normally give the secret to his brother. But because Jasper's brother is now dead, I believe he is to give the secret to the eldest son of his brother."

"Who is that?"

"John Kahale junior. Thos's cousin who is two years younger."

"Where does John Kahale live?" I asked.

"In Kauai. A little town called Kapa'a."

"What does he do for a living?"

"He's a helicopter pilot," Janeen said. "Gives tourists rides around the island and into the crater of the volcano. Mount Waiale'ale." She pronounced it Why-alay-alay.

"Isn't that supposed to be the wettest spot on earth?"

"Yes. Rains all the time. I lived in Kauai for ten years and it seems like I only saw the top of the mountain a few times. The rest of the time it was in the clouds."

"Janeen, you said that Thos hadn't designated what three things he wanted put in the sacred cliff. Will you and Jasper and Shelcie decide together?"

She stopped walking and stood stiffly as if gripped by a new awareness of the finality of her son's death. "I think Jasper already decided."

"Any idea what those items might be?"

There was another long pause while she stared into space. She finally shook her head.

NINE

W e'd come back to Janeen Kahale's house and stood outside near the kitchen door. I asked Janeen for the addresses of some of her relatives, her ex-husband Jasper, and the young man next in line to learn the location of the secret shrine, Jasper's nephew John Kahale junior. She went inside and came back out a few minutes later. She handed me a piece of paper with names and addresses on it. I told her I'd let her know as soon as I had learned anything new.

We both looked around to see if Phillip was nearby. There was no movement in the snowy woods. Just snowshoe tracks that disappeared into the trees.

Janeen grabbed a rope that hung from a ten-inch bell on the corner of the roof eave. She rang it several times. We waited.

Phillip's independence was impressive in an era when most kids seemed to stay inside and watch TV or play video games. Although I'd only been in the living room of the Kahale cabin, I saw no TV and there were even a few books. Janeen deserved credit for not giving in to all the brain-numbing toys of the era. Of course, Phillip's bedroom may have had the standard electronic distractions, but I doubted it. The kid carried an abacus in his pocket.

In a minute we heard sounds of movement in the forest. Phillip came into view, running on his snowshoes just as he had been when he left. Janeen and Phillip hugged when he returned and he whispered something in her ear.

I said goodbye and returned to Spot and the Jeep. I stopped

on my way out and rang Jerry's doorbell, but there was no answer. So I headed back down Spring Creek Road, thinking about the secret cliff shrine.

I was certain that many people would have a desire to find and examine the contents of the Kahale shrine if they knew of its existence. And once someone found the shrine, how tempted would they be by any artifacts with value? If the value was high enough, would someone kill for it? So far, it was the only thing I had to go on.

As to whether anyone could have discovered the shrine, the answer seemed obvious. Secrets are hard to keep. Any number of Kahales may have leaked the knowledge over the years.

I pulled out my phone and dialed Captain Mallory of the South Lake Tahoe P.D. This time he answered.

"Mr. McKenna, keeper of the dog," he said when I identified myself. "How is that hound anyway? Has he found any more mountain lions?"

"If so, he's learned not to drag them out of the woods. Tell me, Mallory, I'm wondering what you know about the Thos Kahale murder."

"Not much. Out of my jurisdiction. The El Dorado County Sheriff's Office is in charge. They're talking to me as a professional courtesy, but you know I can't divulge details of an investigation."

"What if I addressed you as sir?"

"That might help."

"Or Captain Mallory, sir?"

"Much better. People ain't even afraid of cops anymore. Never mind, respect them. Anyway, there isn't much to tell. In fact, we know nothing about this Kahale murder. But maybe soon."

"How soon?"

"Got a diver in the water looking for the slug. Should be running out of air in another thirty minutes or so. Maybe we'll learn something then."

"You're at Rubicon Point?" I asked.

"Yeah. At the Rubicon Lodge. Come if you want."

"I'll be there," I said and hung up.

When I got to the highway, I turned left toward Emerald Bay. I drove by where one of the forest fires had claimed a victim last fall, around Emerald Bay and the rock slide where Jennifer Salazar's sister was killed years before, and on past the granite outcroppings of Bliss State Park.

The turnoff to the Rubicon Lodge was marked by a small wooden sign. Apparently, the lodge's elite guests know of its location or they are delivered by knowing limo drivers.

I headed through a thick fir forest down a lane walled by snow and pulled up in front of a grand log building that had been used in one of the most memorable Marlboro ads. Wood smoke rose from a large cobblestone chimney, the smoke's piney aroma giving the lodge and the woods a cozy, welcoming flavor. As I headed for the lodge, I scanned the parking lot for the vehicle the El Dorado Sheriff's divers would use, but saw only a dented panel van that said Meyer's Commercial Diving and Salvage. I headed inside.

The thirty-foot-tall lobby was made for giants. It had huge leather chairs and couches sprawled in groups near a stone fireplace so big you could barbecue a moose in it. On the wooden floor were deep red rugs. On the walls were trophy game heads. A bear and a mountain lion stood on the lake side. They both appeared to snarl across the lobby at another bear and a large twelve point buck on the mountain side. On the fireplace mantle paced a stuffed wolverine and two coyotes.

I glanced around and noticed that the only people in the lobby were standing at the lake-side windows staring out through the little panes at a group of people down by the water. I walked toward the windows, glancing back at the collection of dead animals.

"Good afternoon, sir. Are you a hunter?" The voice was soft and husky, as though the vocal cords had been damaged years ago.

I turned to face a bear of a man, nearly as tall as me and much wider but without visible fat. He had a rough red complexion under a thick shock of white hair combed straight back. His moustache was equally white and bushy as a fox tail. I could see that he had to shave his cheeks almost up to his sad eyes and his neck down to the top of his chest. His blue eyes were so watery it looked as if he'd been crying. I guessed him to be about 60.

"No, I haven't had the pleasure," I said, trying not to sound disapproving. After all, like most people, I eat meat. Besides, it is not a good idea to critique other people's hobbies. Some people would find my study of art pointless as well.

The man reached out a hand that was the size of a bear paw and had nearly as much fur on it, white fur like a polar bear. "Brock Chambers."

"Owen McKenna." We shook, giving each other a healthy squeeze.

"Good to meet you, Owen. Do you have a room reservation? Or perhaps you are here for an early dinner?" He sounded hopeful as he gestured through an opening to another huge room filled with round rustic tables covered with white linen and what looked like fine crystal. Only two of the tables had diners at them.

"No, actually I'm here to meet with Captain Mallory of the South Lake Tahoe Police."

Brock Chambers frowned. "Oh, that business." He glanced toward the lake. "They're outside."

"Thank you," I said. "Are you the owner of the lodge, Brock?"

"Yes."

"You must be proud of such a handsome establishment. I can assure you I'll be back to enjoy your restaurant in the future. Perhaps a room as well."

"We'd be pleased to have you as a guest," he said, his professionalism unable to mask what seemed a deep sorrow. He smiled like a perfect gentleman as I walked away.

I pushed out through large French doors and walked down a shoveled walk toward the water. Two El Dorado County sheriff's deputies were in the snow examining footprints in an area roped off with yellow crime tape. Mallory stood at the end of the pier looking out into the water, scanning back and forth. He lifted a can of Coke to his lips and took a long drink. The late afternoon sun was shining on the snow-clad mountains across the lake. The contrast between the brilliant white snow and the deep blue of the water was dramatic.

I joined Mallory at the end of the pier.

"The diver still out there?"

He looked at his watch. "Yeah."

"Why a commercial diver instead of the sheriff's dive squad?"

"El Dorado Sergeant Richter is in charge of this investigation. He thinks no way would divers find a slug under water. Said it would be a waste of taxpayer's money. I asked if I could send a diver down, and he said if I had money to burn, go ahead." He looked out at the water. "I know a diver who works cheap."

"How is it you're here, anyway?"

"I busted a gang-banger in town a few weeks ago and he had a little carved totem in his pocket. I called Richter to ask if he'd seen anything like it. When Richter's men found a totem floating near the body, he called me to come and look."

"I also found one behind Janeen Kahale's sink." I pulled it out of my pocket and handed it to him.

Mallory turned it over in his hands. He chewed on his cheek, then pointed down the beach. "Body was found just over there, where the forest comes down to the water. Corpse washed up right next to where his clothes had been neatly piled. There were two sets of tracks in the woods. One set matched the boots of the victim. Other set may be our shooter. They haven't found a shell casing. The diver is looking for the slug. But that scuba tank's gotta be getting pretty near empty. A guy could start to worry."

This seemed out of place for someone who had never seemed

to worry about anything in his life.

Mallory pointed out at the water. "Here we are. Bubbles. Had me going there a minute."

An arm broke the surface. The diver swam toward the dock. Mallory and I reached out as the diver carefully positioned a large swim fin onto a ladder rung. We grabbed the diver's elbows and heaved.

Even with the scuba tank, the diver was about half the weight and size I expected, and the curves were unmistakable in the black neoprene suit.

She pulled off her face mask and breathing hose, disconnected a hose that attached to her suit, then unstrapped her tank and set it on the pier. There was a small tank hooked on her belt. It wasn't much bigger than Mallory's Coke can. She left it attached.

She peeled off her gloves, then bent down and removed her swim fins. Her black hood was last. She shook her blonde curls until they bounced about her face. She was beautiful and could have been a model. Maybe she was.

Mallory stared at her, unquestionably more interested in her than in what she may have found on the bottom. Now I knew why he'd been worried. Mallory was of a chivalrous old school. He wouldn't stress over a male diver.

"How does your hair stay so dry in a wet suit?" Mallory asked in a hard voice. His frown, permanently in place ever since he quit smoking several years ago, was deep enough to hold pennies in the folds of skin.

"This type of suit is sealed and pressurized by air from the tank," she said. "Keeps me dry and warm. Although I also wear a wet suit for extra warmth." Her voice had just enough Southern Belle in it to make it seem unnatural for her to be dressed in anything without lace trim.

"I don't get it," Mallory said.

"The wet suit goes under the pressurized suit. See?" She grabbed an edge of the black suit at the base of her neck and pulled down. Peeking out was the trim of bright green fabric.

She pulled it out a half inch. "A wet suit is designed to let water in next to your skin where it eventually warms up. But this lake is so cold, you'd die of hypothermia even with a wet suit. So we wear a pressurized suit over it to keep the water out. The wet suit never gets wet. Some people wear long underwear under the pressurized suit. But I like this wet suit because it fits perfectly."

"So I see," Mallory said. "What if you poke the suit on a sharp rock or something and spring a leak?"

"Then I'll leak air out, not water in. Replacement air comes from the tank through this valve here and into my suit. If I get a leak, the air will bubble out."

"Maybe we should peel it off and check," Mallory said. "Make sure you're not getting hypothermia."

"Don't worry, I'll be okay."

"Right," Mallory said. "Oh. You should meet Owen McKenna. He's the dick hired by the victim's mother. Doesn't look it, but he's okay. You can even answer his questions after you answer mine."

She stepped toward me and shook my hand. "Morella Meyer of Meyer's Commercial Diving and Salvage."

Up close I could see that her eyes, which were a bright viridian and crinkled enticingly at the corners, did not line up. They pointed somewhat outward from one another. First the left one looked directly at me, then the right. "Pleased to meet you," I said, deciding that the left eye was lined up more in my direction.

"Don't let it bother you," she said, "but you're looking at my glass eye."

"I am?"

"Yeah, I'm in residence over here. This one." She tapped at her temple next to her right eye which seemed to be looking off to the side of my head.

"Oh," I said, finding it awkward to look at that eye when it was staring into space and the other was looking directly at me.

"My problem, too," Mallory said as if reading my mind. He turned to Morella. "So, did you find the slug?"

"No. Sorry. I swam a grid pattern, but saw nothing."

"You think it could have been there and you maybe missed it?"

"No doubt about it," Morella said. "You said it was only about this big." She held her thumb and forefinger about an inch apart. "And it would be all munched up, right?"

Mallory nodded. "Yeah. The slug would have been deformed blasting through both sides of the skull. It wouldn't look much like a bullet, more like a flattened chunk of metal."

"So I looked for anything metallic. Of course, given the sandy bottom, it may be impossible to find," Morella said. "I could have swum right over it, but if a slug slipped under a little sand when it hit bottom I wouldn't have seen it. All I found was this." There was a long pocket on her thigh. She popped open a Velcro flap, reached in and pulled out a toy dagger. She handed it to Mallory.

He flexed the rubber blade back and forth and rapped his knuckle on the tin handle. "Scary," he said. "This all you found?" disappointment obvious in his voice.

"Sorry."

"Is it dark down there?" Mallory asked.

"No," Morella said. "Even if I'd gone to one hundred feet it would still be fairly bright. Now, down at two hundred feet near the edge of the drop-off would be another matter. It would get very dim. Of course, the sun is close to setting, so we're through for today."

"How deep did you go?" Mallory asked.

"Sixty feet. A little more for a bit," she said. "Not too smart considering the time involved."

Mallory scowled. "How come no deeper?" he said, irritation in his voice.

"Mallory," I said. "I mean, Captain Mallory, sir."

Mallory shot me a quick look.

"She can't because of the no-decompression limits," I said. I was thinking back several years to my last dive, flirting with the giant rays off Grand Cayman. "If she goes deeper, she's able to spend much less time searching. Otherwise she'd get the bends."

Morella was nodding. Her eyes seemed to be taking in most of the terrain to either side of me. I couldn't remember which eye I was supposed to look at.

I turned toward Mallory. "She can spend about sixty minutes at sixty feet without having to decompress. Any deeper and she wouldn't be able to spend more than a few minutes down there." I turned to Morella whose face showed relief at my interjection. "Did I get it right?"

"Absolutely," she said. "Much deeper and you go down and come back up with no time on the bottom at all."

Mallory looked suspicious. "So what are the bends, anyway?"

Morella looked at me with a touch of a smirk on her face. "Seems like you know the captain better than I. Should I give him the details or just tell him that it hurts like hell?"

"He's always struck me as a detail man," I said.

She addressed Mallory. "Each thirty-three feet of depth adds another atmosphere of pressure which is nearly fifteen pounds per square inch. The more pressure, the more nitrogen from the air you breathe dissolves into your tissues and blood. If you go down too deep, for too long, and then come up to the surface where the pressure is dramatically less, the dissolved nitrogen bubbles out of your blood just like when you pop the top on a can of Coke and the carbon dioxide bubbles out."

Mallory glanced down at the Coke in his hand. "What happens then?" he asked.

"In a bad case, the bubbles block the blood flow to your brain and heart and you die."

Mallory looked like he needed a stiffer drink. "Sixty minutes at sixty feet, huh?"

"Actually, it's a lot less in Tahoe," Morella said. "It's the high altitude factor. We've got about twenty percent less air pressure than at sea level. I don't know if you've ever noticed, but when you pop open a Coke in Tahoe, it bubbles about twenty percent more than it does in San Francisco. Same with the nitrogen in your blood. A sixty foot dive in this lake is like a seventy-five foot dive at sea level. The bottom line is that we can't go as deep in Tahoe, nor can we stay down as long."

Mallory turned, paced a few steps down the pier, then came back. As I watched him I noticed movement in one of the windows of the Rubicon Lodge. Brock Chambers was watching us. When he saw me looking he pulled away. Mallory drank the last of his Coke and crushed the can in his hand. "If you wanted to search deeper, how would you do it?"

Morella pointed to her tank which lay on its side on the pier. "If I went down with two of those tanks, I could spend a little more time at a greater depth. But most of my extra air would be used up making the decompression stops."

"Meaning?"

"On my way up I'd have to stop at a certain depth for a period of time, then rise farther and stop at a shallower depth for another period of time. The decompression stops let the dissolved nitrogen in my system out slowly so my blood doesn't bubble."

Mallory grunted. He turned and looked out at the lake which was turning a deep blue-black in the setting sun. The backdrop of snow-covered mountains was now lit with a golden alpenglow. Turning back he said, "You make it sound like searching any large area deeper than a hundred feet is impractical."

"Definitely," Morella said. She faced Mallory squarely, aware that he didn't want to hear this. Her walleyed eyes flashed in the last of the sunlight.

"Tell me about the bottom of the lake," he said. "What is it shaped like off this point?"

"Rubicon Point is one of only two places in Lake Tahoe where the bottom drops off so steeply," Morella said. "The other is up near Incline Village. Here at Rubicon is the steepest underwater cliff in Tahoe." She turned and pointed at the water. "Just off the end of this pier the bottom goes down at a steady angle until it reaches a depth of two hundred feet. That point is less than a quarter mile offshore."

"What happens there?" Mallory asked.

"At that point the bottom drops off straight down."

"How far?"

"One thousand two hundred feet. Remember, Lake Tahoe is the tenth deepest lake on the planet. Where Rubicon Point drops off under water, it is one of the more spectacular cliffs in the world, in or out of the water."

Mallory stared at his feet, then looked out at the deep blue of the lake. "Any slug that fell off that underwater cliff would be completely beyond the reach of any diver?"

"Correct," Morella said. "You'd need a deep sea submersible to get down that far."

"Like those steel spherical things on TV?"

"Exactly," Morella said.

"Anybody in the basin got one of those things?"

"Actually, there is a remote-controlled one aboard the research vessel that the University of California at Davis uses to study the lake. But its video camera doesn't have the resolution to pick up a small object from any distance."

"What about a submarine?" Mallory asked. "Something people could go down in?"

Morella shook her head. "There isn't one. Even so, you could never find anything tiny from a sub unless you knew exactly where to look for it. Think of when they search for the black boxes from airline crashes. It often takes days to find them, and those boxes are relatively large. No such luck with a bullet."

Mallory frowned. "It sounds like you're telling me that there isn't any chance at all of finding the slug."

"If it is deeper than fifty or sixty feet, then yes, I believe that is correct," Morella said.

"And if it is less than fifty feet deep?"

Morella turned toward the water and held her hands out, palms facing each other about two feet apart. "You said I should concentrate on this area just out from the side of this dock. Based on what I saw of the bottom, I could spend another tank's worth exploring. More than that much time would be pointless."

"When could you do the next dive?" Mallory asked.

"How about first thing tomorrow morning?"

"Okay," Mallory said. His cellphone rang. He held up a finger as he answered it. "Just a minute," he said into the phone, then spoke to Morella. "If I'm not here when you go in tomorrow, call me at one of those numbers on my card. Whether or not you find anything." He was trying to use his official, stern voice, but it had little effect on Morella.

She grinned. "Yes, sir, officer." She gave a little salute, but Mallory was already turning and walking up the pier, talking on his phone.

TEN

"Can I help you with your tank?" I asked.

Morella looked at me with her wild eyes. "Is this one of those help-the-little-woman things?"

"Of course," I said.

"Good," she said. She reached down and picked up her swim fins. "Been a long time since anyone carried a tank for me. They weigh a ton."

I picked up the tank while she grabbed her other gear, and we trod up the pier, around the side of the lodge on a shoveled sidewalk and over to her van

"So what happened to the buddy system? I thought divers were always supposed to go in pairs for safety."

"They are. But I have to make a living. I couldn't possibly afford an assistant. Besides, I always have my spare air." She patted the little tank strapped to her waist. "You're not going to call the scuba police, are you?"

I shook my head. "I know you were looking for a slug down there," I said. "But I'm wondering if you saw anything else."

"Such as?"

"I don't know. Anything out of place. Any item that looks as though it hasn't been down there long."

Morella frowned and shook her head. "Nothing that I recall besides the toy knife. Do you have reason to suspect that anything else would be down there? If I had a clue what I was looking for, I'd be more likely to find it."

"I have no idea," I said. "But in a murder investigation, one looks for anything out of place. The more imaginative the search, the better."

"Wow, that's great, imagination as part of a murder investigation. And here I thought you'd be a 'just the facts, ma'am,' kind of guy." She looked up at me, her grin mischievous. "But as Einstein said, 'Imagination is more important than knowledge.'"

"Ah," I said. "Is the scuba diver revealing an interest in physics beyond what one needs for diving?"

"It's how I got into diving in the first place. I was majoring in physics at UCLA. and realized that even though I was getting good grades, I didn't have the brainpower to pursue it as a scientist. The physics jocks are very intimidating. So I sort of took an inventory of my other interests and scuba diving seemed a way for me to indulge myself in both physics and sport. I took the various courses and eventually became an instructor before getting into the commercial side of diving. I've been doing it professionally now for seven years."

We got to her van and she slid the side door open. I set the tank into a rack that held several others while she peeled off the rest of her black dry suit. The tight wet suit underneath glowed an eerie green in the shadowy light between sunset and twilight and made her look something like a comic book superhero.

"On your dive tomorrow," I said, "while you're looking for the slug, will you please keep an eye out for anything unusual?"

"Which eye?" she said, mischief in her grin.

"Oh, sorry, I forgot."

"I was kidding," she said and gave me a little smack on my arm.

I looked again. Even now I couldn't tell which of the wayward eyes was seeing me and which was not.

"Don't worry," she said. "It happens with everyone. If I do find anything, how do I reach you?"

I gave her my card.

"I'll get you one of mine." She opened the passenger door of the van. A day planner was on the seat. She flipped to the back page and slid my card under a paper clip. A see-through pocket next to it was empty. "Am I out of cards?" Morella said. "I can't be. Let me look in my purse." She got it out from under the seat and dug inside.

I was looking at the facing page of the day planner which held a small pad of paper. A note was scrawled on it. The handwriting was large and very messy, the smeared, blotchy lines those of a cheap ballpoint pen. It looked something like, "Call Strict ASAP after Rubicon dive. Leave message on machine." There was a phone number with the prefix of 543 which was a local South Shore number. But the last four digits were so sloppy I couldn't make them out. Two of them may have been sevens or else ones with long flags at the top. There was an eight. Or maybe it was a five drawn in one stroke like an S, only with an unruly ink trail attached. Looking at the 543 prefix, I could see that the five there also had a trail which could have made it a weak eight. In fact, I realized that the only reason I thought it was a five instead of an eight was because it would then match a local prefix.

"This person you're supposed to call after your dive," I said. "Is it about what you found on the bottom?"

Morella looked up from her purse. I pointed at the day planner.

"Oh, that," she said, discomfort intruding into her tone for the first time since I'd met her. "That's nothing." She reached over and shut the book. "It was another dive, anyway. Last week."

"You were diving in Tahoe last week? In that long snowstorm?"

If she hesitated it was for only the shortest moment. "No, no. Down in Folsom. The reservoir. I was inspecting the dam. Routine stuff." She turned back to her purse and pawed through it some more. "Here it is." She turned and handed me her card.

"Your note says, 'Rubicon dive.' That wouldn't be Folsom would it? It must mean this dive, Rubicon Point at Tahoe."

"You must have read it wrong. It doesn't say Rubicon. It says Folsom." The lightness had gone out of her voice and her eyes narrowed.

"I'm sorry," I said. "Didn't mean to pry."

"Not to worry. Like I said, it's nothing." She gave me another smile, this one forced. "If I find anything, I'll be sure and call."

She got into the driver's side of the van, shut the door and started the engine. I stepped aside as she drove away.

Back in my Jeep, I wrote down all the possible combinations of the numbers I had seen as Spot leaned his head over the front seat, stuck his nose into my jacket and sniffed out faint hints of lodge and lake, stuffed trophy animals and green wet suits.

I started the Jeep and turned out of the lot. A movement in my rear-view mirror caught my attention. I slowed to a stop and watched in the mirror. Brock Chambers appeared to be arguing with another man over by the service entrance to the lodge. He was backing up, looking small and defeated. His face may have looked red before, but it looked even redder now.

I wanted to know who the other man was, but he was facing at an angle away from me. All I could see was that he had long blond hair that hung straight down past his shoulders and a bushy strawberry blond beard. Despite the weather, he wore a sleeveless shirt that showed hard arms. He looked very much like a picture book version of a Norwegian Viking. I wanted to back up and get a better look, but then I would become obvious to Brock and something made me think that it was better he didn't think I was interested in him at all.

I looked once more in the mirror, then drove down the lane, turned left on Highway 89 and drove back toward South Lake Tahoe.

ELEVEN

That evening I sat with Street in front of the gas fire in her condo. Spot sprawled on the floor as if he were going to mold himself into it. His front legs were wide apart, head down so low that his jowls spread onto the carpet.

Street was wearing a burgundy velour lounging outfit that probably wasn't legal attire more than ten feet from a bedroom. If Rodin had seen her, he would have stopped sculpting nudes and draped all his figures in velour.

We had opened a Ravenwood Zinfandel. Street was making her standard seven drops last an hour, while I had a couple of glasses. I told her about Morella Meyer and the note that said she was to call someone named Strict after her dive.

"And she acted suspicious when you asked her about it?" Street said.

"More tense than suspicious. Almost irritated."

"Maybe there's an officer named Strict on the SLT force."

"I don't think so. I've seen the roster a few times and I think I would have remembered such a name. Besides, she'd logically be calling the person who hired her, and that was Mallory. But I'll call Mallory and ask him just to be sure." I picked up Street's phone and dialed Mallory at home.

"Sorry to bother you," I said when he answered.

"Why?" Mallory said. "Just because you're interrupting my favorite show?"

"Just a quick question. Was it you who hired Morella Meyer or was it someone else?"

"Me. Why?"

I ignored the why. "Which phone numbers did you give her to call you?"

"Just the ones on my card, of course. I didn't want her bothering me at home."

"I don't have your card handy. Can you tell me which numbers those were?"

"If you tell me why you're asking."

"I'm sure it's nothing," I said.

"Yeah, right."

"If it turns out to be something, I promise you'll get it all. If not, I don't want to waste your time."

Mallory grunted, then rattled off three numbers which I presumed were his office, his cell and dispatch.

"Thanks," I said. "One more thing. Anybody on the force named Strict?"

"What kind of a name is that?"

"I don't know. But not a cop name?"

"No," Mallory said, the gruffness in his voice indicating that he thought I was wasting his time.

I thanked him and hung up.

Street said, "Maybe Strict is Morella's nickname for Mallory. It fits."

"True. But do the numbers fit?" I wrote Mallory's numbers next to the various combinations I'd surmised from Morella's messy handwriting. Street came up with a couple more possibilities based on how numbers could be formed. Even so, we couldn't make anything match up. Either my memory was unclear, or else Strict was someone other than Mallory.

Street sipped another drop of wine. "You're thinking that Strict may be someone connected to the murder rather than someone connected to the police."

"It's possible. Morella may be collecting two fees for one job."

Street tapped her finger on the paper next to the phone

numbers. "You could call all of these possibilities and ask to speak to Strict."

While I ruminated on that, Street thought better of it and shook her head. "No, maybe that is a bad idea. Not only don't we know if Strict is a real name or some other kind of moniker, we don't even know if it is a man or woman. If Strict is the bad guy then a phone call would just tip him off and make him go deeper under cover."

"I'll run these numbers through the reverse directories and see what I can find out. If none of them connects to a name, I can always prevail on a colleague in San Francisco who has connections in the phone company."

"A cop you used to work with?"

"Yeah. Upton. But I still owe him a favor so I don't want to bug him until I've exhausted any other possibilities."

"Isn't he the one who helped you after..." Street stopped.

"Yes," I said. "After the shooting at the bank, I became an automaton going through the motions, numb from the neck up. Upton steered me through the inquiries and sat next to me during the long hours while the various commissions interrogated me. Without him, it would have been even harder."

Street put her hand on my arm and we sat in silence for a minute. She said, "You spoke to Janeen Kahale again today?"

"Yes." I drank some wine, then told Street about my afternoon with Janeen Kahale and her grandson Phillip.

When I was through, Street said, "Do you think that other people would have found out about the Kahale tradition of putting sacred items in the family shrine?"

"Absolutely. Janeen said that it was talked about freely. But she also said that the younger Kahales never paid much attention to the whole idea. Even so, I have to think that when other people heard about it they would be intrigued."

"What about the location?" Street asked. "Wouldn't that secret have been discovered by others?"

"Hard to say. You know how some people are. Tell them that

something is a secret and it just ensures that they pass it on sooner rather than later."

"Isn't that the truth," Street said.

"But in this case, it is a father/son thing, with only the two of them ever knowing at any one time. And it sounds like the location is not something that one could simply convey by telling. Those cliffs are huge. Apparently, the father has to personally take the son there. Janeen said it is a two or three day experience. That kind of ritual would be powerful and very effective in convincing the son of the significance of keeping the location private."

"The ultimate bonding between father and son."

"I would think so," I said.

"What about those fathers and sons who don't get along or even hate each other? The Kahale family must have had its share of strained relationships over the generations since this tradition was started."

"Certainly," I said. "And I have to think that here and there someone gave their best friend or their spouse a good idea of where the secret place was. Or even took them there and showed them the cache of goods. But my hunch is that almost no one knows of the place outside of Janeen's ex-husband Jasper. According to Janeen, now that her son Thos is dead Jasper will pass on the secret to his nephew John."

"Why are you so sure that almost no one else knows?" Street asked.

"Because of Thos's murder. I think that Janeen Kahale knew her son quite well. And from our discussion it seems that the only thing about his life that might draw in a killer is this secret. If the killer forced the information out of Thos, he probably killed Thos to cover his tracks. The very fact that Thos was killed suggests that Thos betrayed the secret, a secret that only Thos and Jasper knew." I said. "Turns out there is another death that may connect as well."

Street cocked her head.

I told her about how shortly after Jasper's father died of

cancer, his brother died in an auto accident on the road to the top of the Na Pali cliffs.

Street seemed appalled at the implication. "You couldn't fake the father's cancer, but you think that the brother knew where the shrine was and got killed because of it?"

"It's possible, although Janeen didn't think Jasper would have broken tradition and told his brother the location. So I have another theory.

"Let's assume," I continued, "that someone learned about the shrine and wanted to discover the location. He doesn't want to wait for a Kahale family member to die so that he can secretly follow Jasper to the shrine. Who knows how long that would take?"

"You're saying that this predator caused the accident that killed Jasper's brother just so that Jasper or Thos could be followed to the cliff?"

"Right," I said.

"If Jasper's father died of lung cancer, the bad guy could have followed Jasper then."

"Maybe he didn't know about the shrine then. Or maybe it was that event and the subsequent trip to the shrine that got talked about and alerted this guy in the first place."

"You have an imagination, I'll give you that."

"Morella Meyer just told me that imagination is more important than knowledge."

"She's quoting Einstein?" Street said.

"How'd you know Einstein said that?" I asked, astonished. Street never failed to surprise me.

"I learned about more than bugs in college," she said.

"So I see."

Street looked at me with amusement. "You're pretty convinced of this wild idea, huh?"

"Why do you say this is a wild idea?" I said. "Oh, you think that there are other reasons that cause people to get murdered besides secret shrines on the cliffs of Kauai."

"Well, now that you put it that way, probably not." Street grinned. "But it is a possibility. I remember reading about one or two murders in the paper over the years where there was no mention at all of shrines or sacred cliffs."

"It's usually in the follow-up article the next day," I said. "Remember, a detective has to be good at follow-through." I put my hand on her thigh. Her muscles were firm under the soft velour.

"You mean, you never just start something and then drop it before you've completed a full investigation?"

I turned sideways on the loveseat and gently traced the line of Street's jaw from her ear to her chin and then down her perfect neck to the hollow of her throat. "Never," I said. The top to her outfit had some buttons that never got hitched. That made it easy to trace lower.

"What if your investigation suggests that you make a closer examination?" Her breathing was audible.

"I keep at it until I've uncovered everything."

Later, I watched from her bed while Street slipped into a nightgown. She pulled a brush through her hair and saw me looking at her in the mirror. "I feel like a spotlight is trained on me," she said. "You're giving me one of those intense stares again."

"If I looked like a cross between Audrey Hepburn and a Formula One race car, you'd give me an intense stare, too."

"Don't," Street said. "I need to concentrate on finishing some homework this evening and then getting a good night's sleep."

I remembered that just yesterday Street had announced she was going solo again. I was expected to go home to my cabin and sleep alone for the first time in months. An ache grew in my solar plexus.

Street continued, "I'm supposed to turn in my bark beetle counts to the Forest Service tomorrow and I'm nowhere near ready."

"Can't you call them and tell them the data isn't analyzed

yet? Maybe say that you have to go on a sudden unexpected vacation?"

"I would if I were going on vacation."

"Which brings up something I forgot to ask you. Would you like to go to Kauai with me?"

Street stopped brushing her hair, dropped her arms to her sides and faced me. "When did you have in mind?"

"Tomorrow morning."

Street stared at me. Finally she said, "Thos was killed here in Tahoe. Shouldn't you be investigating here?"

"Mallory and a bunch of cops are investigating here. I'd be retracing their steps. Thos lived in Kauai. The other people who have died and were connected to Thos were in Kauai. And the only unusual thing in Thos's life that I've learned about is the shrine which is in Kauai. Makes sense I should start there. Maybe you and I could vacation a little when I'm not detecting."

Street turned and picked up the phone. "This is why the Forest Service installed voice mail," she said, dialing.

TWELVE

Street decided that since I was already in her bed, I might as well spend one more night with her. We didn't talk about the man who'd been watching my cabin from the clearing in the woods, but it probably played a part in her decision. I was grateful either way.

The next morning I took Spot home to feed him. When I let him out of the Jeep, he ran toward the cabin, but stopped short of the door and stuck his nose into wind-blown snow. He sniffed, pushing snow around with his snout. Then he moved a couple feet away and did the same. His tail was held high. Like a search dog, he was alerting to a scent. He moved another couple feet, plunged his nose back into the snow. He was obviously smelling a recent visitor, but any footprints were obscured by snow. It wasn't blowing now, but I remembered wind when I woke up. My visitor had come prior to that.

I looked for a card or note shoved into the crack of the door. There was none.

Spot didn't come to the door. He moved sideways toward the bedroom window. His movements became agitated, and he started panting. I followed him as he frantically sniffed the ground below the window. Next, he ran around the far side of the cabin and inspected the ground near the kitchen window.

"What is it, Spot? What do you smell?"

Spot jumped up, front paws on the kitchen windowsill, and sniffed the perimeter of the glass.

"Where else, Spot?" I walked down the back side of the cabin toward the deck. "Do you smell him on the deck?"

Spot came toward me, sniffing the air and the snow. Then he turned back and once again zeroed in on the kitchen window.

After a minute, I took Spot around the cabin and then through the four small rooms inside. He alerted to nothing else. That meant my visitor had not walked up to either the front door or the deck door and instead had only inspected the windows.

I fed Spot, then dialed Diamond Martinez. While I listened to the ringing on the other end, I gave a tap to my Calder mobile. Diamond didn't answer, so I dialed his pager and entered my number. The mobile still danced. A striking blend of art and engineering. Balance. Nearby, Rodin's lovers were still reaching for each other. Passion.

Diamond answered my page by showing up at the door to my little cabin fifteen minutes later.

Spot gave a single, deep woof at the knock. He pushed his snout out the door as I opened it. When Spot saw that it was Diamond calling, he shouldered me aside and stepped out to greet the sheriff's deputy, his tail beating the doorjamb like a Zydeco percussionist.

Diamond held out his hand for Spot to sniff. I often thought that one whiff of a hand told a dog a chronology going back several days.

"You learn anything about the Kahale murder, yet?" Diamond asked.

"I was going to ask you that," I said, "you being an official law enforcement officer."

"Naw. Douglas County has its hands full watching the sage brush grow. Besides, we Nevada types like to keep our distance from California. Lotta crazies over there." He bent his head toward the west side of the lake. Spot nosed Diamond's hand around until Diamond gave in and gave him an aggressive head rub with both hands. Spot leaned into it and Diamond had to move a foot back to brace himself.

"In Mexico we'd put a sheriff's badge on this dog and have

him sit at the entrance to town. Scare off the riffraff."

"I was thinking you could test-drive that very idea this coming week. Take his largeness down to Douglas County headquarters and teach him to play good cop to your bad cop. What do you think?"

Diamond looked up at me. "I think you sound like another gringo who can't be trusted. You're looking for a dog sitter. Why not come right out and say it? The least you could do is entice me with a bottle of scotch."

"Sorry, I forgot that bribing an officer of the law is de rigueur in Nevada. But what happened to tequila?"

Diamond shrugged. "Scotch is better. When you gonna be leaving?"

I turned and looked at the clock on the kitchen wall. "In about twenty minutes."

"And you'll be back in...?"

"I don't know. A few days to a week, maybe."

"You and Street eloping?"

I glanced at the Rodin sculpture. "I would if she would. I'd even put up with a real wedding."

"Me too, girl like that," Diamond said. "You got a location picked out for this impromptu vacation, or are you just going to go to the airport and see where the next flight is going?"

"Kauai," I said.

"One of the Hawaiian Islands."

I nodded. "You know my cell number," I said. "And you remember where I keep the spare house key."

"You want me to do your dishes, too?"

"Sure. But more important, the bathroom could really use a new coat of paint."

Diamond turned and pulled on Spot's collar. "C'mon, Spot. Let's see how big the back seat is on a Douglas County Explorer. And no drooling."

Spot eagerly walked away with Diamond, his tail held high. He got into the Explorer without a single look back at me.

Whatever happened to that one-man, devoted dog stuff?

I called out to Diamond.

He couldn't hear me through the window. He hit the button to roll it down. "Que dites-vous?"

"What are you saying?" I said.

"No, that's what *I* said. It's French for 'what are you saying.'"

"What happened to English?" I asked.

"Getting pretty good at that. Trying to learn Francais."

"Oui," I said. I gestured a lot to make up for what I didn't know. "I wanted you to comprendre we had a monsieur over in that clearing." I pointed. "Watching us. Deux nights ago."

"Bad guy?"

"Maybe. And this morning Spot smelled someone who didn't come to either of my doors but spent some time at my windows."

Diamond frowned. "I'll be attentif," he said as he drove away with my dog.

I went inside, rewound my answering machine tape, put out the trash, and took another look at the Calder mobile and the Rodin bronze. Rodin's female figure was lithe and perfect. Street was thinner, too thin, she always said, but she and the Rodin figure shared a lushness of curve. I touched one wire of the mobile and it danced away from me. I touched another and it too made a quick escape. At least, Street would be at my side every night in Hawaii. I threw some clothes in my bag and left.

I drove down the mountain, picked up Street a few minutes later and, after she reassured me that she had packed both the black one-piece and the red string bikini, we headed to the Reno Tahoe airport.

We checked the various morning flights, trying to figure out the best connection to Kauai. We compared arrival and departure times and concluded that the best way to go was to take a flight that was leaving immediately for Burbank and then take a shuttle to LAX. If there were no delays, we'd be able to catch a

United flight direct to Lihue, Kauai and avoid the inter-island hop from Honolulu.

Thirty minutes later, the jet left Reno, arced up over the mountains and climbed into the sky over Lake Tahoe. The deep blue of the lake was set off by the dazzling white of the snow-covered mountains. At the edge of the lake was the jagged face of Mt. Tallac. I could just about see the little house where Janeen and her grandson Phillip lived.

The plane turned south and in a few minutes we crossed over Yosemite Valley. We could see some of the world's highest waterfalls plunging down next to the largest granite walls on the planet. Half Dome had a cap of snow and stood like a benevolent king in a white beret looking over his magical kingdom. Our plane crossed out over the broad, flat Central Valley and began our descent into the Los Angeles area.

It was one of those perfect smogless days when one could see the blue Pacific even as we came down into Burbank. The contrast between the winter air of Tahoe and the warm air of L.A. was wonderful.

The shuttle seemed to be running late, but we made it across town to LAX in time for the late morning flight to Hawaii. The jet was packed. Fortunately I had an aisle seat so that I could periodically stretch my legs, much to the chagrin of at least one flight attendant who looked at me as if my extra length were something I'd contrived just to be a troublemaker.

While Street read, I used the phone in the seatback in front of me to do some exploring for lodging and finally found a condo on the east shore of Kauai. They'd had a last minute cancellation and thus could fit us into a sold-out season. I made reservations for the coming week, figuring that even if I reached nothing but dead ends in a day or two, Street and I could still use a vacation, walking the beach and sipping colored drinks with little umbrellas in them.

When we stepped out of the plane in Lihue, Kauai, the humidity was heavy and the air was thick with the powerful scents of tropical flowers.

"Get a whiff of that," I said.

"Unique aromas from unique flowers," Street said. "Hawaii is the most isolated island chain in the world. As a result it has an entire ecosystem of plants and animals that exist nowhere else."

I inhaled a long breath through my nose. "I suppose there are unique bugs as well."

"With unique aromas, too," she said.

"Aromas," I said. "My favorite euphemism for the odors of bugs."

"You know, you're very predictable when it comes to insects."

"Predictability," I said. "Good quality in a man, don't you think?"

"Not if it means you disrespect the bugs." Street's training as an entomologist made her constantly aware of, and empathetic with, a world of creatures that the rest of us swat at and step on.

"I respect insects. Especially some of the Hawaiian ones. I seem to recall something about poisonous centipedes."

"Actually, centipedes are the most dangerous thing on the islands. But they aren't insects. Centipedes are the same Phylum, but a different class. Chilopoda, I think. A completely different animal."

"I always get that wrong," I said. "From now on I'll just call them creepy crawlers."

"That, as applied to centipedes, I'd agree with." Street hugged herself and seemed to shiver in the tropical air. "Did you know that centipedes are carnivorous? They kill their prey with a venomous bite."

"If they bite a human, is it fatal?"

"Not usually. It falls into what I call a category five bite, which is to say it probably won't kill you, but you'll spend some time wishing it had."

"Is there an antidote?"

"No. With category five bites, the best treatment is liquor.

Lots of it, for several days running."

"Maybe we should stop at the airport bar and get some drinks now, just in case."

"I don't think this little airport has a bar."

I looked around and didn't see one. "Do you know what places to avoid if you don't want to be centipede dinner?" I asked.

"They hang out in the jungle. Dark, wet, leafy kinds of places."

"Like the Na Pali cliffs I want to go explore?"

"Yes."

"Well, I'm lots bigger than a centipede."

"Not as much bigger as you think," Street said. "Centipedes can grow to a foot."

"Excuse me?" A small wave of discontent rose within.

She nodded, her face somber in the glow of the late afternoon sun.

A palm-covered walkway took us across to the rental car offices. In the distance was a thunderstorm, its thrusting cauliflower head glowing pink in the approaching sunset.

The woman at the counter gave us our car keys along with a map and directions to our condo. We stopped at a market and picked up basic provisions, Sierra Nevada Pale Ale, wine, some fixings for dinner and breakfast. Then we headed north up the coast.

We turned down a lonely road, came to a small sign that announced our lodging and soon were ensconced in a second-floor luxury condo a few yards from the beach.

After we'd cooked a delicious dinner of fresh-caught tuna with bread, salad and a Pinot Noir from Oregon, Street opened the slider. The ocean breeze made the curtains billow enticingly. Street slipped past them and walked out onto the lanai. I snuggled up behind her at the railing.

Nightfall had come. The moon was bright, yet the rest of the sky, free of the glow of civilization, was black with a million stars. Below us was the graceful blue oval of the swimming pool, lit with underwater lights. Above it shimmered a canopy of palm trees, their fronds glistening and clicking as they waved in the wind. Around the pool stretched a spacious lawn and, beyond it, the ocean.

Street turned, leaned her back against the railing and said, "This is so special, you should probably commemorate it by kissing me."

Which I did.

The heat of her high metabolism was significant.

As if in answer to my thought she said, "It's so warm here a girl hardly needs any clothes," she mumbled through our kiss.

"Really?" I said. "Maybe we better check it out."

Which we did.

THIRTEEN

Street was in the tub the next morning when I padded into the bathroom. I took a long look at her. "If you'd been Degas' model he never would have painted ballerinas. He would have just stayed with bathers."

"For that matter," Street said, "you could model."

I glanced at myself in the mirror and quickly sucked in my stomach. "Oh, yeah?"

"Yeah. For one of those butt calendars."

"Street, my sweet, I didn't know you were aware of such things."

"That art you study in your books. It's all there. Line and form and such."

I tried to look around and back at my butt. I turned for a better angle in the mirror. "Think there's any money in it?"

"Depends on how good you are at posing," Street said.

"Which do you like?" I tried a pose. "Like this?"

Street giggled.

"Or like this?"

Street's giggle became a hearty guffaw. "Okay, maybe it's not the best idea," she said.

I turned away, wounded. "If you want me, I'll be on the lanai." I did an Elvis-style hip thrust and strutted out of the bathroom.

We drank our coffee out on the lanai and had a breakfast of mango and pineapple.

Street wore a pair of yellow shorts and a white blouse that didn't quite cover up her midriff. Her feet were up on the lanai railing, her ankles catching the sun. I didn't know what to stare at.

"Did you hear that loud clicking last night?" she said. "It sounded like someone was tapping on a window with a key. I got up, but saw nothing."

"Sorry, I was sleeping."

"Not fair," she said. "Whenever we have energetic romance you sleep like the dead and I'm awake half the night."

"Energetic romance?"

"You would call it raw, raucous sex?" she said.

I grinned at her.

Street picked up our coffee cups and filled them from a pump-action thermos. "Anyway, you wouldn't believe the sound. So I came out here on the lanai and discovered the clicking noise came from geckos."

I gave her a questioning look.

"Geckos are little lizards that eat cockroaches."

I thought about that. "My new best buddies."

"So what is your plan for today?" Street asked.

"Today I look up Thos's father Jasper and Thos's cousin John Kahale junior."

"John junior is the one who is next in line to learn the location of the sacred cliff shrine?"

"Yeah. Janeen said that because Thos was their only son, Jasper would normally tell his closest brother, John senior. But because he died in the car accident, Jasper must now tell his nephew John junior instead. Janeen didn't know if Jasper has told him yet, but I wouldn't be surprised if he had. Being the only one with the knowledge of the shrine's location would be scary. Hundreds of years of family tradition would be dependent on you being very careful not to have a sudden accident."

"Look both ways before you cross the street," Street said.

"Right. Do you want to come along with me, or are you

going to sit here and look beautiful all day?"

"Why don't I explore the beach?" she said. "It looks like it goes for miles. When you've got something on the agenda that you know will be exciting, I'll tag along."

"Are you going to do your beach exploration in one of your swimsuits? If so, I'll be forced to come along and fend off the modeling agents and onlookers."

"How about I wear baggy shorts and a baggy shirt?"

"Good idea," I said, then went inside to make inquiries.

I got Jasper Kahale's number through Information. He said he'd see me after lunch at his home in Poipu on the south side of the island.

Next, I called the helicopter company that John junior flew for. The woman who answered said he was off today and the next. I booked his first flight the following morning.

When I was done on the phone, I found Street reading Michener's Hawaii. I gave her my schedule and asked if she'd like to join me on the helicopter ride.

"Day after tomorrow at nine o'clock. Just you and me," I said. "A private carriage ride."

Her eyes widened. "Would he take us to the shrine?"

"I don't think he'd tell us the location, but I don't see why he wouldn't give us a tour of the Na Pali cliffs in general. From the brochure the rental car company gave us, it seems that all the helicopter companies go to the cliffs."

"I'd love to go." She was sitting back on the deck chair. She bounced her toes against the lanai railing. The movement made her calf muscles flex. My heart thumped. She must have seen me notice.

"What are you staring at now?" she said.

"Maybe we should cancel all these plans and concentrate on – what did you call it – romantic energizing?"

"No, I didn't call it that, and you have work to do." She waved me away with her hand. "Go. Now. Away. Do your work. We can energize some other time." She picked up the Michener book.

FOURTEEN

I drove by several expensive resort hotels on the south side of Kauai to get to Jasper Kahale's house, a small, neat box made of concrete block. The house was painted bright turquoise with dark green shutters. It sat directly back from a great beach, a wide swath of white sand with crashing waves the same color as the house. A narrow, cracked sidewalk led around to the side where I knocked on a green door that had prickly pear cactus growing in the dirt on either side. I watched the waves for a long minute before I finally heard noises on the other side of the door. The knob turned and the door opened.

The short, broad man standing in the dark entry was older than his ex-wife Janeen by a decade or more, yet his dark and supple Hawaiian skin had few wrinkles. He wore an orange, floral Hawaiian shirt. The shirt hung over baggy blue shorts that seemed to be slipping off his large belly. His legs were as sturdy as Koa trees and his bare feet were wide and gnarled. Despite his age he still looked very strong.

"Aloha," he said with a sad smile.

"Mr. Kahale, I'm Owen McKenna. Thank you for seeing me."

He stepped out into the sunlight and leaned his head back to look up at me. He shook my hand, holding my forearm with his left hand. "Call me Jasper. Everyone does. Mr. Kahale was my father." He smiled, but it didn't hide his sadness. He still held onto my hand and arm. His own arms were scratched in several places.

"Good to meet you, Jasper. Tell me, these cactus plants next to your door, aren't they unusual in the tropics? I thought Hawaii would have too much rain for cactus."

"C'mere, Onan," Jasper said, finally letting go of my hand.

"Owen."

"Owen," he repeated. Jasper turned, reached a thick hand back up to my elbow and steered me out toward the beach that was his backyard. He walked stiffly and had a slight bend in his back so that he leaned a few degrees to the left.

When we were away from the house, he pointed inland toward where the land rose up to thick clouds. "See all those clouds? They cover the summit of Mount Waiale'ale. That's our volcano. Rainiest spot on earth. Four hundred and fifty inches a year. But the trades that carry all the moisture come from the other side of the island." He turned and looked up at me, his eyes searching mine.

"So when the winds blow up the mountain from the other side they drop all their rain, right?" I said.

He nodded. "By the time the air gets back down to this side of the island it is drier than..." He faded off, then seemed to wake with a start. "They call it a rain shadow."

"I follow," I said. "This side of the island is a desert."

"Not a desert, but arid. Yet up there is the wettest place you'd ever hope to see. Just a few miles apart. Amazing, huh?"

"Amazing," I agreed.

"Omen, what can I get you to drink?"

"Owen."

"Right. Owen. What can I get you to drink? I've got Mountain Dew. You want a Mountain Dew?"

"Sure."

I followed him inside. It was dark and cool in the block house and the roar of the waves was diminished.

The inside of the little house was as neat as the outside. There were two faded blue wicker chairs arranged side by side. In front of them was an old TV on a rickety metal stand with plastic wheels, a loud game show filling the house with commotion. A wicker couch sat near the end of the room and behind it was a black surfboard with yellow stripes. A bulletin board was covered in faded, curled pictures of children, most of a boy at a variety of ages, some of a girl, all when she was quite young. No doubt they were Thos and Shelcie.

"Have a seat," Jasper said. He punched a switch on the TV and the screen went dark, clicking with static discharge. "Owen, right?"

"Right," I said.

Jasper walked into the kitchen area from the living room. I browsed the pictures on the bulletin board.

Thos's pictures were mostly of sports, riding his surfboard down a large curling wave, launching his bicycle into the air off a dirt jump, racing down a steep road on his Roller Blades.

Balance.

Shelcie's pictures showed her acting or acting up. She sat in front of a chocolate cake, her face covered in frosting so that only her huge grin and eyes showed through. In another photo she was a little girl dressed up in women's clothes, putting on lipstick in front of a mirror. In a third, she stood at a mouth-high fence post out in a field, the post being like a microphone stand. Her arms were stretched out like Judy Garland's, her head was back, eyes closed. Maybe she was singing Somewhere Over The Rainbow.

Passion.

"Those are my boy and girl," Jasper said. "The best little kids you could have. But then, kids have a way of growing up on you. Do you have kids?"

"No."

"Well, you can never predict what will happen to them when they grow up. Every parent eventually finds out that no matter how hard you try, there are some hard shocks coming down the road. You think you have it all figured out..." Jasper's voice trailed off.

I turned to see him staring, unfocused, toward the bulletin board.

He gave a little jerk and resumed talking. "Believe me, you're not ready for it when it happens."

I sat down in one of the wicker chairs as he got out two glasses, filled them with ice from a shallow bucket in the top compartment of an ancient refrigerator and then carefully poured yellow-green soda from a large plastic bottle. The soft drink fit well into the tropical color scheme of the room. Jasper brought the drinks out, handed one to me and, still listing sideways, sat down next to me in the matching wicker chair. We were side by side facing the dark screen of the TV.

Jasper took a drink. "You said on the telephone that you've come to talk about my boy."

"Yes, sir, if I may."

"He was a good boy," Jasper said, his words suddenly thick. He tried to clear his throat. "I don't understand why..." He stopped and coughed and wiped his eyes with the back of his hand.

"I'm sorry about Thos," I said, turning in my chair toward him.

Jasper was still facing the blank TV. He cried softly for a minute. "Is your drink okay?" he finally said.

"Yes, thank you."

"You said you are looking into his death. Why?"

"Because your ex-wife hired me to. She thinks that I can concentrate on his murder in a way that the police cannot."

"Janeen," he muttered softly. "I still love her. Every day I feel bad that it didn't work out. I feel like not only did I cause her to divorce me, but that something I did set in motion a chain of events that led to Thos's death." Jasper was staring unfocused at the dark TV screen.

"What do you mean?"

"Nothing specific. It just seems that if you traced back everything in Thos's life you'd come back to me. If I'd done something different, given different advice maybe..." his voice was thick. "I don't know." Jasper shook his head back and forth.

"Why didn't your marriage work out?" I asked. I'd already heard Janeen's side, but sometimes people have dramatically different views.

"I never quite knew why. I tried hard to make her happy, but she said I wasn't right for her. It tore a hole in me when she left." He drank his soda pop. "Seemed like I didn't do such a good job at work after that. The promotions I should have gotten went to other, younger men. They said they wanted me to stay on, but I knew better.

"They made me a decent offer to take early retirement. Of course, social security is a lot less when you do that, and half my pension still goes to Janeen. But I don't mind. She deserves it. She was a good wife while I had her and a good mother and I bear her no ill will. She is raising Shelcie's child. It only makes sense that some of my money would go to that. Besides, this place is paid for and I don't have need for much.

"You said you were a detective, Owen. So maybe you know if I'm wrong about this. Some murders, maybe it is for money or something, and maybe it means the victim didn't do anything wrong to become a target, right? From what I heard about Thos, getting shot in the lake, his wallet still in his pants on the shore, it sounds like he was involved in something bad, doesn't it?" Jasper Kahale turned in his chair and looked at me. "Am I right?"

"I don't think that is the case, Jasper. From what I've heard Thos was a fine young man with a thriving business." I sipped my drink. "Were you close to your son? Did you see each other much?"

Jasper looked toward the wall. "Almost every Sunday night when he was on the island. We'd have dinner. Thos usually picked me up and he'd take me out to a restaurant. Sometimes he'd drive us up to the north side of the island where he lives. We'd stop at his place first for drinks, then go to a restaurant in Princeville. He knew them all, of course, because he sold them wine. Thos was a good son. It was a precious thing for me with so many of my old friends having gone to see Lono. Now Thos has made his journey, too."

"Lono?"

"Lono is our god." Jasper paused and seemed to disconnect from our conversation. Once again, he gave a little jerk of his head and resumed talking. "Lono comes from the sea and is responsible for all the good that Hawaiians have in their lives. The plentiful harvests, the fish, the perfect weather, even the sunsets. You may have heard of him in regards to Captain Cook."

"Sorry, my history of Hawaii is weak," I said.

"Lono comes twice a year, always from the sea. When Cook discovered Hawaii, as you white people say, his arrival coincided with Lono's timing. And because my ancestors had never seen large square riggers or men with pale skin, they got confused and thought Cook was Lono."

"No doubt, that made things easier for Cook," I said.

"Yes." Jasper drank more Mountain Dew. "Hawaiians are naturally peaceful and friendly anyway, but thinking Cook was our great god made my people very giving of favors, even down to our young women joining Cook's men on his ships. In return, Cook's men gave the islands venereal disease. In a few years V.D. had spread throughout the islands."

"What a legacy to leave behind," I said.

"Actually, V.D. was only one of several deadly diseases brought here by white men." Jasper turned to look at me directly. "My family knew Captain Cook."

"Really," I said.

"When Cook discovered Hawaii, it was the island of Kauai he came to first. I always heard about it from my father. Captain Cook met one of my great, great, great, great grandfathers. My ancestors invited Cook and some of his men over to a big pork roast on the beach. Of course, they still thought Cook was the god Lono. Two days later Cook invited them onto his ship where he gave them a piece of tableware."

"You mean like a fork or a spoon?"

"Right. Hawaiians never had metal. The only place they'd seen metal was nails in old pieces of wood washed up from distant shipwrecks. So any metal fascinated them."

"Could Cook's tableware have ended up in the cliff shrine?"

"How did you know about... Oh, Janeen told you."

I nodded.

"I don't know what happened to Cook's gift. But who would care? The only really valuable thing my family ever had is gone," Jasper continued.

"What was that?"

"A gift from Mark Twain."

At this my doubts about Cook's visit grew ten times stronger. "Your family knew Mark Twain?"

Jasper nodded. "Twain came to Kauai about a hundred years after Captain Cook. My family was educated by then and spoke some English. They had heard of this young writer who was coming to Oahu in March. This was back in eighteen sixty-six. After Oahu, he came here to Kauai. They invited him to dinner and he accepted. The next day they took him up Waimea Canyon. He ended up staying with them for a few days. It was a big celebration."

Jasper's stories were beginning to sound like one of Twain's tall tales. Then again, I remembered reading about Twain visiting Hawaii. Further, unlike Captain Cook, Twain spent time in Tahoe while working for the newspaper in Virginia City. Mark Twain and the Kahale family shared that much, a connection to both Kauai and Tahoe.

"Twain gave your family a gift?"

"Yes. It was similar to when Captain Cook came to dinner. A couple days after Twain had spent time with my family, he returned with a thank you gift. I never saw it because it was lost a few years later. But I heard about it from my grandfather. He remembered it well."

"What was it?"

"It was a leather notebook, dark brown with the letters

MT embossed on the cover. Twain used the notebook for his newspaper letters that he sent back to California."

"Did you read that about Twain? That he wrote letters back to a California newspaper about his Pacific travels?"

Jasper looked startled. "Me? I've never read anything about Twain. I just remember what my granddad said. My granddad was a boy at the time and he had admired the notebook when Twain came to dinner. So when Twain came back he had torn out the pages with the newspaper letters. He gave the rest of the notebook to my granddad. Of course, my granddad thought it was the greatest thing, getting a notebook that had belonged to a famous writer. What he didn't realize until the next day was that there was writing inside."

"A letter?"

Jasper shook his head. "No, a story."

FIFTEEN

Jasper said, "Twain's story was called The Amazing Island Boy And His Trick Wood. It was about a boy my granddad's age who had a stick of Hawaiian Koa wood he claimed was magical. He could cast a spell with it. He used it to trick his gullible friends out of money by getting them to pay to be put under a spell."

"What happened to the notebook?"

"My granddad kept the notebook in a little box next to his bed. The year he turned twelve a hurricane struck in the night. A storm surge flooded their thatched hut. They ran out and hung onto a palm tree as their house washed out to sea."

"Could your granddad have grabbed Twain's notebook and held onto it as he escaped the hurricane?"

Jasper looked startled. "I suppose so, but if he'd kept it he would have proudly showed it to everyone, wouldn't he?"

We were both silent for a moment. Finally, I said, "Jasper, did your son have any enemies that you know of?"

Jasper shook his head. "No. None at all. Now don't get me wrong. He wasn't the friendliest boy. Once I told him he should get out more and he said, 'Dad, I'm not a party animal like you.' Then he told me he spent his spare time alone dreaming up the next phase of his business."

"What was that?"

"He wanted to start a vineyard and winery in California. But he said he needed a lot of money first, so it was going to be awhile." Jasper was silent for a moment. "I still don't understand that, people who like to spend time alone. But then, look at me. I like to be around people, yet here I am almost always by myself." His eyes went vacant for a moment, then his head jerked again.

"Even so, Thos didn't have any enemies. I even wondered if maybe he stole some other boy's girl. Thos was handsome and polite and could get a gal's attention. But it wasn't his way. No, whatever he got involved in, it was something else."

Jasper put his hand on my forearm. "My boy was a man of honor, Owen. I think he got into a moral dilemma. Maybe he learned something he felt he had to bring to the authorities. Maybe he got killed for it."

Jasper drained the last of his drink and chewed on an ice cube. "Or else someone wanted a piece of his business. Thos told me that some of the wine deals were real money makers. He said there's a company that owns eight restaurants in Honolulu. They'd order five hundred cases at a time. Then Thos had the wineries in California, what's it called? Drop-ship. Thos never touched the wine. But he made the sale and did the billing. He'd pocket something like ten thousand dollars on five hundred cases.

"And recently, he's started his own brand. Pacific Blue. I forget exactly how it works, but he's lined up a supplier, some big winery in Mendocino County. It's called private labeling. Thos puts his Pacific Blue label on it. He's even got a Polynesian logo, kind of an art thing." Jasper was talking as if Thos were still alive.

"Anyway, maybe someone wanted to take that business away from him."

"I don't know, Jasper. It doesn't seem like a motive for murder. I know from my small detective agency that the expenses generated by any small business are substantial. Ten thousand from a single sale would seem like a lot to a man on a salary, but it is just another opportunity to pay the rent, utilities and payroll taxes. I don't think that kind of business is worth killing over."

"Yeah, I suppose you're right."

"What happens to Thos's business?"

"He told me he was leaving it to me. I told him that was

crazy. How could he die before me? But there it is. Thos wanted it that way. All because I was interested in what he did. Maybe I'll give it to his employees. There's a General Manager name of Brian Malone and a few workers. Malone's a nice guy, but too meek to run a business if you ask me."

"Where does Malone live?"

"Princeville. Not far from Thos."

"What about Thos's townhouse?"

"It's to be sold with half going to Shelcie and half to a trust for her son Phillip."

"Jasper, what about the cliff where your family puts sacred items of the deceased? I'm wondering if someone might have forced Thos to tell them the location and then killed him to cover it up."

"Why? So they could sneak up there and steal knickknacks and such? That's ridiculous."

"Isn't there anything valuable in the family shrine?"

Jasper took a long time answering. "I can't say."

"You can't, or you won't?"

"Both," Jasper said. "I can't because I've never gone through all the stuff left there over the centuries. But if I did know what all is there, I wouldn't tell anyone. It would violate the rules. I explained them to Thos. But now that he's dead, I had to take my nephew John junior to the shrine two days ago and explain it all to him." Jasper's voice was thick again. "It was difficult, let me tell you. I put Thos's sacred things in the cave."

"Janeen said Thos didn't designate any items."

"No. I had to choose. I took the three biggest surfing trophies because those were what he was proudest of. John junior carried them in a pack because they were heavy."

"Can you give me an idea of the kinds of things that are in the shrine? Would that violate the rule?"

Jasper thought for a minute. "It's mostly just junk up there. And it's been pawed over by countless animals. Anything fabric rotted long ago. Some stuff's been dragged away or half eaten.

Little critters have made nests. It's a mess if you want to know the truth."

"Is there any protection from the elements?"

Jasper nodded. "Sure, if you mean rain and wind. It's in a cave that goes back into the cliff about fifty feet. A volcanic tube from when the island was formed. The opening is overhung with jungle so no one would ever see it. There's a split in one side of the tube. Between the split and the main opening, some light gets in so you can see a little. Rain and humans are kept out. But animals and bugs and humidity and rot have been present from the beginning." Jasper shook his head. "No protection from any of that."

"How long has your family had the shrine?"

"As far as I know, it was started when my first ancestors arrived."

"Before Captain Cook came to the islands?"

"Long time before. Cook came in the seventeen hundreds. My family arrived about five hundred years before that."

"From Polynesia?" I asked.

"Yes. They built huge canoes for journeys that went thousands of miles across the open ocean. They were navigating by the stars and had settled most of the islands in the Pacific back when your ancestors were still in the dark ages."

"How did the Polynesians find Hawaii with it being the most isolated island chain in the world?"

"Birds."

"I don't understand."

Jasper pushed up from his chair and refilled his glass. He gestured toward me with the bottle. "Want some more?"

"No thanks."

Jasper came back and sat down. He sipped his drink. "My ancestors knew from their travels that the ocean to the north was largely empty. But there were birds that flew that way. Even when the people were far out at sea they saw birds fly past them going north. They knew from the kind of birds and from the season that they weren't migrating to a cold spot. That meant there was land to the north. Temperate land.

"So they mounted a major expedition north and brought enough food and water and people to start a new colony. They also brought goats and pigs and all of their special plants. They sailed and paddled and navigated by the stars at night. Sure enough, they found the Hawaiian Islands right where they expected."

"Jasper, did the Polynesians have gold or other precious stones or metals?

"You're wondering if there's gold in my family shrine? The answer is no."

"There must be some valuable jewelry."

"Like I told my brother John..." Jasper's words faded. Then he gave his head a single shake as if coming out of a trance.

"What did you tell your brother?"

Jasper looked at me for a moment. "Nothing," he finally said.

"Jasper, it is important that I know if you gave anyone any information about the shrine or its contents. It could help me find Thos's killer."

"I can tell you there's nothing valuable there. Anyway, you're asking too many questions about our sacred place. It can't be laid bare for anyone. My ancestors deserve some privacy."

"Is there any way I could convince you to show me the shrine? I'd promise never to tell anyone."

Jasper shook his head.

"I could go there blindfolded. That would guarantee its location would remain secret."

"No," Jasper said.

"But what if the shrine caused someone to murder your son?"

"No. Showing anyone else would violate the sacred trust my father taught me about. And Thos would still be dead. Besides, I don't believe that Thos was killed for any reason having to do with the family shrine."

I stood and walked over to the bulletin board and looked at the snapshots. One showed a young Thos and Shelcie standing with a weathered man in the stern of an old wooden fishing boat. He looked like an even wider version of Jasper. His height may have been greater than his width, but not by much. Yet, as with Jasper, his girth seemed less like obesity and more like the muscles of a Suma Wrestler. "This man, was he your father?"

Jasper nodded. "Alvin Kahale. The Tuna Terror, the other fishermen called him. He had taken a tuna skeleton and poured some kind of glue over it so the bones stuck together. He strapped the skeleton to the stern of his boat and it stayed there for years, gradually shedding bones here and there. The boat, the skeleton and my dad all fell apart at about the same rate."

"I think Janeen told me your father died of lung cancer. Is that right?"

"Yes. He liked his cigars."

"It was fairly recently?"

Jasper gazed at the wall.

"Jasper?"

The man gave a start. "A month ago." His voice sounded pained. "He lived with me the last couple years. Then he went to the Holy Cross Medical Center. He hated it. But he had too much pain. He needed morphine. What does that have to do with Thos?"

"Nothing. I was just curious. What about your brother? That was even more recent, wasn't it?"

"Yes. Car accident a week after my dad died. You're not suggesting his death is connected to Thos, are you?"

"Like I said, I'm only asking questions. The more I learn about Thos and his family, the better I will be able to see into his life and learn why he was killed."

I could tell that Jasper was getting tired. I asked if I could call on him again. He nodded.

"Mahalo, Owen."

"You're welcome," I said as I left.

SIXTEEN

I was at the Holy Cross Medical Center at 9:00 a.m. the next morning. The receptionist smiled at me as I approached.

"Good morning," I said. "My name is Owen McKenna." I opened my wallet and showed her my license. "I'm a private investigator looking into a matter connected to Alvin Kahale. I understand he spent his last days in your hospital." The woman's smile went flat. "I would like to speak to his physician. Can you please tell me who that would be?"

The woman stared at me for several seconds, then pulled out a chart and ran her finger down it. "That would be Dr. Fujimoto." She scanned an appointment book. "The doctor has a cancellation at ten-thirty. He may be able to speak with you for a few minutes at that time if you'd like to come back then."

"Thanks. I'll be here."

I strolled up and down the corridors and rode the elevator, looking like a casual visitor as I noted the lack of security. There were several doors on each of two floors. None of them was locked. Outside each exit door was a single security light on the wall above. Except for the parking lot, it appeared the nearby grounds would be dark at night. The few people on staff had their hands full with medical duties and did not seem to notice my movements. I was back at the reception desk at 10:30.

"He should be here any minute now," the woman said.

A moment later, a small man around 30 years of age approached from around a corner. He wore a white coat, walked fast and carried two clipboards thick with papers.

"Doctor," the receptionist called out. "This man is Mr. McKenna and he wants to talk to you for a minute."

The doctor looked up at me, then made a point of looking at his watch. "I'm sorry, I'm very busy. If you'll call my office…"

"Certainly," I said. "But first I have a quick question. My name's Owen McKenna. I'm a private investigator looking into a murder that is connected to Alvin Kahale." At the mention of the word murder the receptionist inhaled sharply. "I understand you were the attending physician at the end?"

Dr. Fujimoto looked at me with suspicion. "And your question is…"

"He died of lung cancer, is that correct?"

"Yes."

"Was there anything suspicious about the death?"

The doctor sighed. "I just acknowledged that he died of lung cancer. Short of learning the motives of a very nasty tumor, no, there was nothing suspicious about it."

"Could someone have hastened his death?"

"You mean slipping sodium pentothal into his IV drip like on TV? Of course. We do it all the time. That way, the most lucrative part of our payment from the insurance company is cut short." His derision was thick. I wondered why.

"Doctor, while waiting for you, I've been through the entire hospital, in and out of two separate supply rooms and through the staff lunch room without anyone noticing. The outer doors are all unlocked and there is little or no lighting on the grounds. There seems to be no security."

"Last I looked, this wasn't South Central L.A., but a tiny hospital on a small island in the middle of the Pacific." A door next to us abruptly opened and a female nurse came out. The doctor glared at her.

"Oh, excuse me," she said as she hustled away.

"How long would a patient in Alvin Kahale's condition be expected to live?" I asked.

"Listen, Mr. Detective, you're not a lawyer and this is not

a deposition. I have no more time for your insinuations." He began to walk past me.

I put my arm out in front of him and leaned against the wall. "If you don't answer my questions, I'll get a lawyer and you'll get a summons for a deposition."

Dr. Fujimoto sighed again. He was good at sighs. "He was on life support. We expected him to die at any moment."

"But if he had lived longer, you wouldn't have been surprised?"

"Perhaps not."

"How long could he have lived on life support before you would have been surprised?"

"At four months I would have called in my colleagues to check out the amazing living vegetable."

"So you believe he died of natural causes."

"Look, I don't understand why you are pursuing such a ridiculous idea. The man was dying. He had a month or two at the outside. Why on earth would someone murder a dying man?"

"Good question, doc." I turned away from him and pulled out one of my cards. I picked up the pen that was chained to the receptionist's desk and jotted down the name of the condo where we were staying. Dr. Fujimoto hurried away down the hall. I handed the card to the receptionist. "If you or the doctor think of anything unusual regarding Alvin Kahale's death, please give me a call. Another life may depend on it," I said as I walked out. It was a lie, but it sounded good. Then again, maybe it didn't sound good. But maybe it wasn't a lie, either.

Street was gone when I got back to the condo. Looking around for any note she may have left, I noticed that the message light on the phone was blinking. I dialed the front office. "I have a message?"

"Yes. Well, not really. A woman called just a minute ago. She didn't leave a number. She said she'd call back at one o'clock."

"Thank you. I'll be here at one."

I opened the refrigerator for a Coke. I was reaching for the six-pack when I stopped. It was on the top shelf, but had been moved from the right side to the left. I remembered the position from when I'd gotten a can the day before. It looked like the six-pack had been moved as if to see whether anything was behind it. I didn't think Street would have moved it because she didn't drink soda. There was nothing else on the top shelf and Street had put away the groceries we'd purchased, so she'd know there was nothing behind the Coke.

I left the Coke where it was and walked around the condo. It was obvious that the housekeeper hadn't been through yet because the bed hadn't been made. I couldn't tell if anything else had been shifted. I picked up the phone and dialed the office again.

"The housekeeper who does our unit," I said when the desk clerk answered. "Has he or she been here, yet?"

"No, sir. I'm so sorry. We are short on staff today. Perhaps three o'clock? Will that be okay?"

"Three o'clock will be fine. Is there anyone else who came into our unit this morning?"

"No, sir. We had a plummer up to the unit next to yours, but not yours."

"Thank you."

I was still looking around the condo when the phone rang at five after one. "Owen McKenna," I answered.

"Mr. McKenna, I work at the Holy Cross Medical Center." A female voice, very high, Asian accent, frightened. No woman I'd spoken to there unless she was trying to disguise her voice.

"Are you a nurse?"

"I don't want to say. I'm calling from a pay phone."

"You want to tell me something about Alvin Kahale's death," I said.

"Yes. I overheard something the day after he died. A nurse was talking to Dr. Fujimoto. In whispers. The nurse was on duty when Mr. Kahale's monitor gave the signal that his heart stopped. It was five in the morning. There was a no-resuscitate order on the patient. The nurse said he went in and found Mr. Kahale's pillow moved out from under the dead man's head. The pillow had been in place earlier and no one else had been on the floor. So he told Dr. Fujimoto he didn't think the man could have moved his pillow as he died."

"What did the doctor say?" I asked.

"The doctor said he agreed. The man was in a coma and could not have moved his pillow."

"What else did they say?" I asked.

"Sorry. I have to go." The line went dead.

Street walked in as I hung up. "What was that about?"

"If I am to believe this caller, Jasper's father was suffocated and the hospital is covering up."

"Do you believe it?"

"It squares with the belligerence of the doctor I spoke to. Otherwise, I have no reason to believe it except for my suspicion that someone is killing Kahales in an effort to learn the location of the shrine. And the direct evidence for that is non-existent."

"Then why do you suspect it?"

"Because Jasper's father Alvin, brother John senior and son Thos are all dead in the space of a month, one a confirmed murder and the others possible murders. Being a detective makes me inclined to connect up the deaths. In Thos's suicide note he mentioned being responsible for three deaths besides his own. Perhaps his grandfather and uncle are two of them. If so, I need another body."

"And the point of the killings?" Street said.

"The killer wants the loot in the shrine. The more dead Kahales from the patriarchal family line, the more trips to the shrine. The killer could try and follow to learn its location.

"By the way," I continued, "have you moved the Coke in the refrigerator?"

"No, why?"

"Just curious. I thought it had been moved. But I suppose I'm suffering from premature senility."

SEVENTEEN

The following morning it was raining hard when we woke up. By the time we checked in at the helicopter tour office in Lihue, the clouds had parted and the sun was streaming down through misty air. Street and I were driven in the company's van out to the airport helipad where John Kahale junior was doing his preflight check, walking around the metal bird, doing a visual inspection of all its components.

He was in his early thirties and built much like his uncle Jasper, short and wide with the bulky musculature of a bulldog filling out his brown skin. Like Jasper, John wore a loose, short-sleeved Hawaiian shirt vibrant with bright reds and oranges in a bold, floral pattern. Street and I walked across the wet and steaming tarmac and introduced ourselves.

"Aloha. A pleasure to meet you both," he said, shaking hands, his eyes making a quick detour toward Street's legs and black miniskirt. I noticed that his forearms were scratched and abraded. His trip to the family shrine must have involved a trip through dense jungle.

"You've signed up for the grand tour which takes seventy-five minutes." He looked up at the sky. "The weather was iffy at dawn, but it's shaping up to be a great day." He turned to me. "How much do you weigh, Owen?"

"Two-fifteen."

"And you, Street?"

Street turned and looked at me.

"He needs to know for the helicopter's center of gravity," I said. "Where to seat us and such. Not that you weigh enough to matter."

"My thought, as well," John said, grinning. "But the F.A.A. would have my license if I weren't thorough."

"One-oh-eight," Street said.

"Then we can all sit in the front. Street, you'll be in the middle and you, Owen, right seat."

We walked under the stationary main rotor. The long blades drooped dramatically under their own weight. Street climbed in as John held the door. When she was seated, John leaned in and showed her how to buckle her lap and shoulder belts. He removed a headset and microphone from a cradle on the ceiling and helped Street adjust it over her ears. I was next, climbing into the right front seat and donning my belts and headset. John walked around to the left seat and, after putting on his headset, spoke to us over the microphone system. He went through a safety speech similar to that which airlines use, only his was adapted to the helicopter. He explained how to work the doors in case of an emergency landing, admonishing us not to exit the craft until the main rotor had stopped moving. Once out of the craft we were to stay away from the rear rotor. Last, was the location of the airsick bags.

John started the engine and told us that he was switching off our microphones until we had taken off and flown out of the airspace around the airport. He didn't want us to interrupt him as he spoke to other air traffic in the area. Symphonic music by John Williams came into our headsets.

I watched as he continued his preflight check, glad to see a thoroughness that pilots often lose as they make the long transition from earnest, young students to experienced old-timers.

The huge engine behind the cabin's rear wall was well insulated. Nevertheless, as it revved up, the cabin was permeated with a dull roar, much louder than inside of a passenger jet. The headsets obviously were not just for ease of communicating, but also did a good job of muffling the noise.

John's voice came over the headset for a moment.

"Okay, ladies and gentlemen, prepare for lift-off."

The rotor blades were now just a gray blur above my window. John lifted us off the heli-pad so gently that it took a moment before I noticed that we were airborne. We rose straight up about thirty feet and then drifted backward another thirty feet. John tipped the control stick a tiny bit. The bird stopped floating backward and began to move to the left. He rotated us so that we faced the direction we were moving. We tipped forward and accelerated rapidly, rising up into the sky, over the big airline runway and off toward the sea as music from Raiders Of The Lost Ark filled our headsets.

Having a fixed-wing private pilot's license I was always eager to ride in helicopters and was fascinated by the differences in how they operate. While the helicopter pilot possibly envies how a plane can nearly fly itself, the fixed wing pilot is drawn to the amazing maneuverability of a machine that can hover, fly backwards, and go up and down like an elevator.

In a few moments, John's voice once again came into our headsets. "Our tour of the island goes clockwise by agreement with the other helicopter companies. Best to have us all going the same direction." He then began to describe the sights in front of us. Famous golf courses and hotels near Lihue soon gave way to mountains and valleys. A waterfall suddenly appeared in the jungle plunging down into a perfect lagoon. It was, John explained, one of the places that Jurassic Park was filmed. As we arced up and over Waimea Canyon, John listed some of the dozens of motion pictures that had used the perfect jungles and beaches of Kauai for backdrops.

We rode in silence for a couple of minutes, climbing up above the ridge above Waimea Canyon. Waterfalls draped the canyon walls like strings of pearls.

"My uncle Jasper told me about you," John suddenly said in our headsets. "Said you were looking into the death of my cousin Thos."

"Yes. Your aunt Janeen hired me to try and find his killer."

"Any luck yet?"

I knew that Jasper would have told John of my interest in the family shrine. If nothing else, it would be a warning for John to be on his guard around me. "No," I said. "I have no clues as to why someone would want to kill Thos. From what I've learned, his life seemed ordinary. The only unusual thing that stands out about Thos's life was the secret family shrine on the Na Pali cliffs. It may have nothing to do with his death. But I thought it was worth checking into."

John said nothing.

"I understand that Jasper showed you where it is a couple of days ago."

John looked over at me, wariness and irritation showing. "Jasper always had a loose mouth."

"If Jasper hadn't told me, it would have been obvious anyway, based on the fact that you were next in line to learn the location and from the scratches on your forearms."

John glanced down at his arms, then back up. "Well, don't think I'm going to fly you anywhere near the place. Unlike some people, I'm not the kind to betray a secret."

There was hostility in his voice and I wondered who it was aimed at.

"I am concerned that someone else could be killed for knowing where it is."

"You're kidding," John said. "No one is going to kill me just because I know where a bunch of trinkets are buried."

"Someone killed Thos."

"Thos was not careful," John said the edge in his voice growing pronounced.

"Someone killed your grandfather."

"That's ridiculous. My granddad died of lung cancer."

"He had advanced lung cancer," I said. "But that's not what killed him."

The tiniest movement on the control stick betrayed his tension at my statement. The chopper yawed as we rushed forward above the jungle. The erratic movement gave me a shot of adrenaline. I saw Street's hand grip her thigh.

"The doctor said lung cancer was the cause of death."

"Right," I said. "But there are doubts about it. More doubts now. I spent yesterday morning at the hospital. My questions about the lack of security provoked defensiveness from the doctor and, later, a phone call from a woman who wouldn't give her name. She said she was calling from a pay phone. She overheard a doctor and a nurse talking about your grandfather after he died. Although the lung cancer was about to kill him, he actually died from asphyxiation." I stated it as if it were fact.

John hesitated. "I don't understand."

"Someone suffocated him with his pillow."

John's knuckles grew pale as his hand squeezed the control stick. The chopper flew less smoothly than before. As a sometime pilot, I knew well the connection between smooth flight and a light hand on the yoke or stick.

"Why would someone want to kill my granddad?"

"One possible reason would be that the killer was trying to find out the location of the secret shrine. Maybe he asked your grandfather. Or maybe he pressured or blackmailed your grandfather. Whether he was successful in finding out the information or not, he didn't want your grandfather to be able to identify him."

"So he killed him?" John sounded genuinely surprised. "That's extreme."

"Another possibility is that once your grandfather was dead, Jasper would take his three sacred items up to the shrine. Every time a family member dies, another trip is made to the shrine. At each visit to the shrine, the killer has another opportunity to follow and learn the location."

"Well, following unseen would be impossible. Without giving anything away, I can tell you that part of the path to the shrine crosses the face of a broad cliff. Anyone on the cliff would be in full view of anyone else on it. You can imagine what I mean as we fly off the end of the ridge up here."

With that statement, the helicopter crested the Na Pali cliffs and soared out over a breathtaking drop-off thousands of feet high. Street's intake of breath was audible in our headsets. Below us stretched a vertical face of rock, covered with impenetrable jungle and rippling with huge valleys like lush green window drapery. Far below was the intense blue of the Pacific. The ocean lapped at tiny crescents of beach, nestled in against the cliffs. From a mile above, the white lines of surf looked like gentle waves, although in reality they were no doubt the fierce waves of winter on Kauai's north shore. To the northeast a dense cloud had thrust up against the base of the cliffs. Winds had pushed the cloud up 4000 feet, where it flowed over the top. The mist swirled through the jungle foliage and flowed back down the back side toward Waimea Canyon. While we flew by in blue sky, the valley with the cloud was socked in.

"What if," I said, "the person watched from a distance with binoculars while you crossed the cliff?"

John shook his head. "With great effort, a person could climb to a vantage point to do that, but then they would never know where we went after we crossed the cliff." He angled the control stick and the helicopter began to drop down to the right, into one of the giant folds in the cliffs.

I said, "Suppose, however, that after they watched you cross the cliff, they killed another Kahale like your father and then hustled out across the cliff before you showed up with the person's sacred items. They would be able to follow you from the far side of the cliff to the shrine. After they learned the location of the shrine, they could retreat and wait for another day when you were nowhere near."

John was silent after that.

We dropped farther down toward the ocean, the lush green cliffs now rising above us and stretching for miles up and down the coast.

"I can't see that," John said finally. "Anyway, there is nothing about the shrine that would motivate murder."

"That's what Jasper told me."

"Well, he's right. People designate sentimental objects. Nothing anyone else would consider valuable."

We were flying out over the edge of the water and had dropped most of the way to the sea. The altimeter showed our altitude as 500 feet. The cliffs towered thousands of feet above us.

"From what you described there could be valuables there and no one would even know of their existence."

"What kind of valuables?" John asked.

"I don't know. Maybe a woman on your father's side of the family had a large diamond and asked that it be put in the shrine. Your predecessor may have hidden it well so that future generations wouldn't notice it."

"There is no way that any diamond..." John suddenly stopped talking.

"What?" I said.

John was looking out the window, slightly behind us on the left. "We've got traffic at nine o'clock. Shouldn't be there."

I turned around and looked. Sure enough, there was a helicopter in the sky behind us, about a mile back. I didn't see why another chopper couldn't be in that airspace. "What's wrong with its position?"

"All the tourist pilots have an agreement to keep to a certain schedule and order. This guy's out of place." At that, John hit the switch that kills the connection between his microphone and our headsets. He kept speaking, presumably to the pilot off our left as well as to surrounding chopper traffic. I watched his lips but couldn't make out his words.

After he was through talking and switched our headsets back on, I said, "What does the other pilot say?"

"Nothing," John said. "No response." He again looked over his left shoulder.

I couldn't decide if John was lying or telling the truth.

I watched the other chopper. It hovered in the sky to the side of us, small enough that I couldn't make out the type or color. Nothing about it or its position seemed threatening, and I wondered if John was using it as a cover for his discomfort over the subject of the secret shrine.

I tried to imagine John's thoughts. This was his first helicopter flight since Jasper brought him to the shrine. He would be very curious to see what the area looked like from the air. Yet he had Street and me onboard.

I watched John's eyes as we flew at high speed along the coast. I noticed him make the briefest glance up toward another of the giant folds in the cliff. The undulation in the cliff face was narrow and deep.

"Could we fly into one of these things?" I said.

"You mean the valleys into the cliff face?"

"Yeah. That one we just passed. It looked narrow and deep, but I suppose there would actually be plenty of room for a helicopter to maneuver, wouldn't there?"

"This one coming up is bigger," John said. "You would feel more comfortable in a larger valley." He looked at Street.

"Don't worry about me," Street said. "I'd love to fly into that last one! It would be so exciting. But only do it if you feel up to it."

I stifled a grin at Street's psychological tactics.

"Sure, no problem," John said. He pulled on the stick and the chopper arced around in a tight circle and headed into the valley. The helicopter off to our left continued on without us.

I looked at the airspeed indicator. It read 60 knots. Vertical green walls rose up on both sides of the craft. The canyon curved to the left, then back to the right. It narrowed further, seeming to close in on the chopper.

John flew near the bottom making the sky a narrow slice of blue overhead. He eased back on the stick and we slowed further as we came to the end. "We'll about-face here and head back out," he said. The chopper came to a stop, hovering near the bot tom of the canyon. We slowly rotated.

"Wait," Street said. "Up there. What is that?" Street had her face against the window. She pointed straight up.

I put my head next to the canopy and looked up, but could see nothing but green cliffs reaching for the sky. "Can we go up?" I asked.

John rotated the craft further and we slowly began to rise. He had a strange look in his eyes that I couldn't make out. Resistance and curiosity combined.

"What do you see?" I said.

"I can't tell," Street said. "Something tiny up on the cliff. Light colored. It was moving."

John and I craned our necks to try and see what she was talking about.

"There," I said, pointing. "A climber up on that broad cliff face." The climber was maybe a thousand feet above us.

John saw where I meant. "What in God's name is someone doing up there," he muttered just loud enough that we could hear it in our headsets. Judging from the intensity of John's frown, he knew exactly what the climber was doing, attempting to head to the Kahale shrine.

"How 'bout we go a little closer and check it out?" I suggested.

"Definitely," John said. "It could be someone in trouble." John's jaw muscles bulged.

John maneuvered the chopper so that it went slightly backward, away from the cliff as it rose. For a long time it seemed as if we didn't get any closer, but eventually we gained enough altitude to be even with the climber.

We were about 300 feet out from the cliff. The climber appeared to be a man dressed in white shirt and blue shorts. He was on a cliff face as wide as a football field and five times as high. The cliff face had a trail of sorts that ran across it. It was on this line that the climber half-walked and half-pulled himself along. He used branches of the cliff plants to hang onto, his feet wedged into the narrow trail. A slip would send him falling over a thousand feet to his death.

"What do you make of a climber out here?" I asked John.

"I don't know," he said, his frown deeper than before. "I'm going in closer. I want to see who this guy is."

We eased toward the jungle-covered wall.

The climber stopped and turned to stare at us. John went closer still, pressing the chopper uncomfortably close to the cliff.

I was about to suggest that we head away when John exclaimed. "My God, I've seen that guy. He has long blond hair and a big beard! He's wearing the same T-shirt like before. Where was it?"

I was staring at the climber as we hovered near the cliff.

"I know! I remember now!" John said. "At the hospital. I was visiting Grandfather the night before he died. This guy walked into the room when I was there. He was startled to see me and left immediately. It's the same man, I'm positive."

I took a long look and felt the shock of recognition. I'd seen the man, too.

It was the man I thought of as the Viking. The man who'd been arguing with Brock Chambers outside of the Rubicon Lodge on Lake Tahoe the day that Morella Meyers was doing the underwater search.

John flew even closer. "He's trying to go to the shrine!"

At that the Viking picked up a thick, sturdy stick about three feet long. He swung out from the cliff by hanging onto a jungle plant with his left hand. His right hand made a Herculean toss with the stick and it arced up into the air toward us.

"Oh, shit!" John yelled. He cranked the control stick sideways and the helicopter lurched in the air. But it was too late.

The stick came down from above. The main rotor hit the wood. There was a horrible crunch of metal that sounded like two cars in a head-on collision. An explosion of wood splinters shot past the chopper in the down draft.

The chopper began to wobble to the left. Street gasped. She stiffened and grabbed onto my arm.

John wrestled with the stick. "Goddammit!" he shouted. The chopper started a slow spin. Screeching metallic sounds came from the engine compartment behind us. Our spin increased in speed. We wobbled through the air like an out-of-balance top spinning closer and closer to the cliff as we dropped out of the sky.

"Mayday! Mayday!" John shouted into his microphone. "Alpha Bravo Three Two Niner Niner going down at Na Pali! Mayday!"

John's call for help was cut off as we hit the cliff. A tree branch ripped through our canopy tearing off the windshield. The spinning rotor hit the cliff and broke into pieces. Sparks showered from an overhead panel. An explosion rocked the engine compartment. My ears were deafened and I heard nothing as the craft bounced off the cliff and plummeted toward the bottom of the canyon.

EIGHTEEN

The helicopter bounced against the cliff again. Jungle plants caught on the landing gear. As we ripped away, we went into a slow backward rotation, end over end.

John yelled, "Shit!" several times. Street stayed silent, her hand like a claw on my arm as she braced herself. The chopper turned a backward somersault one and a half times and landed tail first on the bottom of the canyon.

The chopper's tail crumpled as the chopper collapsed down onto it. The impact tore the rest of the chopper into pieces. The piece with my seat attached to it crashed through branches and landed upside down with my face mashed into the gnarled trunk of a tree.

It took me ten or twenty minutes to decide how it was that I hung from the seat. I realized there was a seat belt over my hips. I rotated my face away from the tree and spied the belt buckle up there on my lap. The latch was easy to pull. The belt gave way and my face scraped down the tree bark as I fell to the ground.

I got onto my knees, grabbed a nearby branch and pulled myself to my feet. The jungle tilted, but I hung on. In a minute I could stand without holding onto the branch. Look, ma, no hands. But something gave way and I fell. My face went into leafy muck.

"Street," I called out, my pronunciation garbled by the gooey dirt in my mouth. "Street!"

"Up here," came the miraculous response.

I crawled through jungle toward the voice and looked up. My

vision was distorted. I blinked and tried to focus. The portion of the chopper's floor that held both Street's seat and John's seat was hanging from a tree. Street was still strapped in, hanging upside down. She looked okay, but her face was red.

John was still strapped in as well, but not so lucky. His left arm was missing. A large piece of metal sprouted from the center of his chest, its mangled end red with blood and looking vaguely like a rose. Mercifully, Street was situated such that she was not facing him. I was already thinking about how to get her down in a way that would prevent her from seeing him.

"Hang in there, sweetie," I said in my most reassuring voice. "I'll have you out of there in a minute."

I grabbed onto a woody plant, pulled myself to my feet and tried to walk. My feet didn't coordinate with my brain signals and I tripped and went down. I pushed up onto my hands and knees. I crawled around a big bush and approached the trunk of the tree where she was trapped. All I needed to do was climb the tree and carry her down. I reached up and grabbed a branch. I tried to squeeze my hands like vice grips as I pulled myself up onto my feet. But my hands gave way and I fell again.

My vision was blurry. I tried to do a pushup and get to my feet that way. But my arms slipped on moist leaves and I collapsed face down in the mud. I thought briefly about centipedes. It was my last thought for a long time.

NINETEEN

When I awoke, the jungle was gone.

I lay still. What didn't hurt felt numb. Not a lot was numb.

In time, I had an idea. I moved my fingers. Then my feet. Continuity from head to toe. Life is good.

I turned my head to look around. That hurt. Maybe I didn't need to look. Yes, I did. There was Street.

She was sitting on a vinyl chair reading Newsweek. She still had on her black mini skirt. Her bare legs were crossed, her sandal lightly bouncing from the toes of her raised foot.

"Good afternoon, my dear," I said. The time of day was a guess.

Street jumped up, bent down and hugged me. "Thank God, you're awake. They said you'd be fine, but I..." Her voice wavered.

I grit my teeth and boosted myself to a sitting position. Street helped me lean back against several pillows.

I was in a bed in a small room painted periwinkle. On the window sill sat a potted plant with a single red flower.

Street gave me a hug. "Oh," I said. I tried to shift under her grip. "Easy," I said.

"Am I hurting you? Honey, you need to speak up."

"No. Yes."

Street let go. She sat next to me on the bed.

"Every time we're in a helicopter crash," I said, "I get banged up and you come through unscathed. How do you do it?"

"I don't know. Natural talent, I guess." She tried to force a grin, but it didn't work. It was clear she was very stressed by John's death. "Or else it was that modern dance class I took in college. Never know when such techniques come in handy. But I did get a scratch on my arm. See? And I got some dirt on my skirt." Another attempt at a grin, then tears filled up her eyes.

After a few minutes, I inched my way out of bed, Street helping. They had me in a hospital gown, a short little thing that matched the room and the flower. Street helped me stand up. The gown barely covered my crotch. She peeked through the opening of my gown. "Jesus, Owen, your back and side are the same colors as your face. You poor thing."

To one side of the room was a bathroom.

A look in the mirror told me I should stay away from children and people with heart problems. The skin that wasn't covered with bandages looked pulpy. Some of the colors had darkened toward blue, but others still showed hues of lavender that blended nicely with the periwinkle walls. In my little lavender dress I looked ready for the Easter Pageant.

"How'd we get out of there?" I asked.

"John's Mayday call was heard by another tourist helicopter. They spotted us twenty minutes later. They sent a big military-type helicopter and did the stretcher-on-a-cable thing. You and I went first and they went back later to get John's body." Her eyes watered again. "They said he probably didn't feel a thing."

"How long has it been?"

"They pulled us out of there about noon." She dabbed at her eyes. "It's now three in the afternoon. The doctor said you have a serious concussion. You are not to bump your head anymore. Ever. They examined you for broken bones, but only found cuts and bruises. So they took advantage of your semi-consciousness to stitch up some of the cuts. You were kind of noisy about it while they were sticking the sewing needles in you. How do you feel? You look like one of those monsters in a fifties horror movie."

"I feel like one, too." My head throbbed. My body felt broken.

All I wanted was a handful of pain pills and a six-pack to wash them down. I looked in the mirror. Boris Karloff in The Mummy stared back at me.

The door opened and a dark man dressed in a white shirt and blue pants walked in. He had smooth Polynesian skin on European features. He saw me standing in front of the bathroom mirror. He showed no reaction to my bandaged head. "Good to see you up and about, Mr. McKenna. I'm Frank Kanoa, Lihue Police Chief."

We shook hands. Even that hurt.

"I would like to talk to you. Is this a convenient time or would you like to..." he gestured at my mini gown.

"Why not give me a few minutes to get dressed."

"Good idea," he said.

Kanoa stepped out into the hallway while Street helped me pull on my clothes. It wasn't easy as I had aches and pains to match the bruises. While we were at it, Dr. Fujimoto came into the room.

"You are doing better," he said, his voice brusque. "But don't dress. You will have to stay here at least twenty-four hours."

"Is that the most lucrative portion of the insurance payment?"

His face reddened. "I'm sorry I said that about Alvin Kahale's death." He handed me two pills and a little paper cup of water. "Here, take these. You're going to need them for pain for the next several days."

Tell me about it, I thought as I swallowed. "Anyway, I pay my own bills. So I think it's time I leave. Thanks for your care." I continued struggling with my clothes. I got my pants up and snapped and decided to sit on the bed to rest for a minute.

"May I?" the doctor said, approaching me with one of those lights to look in my eyes.

I nodded.

"Now that you're conscious we'll need you to fill out some forms. Get you checked in before you check out," he said as he inspected my eyeballs. "Any dizziness? Head pain?"

"Both."

"You are lucky," he said. "They informed me that you landed head first which is always a bad idea."

"Hard to plan these things."

"In any event, it is paramount that you do not bump your head."

"So Street has told me."

"Your brain is bruised from the impact. Another impact in the same area could throw you into a coma."

"Message received."

"Your lady friend, here, told me about what John Kahale said. That the man who threw the stick at the helicopter was in the hospital around the time John's grandfather Alvin Kahale died. If there is a connection, then I apologize for being abrupt with you yesterday morning. Perhaps you were on to something after all, although I still believe he died of cancer."

If Dr. Fujimoto were sorry, he didn't sound like it. I had the feeling he was forcing himself to say the words in hopes I wouldn't make good on my threat to bring in lawyers. I knew from my Tahoe doctor friend John Lee that medical malpractice attorneys were a doctor's worst nightmare.

"I will give you a prescription for some medication." He scrawled on a prescription pad, tore off the sheet and handed it to me. "Remember not to bump your head. I can't stress that enough." He left.

"What a cockroach," Street muttered.

She helped me pull on the last of my clothes. "The policeman was here earlier. I told him about what happened. He wanted to know as much as possible about the man who threw the stick. All I could give him was a physical description."

"I can only add one thing to that. I saw the same man arguing with the owner of the Rubicon Lodge where Thos was shot."

"You saw the man in Tahoe?"

"Yes. At the time I thought of him as a Viking, because his

blond hair and beard looked like a clichéd version of a Norwegian."

"Seeing him twice connected to this case certainly makes him look like our killer."

"Yeah," I agreed. "Let's go talk to the Police Chief."

I opened the door and we stepped out into the hall where Frank Kanoa was waiting.

"I met Street a few hours ago," he said. He nodded toward her and gave her a polite smile. "She explained that you are a private cop, and she filled me in on parts of your investigation. We are interested in what you know of this man with the beard and long hair."

"Next to nothing. I saw him at Lake Tahoe a few days ago." I explained where I'd seen him.

Frank Kanoa raised his eyebrows. "We faxed Street's description of the man to every agency at the airport. Security, airline personnel, car rental companies, etc. We eventually learned that a man fitting the description took an inter-island flight to Honolulu. His name is Ole Knudson. We spoke to the gate attendant. He remembered the man because of his long hair."

"Any idea where he went from there?"

"No. He could have disappeared on Oahu. We're also trying to check the passenger lists of all departing flights since then." Frank looked at his watch. "He could be landing in San Francisco or L.A. in a few hours. But if he has an ID under a different name and managed to cut his hair and beard before he boarded a mainland flight, we're out of luck. The attendant verified that Knudson had a photo ID with that name on it. The attendant is sure the ID wasn't a California or Nevada driver's license, because he sees them so often. But he couldn't remember what state had issued it."

"How could Knudson have gotten out of the canyon so fast?" I said. "I understood it was a two or three day hike in and back."

"On a normal route, yes. But if he is a good climber and very strong, he could have climbed straight up the cliff and worked his way back to one of the lookouts on the road above. It would only take an hour or so. He may have left a car there."

"Street," I said. "Any idea where my phone is at?"

"It was in your pocket. It survived the crash." She pulled it out of her bag and handed it to me. "You're worried," she said.

I nodded. "Another Kahale is dead and the Viking is my only suspect. He was in Tahoe before. He may go back there. Could be there are more Kahales on his list."

"Janeen and her grandson?"

"Yes."

"But Jasper is still alive and he's here."

"I can't make sense of it," I said. "But I want to warn them." I hit the phone book function on the phone. It was hard to see the names because my vision was blurred and my head hurt so much it was painful even to try and focus my eyes. I didn't remember if I'd entered in Janeen's number and others connected to the case, but there it was. I hit the call button and waited while it rang. Either I had a bad connection or else Janeen hadn't turned on her answering machine. After two tries with no answer, I dialed Captain Mallory.

He was in his office. "Mallory," he barked.

"It's Owen."

"I thought you were in Hawaii. Diamond said..."

"I am."

"Oh. How's the beach? Golf? Hula girls?"

"Don't know," I said. I filled him in on what we'd learned, telling him about the Viking named Ole Knudson, but leaving out my injuries to save time.

"You want me to baby-sit the lady and her son?"

"Grandson. No, but maybe you could send a patrol unit out there, check up on them, tell them to answer their phone."

Mallory said he would.

I said goodbye and scrolled through the other names I'd stored in the phone. I squinted, trying to see. Every heartbeat sent a pulsing pain through my temples. There was Jerry Roth.

He answered on the second ring.

"I'm wondering if you can do me a favor," I said after I'd identified myself.

"Of course."

"I'm hoping you can check up on Janeen and Phillip. She doesn't answer the phone."

"Is this connected to her son's murder?"

"Yes."

"You think Janeen and Phillip could be next?" Jerry sounded very worried.

"It doesn't make any sense, but I don't want to take any chances. We've identified a possible suspect in Thos's murder. But any danger to Janeen and Phillip is still speculation."

"Who is the suspect?"

I hesitated. "I'd appreciate it if you didn't repeat anything about this just yet."

"Oh, of course not. But if I have an idea of who to watch out for, I'll be better able to look after Janeen and Phillip, won't I?"

"The man's name is Ole Knudson. He has long blond hair and a big bushy beard. Three Kahales have died recently not counting Janeen's son Thos."

"Jesus. The poor woman will flip her britches. I'll run over there right away, then. Soon as I can pull on a jacket." It sounded on the phone like he was already moving.

"Thanks. One more thing, Jerry. I know it's a lot to ask, but I'm wondering if you could put them up for a few days at your house. It'd be easier to keep a watch on them and they wouldn't be quite such easy targets if Ole Knudson does come after them."

"Janeen and Phillip at my house? Well, I suppose. I've got an extra room. Actually, I've got about four extra rooms. This is a big house. But the thing is, Owen, I doubt that Janeen would agree to that. She's quite headstrong. Maybe you should come over and talk to her in person."

"I would, but I'm in Hawaii."

"Oh. I never..." he stopped, surprise in his voice.

"Just make the offer to Janeen," I said. "Meanwhile, I'll still try to get her on the phone and explain."

"Okay. Do you know where this Knudson fellow is?"

"No. He was in Kauai, but he's left and may be heading to Tahoe. I'll be there as soon as I can, but it will still take half a day."

"Well, you can rest assured that if the bloody bugger intends to harm Janeen and little Phillip, there'll be hell to pay."

"Thanks for helping, Jerry. I'll call back soon." I hung up wondering what kind of mismatch it would be between Jerry on his crutch and the muscular Viking. I turned back to Street and the Lihue Police Chief Frank Kanoa. "Janeen's neighbor Jerry is going to check up on them."

Kanoa spoke. "Why don't you take me back through your investigation. Tell me about this case from the beginning." He gestured toward some chairs in the hallway.

I took the hint and sat down. I started with the phone call from Janeen Kahale and took him through the details step by step.

"Let me see if I have this straight," Kanoa said when I was done. "You think Jasper Kahale's father died from suffocation and that his brother's death in the car crash was no accident."

"Correct," I said. "That car accident. What can you tell me about it?"

"Not much. The body was found in his car down a steep incline below the Waimea Canyon road. It looked like he missed a turn in the dark. The vehicle rolled several times."

"Was it a turn that is easy to miss?"

"Yes," Kanoa said.

"So if someone forced him off the road, no one would be the wiser."

"Yes, again." Frank Kanoa picked at a hangnail, then bit it off. "Thos wrote a suicide note?"

I nodded. "In it he claims responsibility for three deaths."

"Did you believe the note?"

"I asked Thos's mother if she believed it. She felt that Thos had told the truth as he knew it in the note. So I assumed that if Thos didn't murder anyone, then he did something that indirectly caused three people to die. I went looking for any deaths that were proximate to Thos. When I found two of them in his family I wondered if they were murder. With the death of John, it is starting to look like an epidemic in the Kahale family."

Street spoke up. "With Grandpa Alvin, Jasper's brother John senior, and his brother's son John junior, that is three deaths. Yet only the first two of them could figure in Thos's note about causing the deaths of three people. So we're still missing one death."

"Right," I said. I turned to Frank. "Have there been any other unusual deaths in Kauai recently?"

Frank pushed his lips out and frowned. "I don't pay a great deal of attention to all the deaths on the island, of course. They are almost always of natural causes. The only recent death that wasn't was a stabbing death about three weeks back."

"Who was the victim?"

"A local tough guy who went by the single name of Napoleon. He was always in trouble. Brawls when he was young, knife fights when he got older. Last time we picked him up, it was for unlawful possession of a Glock Seventeen, stolen in a burglary from a Phoenix cop's home. How Napoleon got it, we don't know."

"Did you find Napoleon's killer?"

"No."

"Recover a weapon?"

"No. The medical examiner said he died from a single stab wound to the chest with a long, thin knife. But we never found it. The most unusual thing about the death was that Napoleon was found right out there." Frank pointed out the front door of the hospital. "Someone dumped him on the grass in front of the door, honked his horn twice and drove off."

"Someone who wanted to save Napoleon's life but wasn't going to risk getting any more involved."

"Yeah," Frank said. "You think it was Thos and that this was the third death he mentioned in his suicide note?"

"Could be."

We spoke for another half hour, going over every detail. "You think Ole Knudson is going to Tahoe?" Frank said at last.

"Yes. I saw him there before, so it makes sense he may head back. If not now, later. Brock Chambers, the owner of the Rubicon Lodge, might know who the Viking is. I'd call, but something tells me to be wary of Chambers. I'd like to confront him in person."

"Then I'll wait until you talk to him before I put his name on my report," Kanoa said. "Of course, Knudson may get to Chambers first. If Chambers is involved in some way, he could be doing a vanishing act as we speak."

"I'll let my friend Mallory of the South Lake Tahoe PD know. Maybe he can convince the El Dorado Sheriff's Office to put a tail on him," I said. "Have you found out how Ole Knudson got around Kauai? Did he rent a car?"

"We're still checking. I'll let you know when we find out."

Street and I walked very slowly out to our rental car which Street had earlier fetched from the helicopter tour office. If anyone saw my lurching and my bandages, they'd look around for the movie cameras with Hollywood logos on them.

"How you doing, hon?" Street said as she held my arm.

"I feel like I've been in a helicopter crash."

When we got to the car, Street eased me into the front seat, then she drove back to our condo. She took the house phone out on the lanai to call about moving our return tickets to the next available flight while I got Mallory on my cellphone.

"I think you should convince the El Dorado deputies to watch Brock Chambers," I said. "The guy who owns the Rubicon Lodge."

Mallory asked a few questions. I gave him the background.

"Thanks," I said. "I'll be back in a day or so."

"Better not wait too long. They're talking about a big storm in the Gulf of Alaska. Supposed to hit us in a few days. From the way the weather guys are carrying on, it'll shut down the passes and we'll be isolated for a time."

"Thanks for letting me know."

Mallory hung up without saying goodbye.

"We're booked on tonight's flight to LAX," Street said when I joined her out on the lanai. "It gets in at five a.m. There's a six a.m. flight to Reno. We'll be in Tahoe by nine in the morning. What next?"

"Next we go back to visit Jasper. He must be reeling in shock over John's death." I found his number and dialed.

"Hello, Jasper," I said when he answered. "Owen McKenna calling."

There was silence on the phone. Then, "My nephew John died this morning in a helicopter crash. They say someone caused the accident on purpose."

"Yes, Jasper. I'm very sorry." He didn't know that Street and I had been on the same aircraft. We could explain later. "I want to come and talk to you about John. Would that be okay?"

Another pause. "Yes."

"I'll be there in half an hour."

TWENTY

Street drove. I held my head. We headed across Kauai, through fields of sugarcane so thick one would need a machete to walk through them. It was late afternoon when we got to Jasper's house.

"Will he mind that I'm coming?" Street asked as we parked outside of Jasper's cinder block house.

"No. It will help. He will be less sad with you around."

We walked very slowly up the side of the house. I felt like I needed a walker and my head throbbed as if a 747 had landed on it. The waves on the beach were gentle and not as loud as before. I knocked.

"Door's open," Jasper called out.

I pushed open the door and stepped into the dark interior. "Hello, Jasper."

"Hello." He sat in his chair unmoving. "What happened to your head?"

"My girlfriend Street Casey and I were in the helicopter with John when it crashed."

Jasper didn't respond.

After a long moment I said, "Jasper, I brought Street along because I told her about you and she wants to meet you."

Street stepped forward, a warm smile on her face. "Hello, Jasper. I'm Street. Good to meet you."

"Well, well," Jasper said. He stood up slowly, pushing on the arms of the chair for assistance. When he was standing he reached out and shook Street's hand. "I know you told me she was good looking," he said, "but I didn't realize she was so beautiful." Although he gave me an elaborate wink, there was no joy on his face. "Can I get either of you a drink? I have Mountain Dew."

We both said no thanks.

"Jasper, we're very sorry about John," I said.

Jasper stopped moving and leaned on the kitchen counter. "They told me what happened, the man throwing the stick. But I didn't know who was with him." Jasper looked out at the surf. He didn't move. "Well, you survived," he said finally. "John would have wanted that. My brother and me, our boys, we're alike that way. Thos and John both had honor. They would go down with their ships. But they wouldn't want harm to come to anyone near them."

"I want you to know that John was a good pilot, Jasper. He flew well and was in no way responsible for what happened."

"But why did the man throw the stick?"

"We're trying to find out. To do that we need to know more about John and Thos. We need to talk to their friends. Can you give us any names?"

"I don't know any of John's friends. As for what was going on in Thos's life, I don't think he had friends who could tell you much about that. He was too private. You can check with them. Let's see."

Jasper seemed to disconnect for a moment. He twitched and then spoke. "Donny Kyono was one. I know Thos golfed with Donny. He lives in Princeville. And Tom Rypel. He's an old surfer friend who lives on the coconut coast near Kapa'a. And Caesar... I forget his last name. Donny will know. Other than that, there were Thos's employees. Brian Malone and the others whose names I forget.

"Call them," Jasper continued. "I think you'll find that Thos wasn't the kind of boy who shared his concerns and troubles. He kept things to himself. Like his mother. Friends were people to go fishing with. Talk about wine. Nothing personal. I asked him once if there was a girl in the picture. 'Thos,' I said. 'What do you and the boys talk about when you go fishing? Do you have girlfriends? You talk about girls?' And he said, 'No, dad, we just talk football. The last surf championship. Stuff like that.'"

Jasper poured soft drink in a glass and carried it to his chair.

"So I got nosier," Jasper continued. "I said, 'What about girls, Thos? Is there a girl you like?' He said that he liked to date, but that there wasn't any one girl he was special on."

"No close friends," I said. "No close girl. Do you think he confided in anyone?"

"Yes, I think so. But I don't know who it was. Do they call them pen pals when it is email? Anyway, maybe he was close to that person, I don't know."

"A woman?" I asked.

"Maybe," Jasper said. "A couple times here and there, Thos referred to his cyber friend. Most of the time Thos would just refer to guys. 'This guy I know.' Like that. So I thought maybe the cyber friend was a woman." He sipped his drink.

"You never asked?"

"No. I kind of hinted around, but if you knew Thos, you knew not to push him on something private."

"You couldn't guess who this person was?"

"No," Jasper said. "Would it be in his computer? You could look there."

"You give us permission?"

"Yes. The cops have already been through his townhouse. Computer, too. Why not you? I'll give you a key. If it'll help you find out what happened to my boy, then I'll be forever grateful. Janeen will be grateful, too."

Jasper got up and rummaged through a kitchen drawer. He pulled out a key and a pencil. There was a small pile of bills on the counter. He opened one, pulled out the contents and set them aside, then wrote on the back of the envelope. Street was sitting closest to him. He handed her the key and envelope. "Here is his address."

"We'll go there now," she said. "We have to catch a plane later. Is it okay if we mail the key back to you?"

"Of course."

We tried to make some pleasant small talk with Jasper before we left, but it did not set him at ease. He grabbed my arm as we were leaving. "Owen, will you find Thos's killer? John's killer?" Jasper looked up at me, his dark, opaque eyes searching mine. "First my father dies of cancer, then my brother in an accident. These things are bad, but I accept that. Now this man is taking what's left of my family, Owen. I don't think I can take it."

I took his hand. "I think we will find him, Jasper. We know his name and what he looks like. It is only a matter of time." I tried to sound confident.

Street hugged Jasper as we said goodbye. We pulled out with Jasper standing in front of his house. He gave a little wave.

TWENTY-ONE

We drove from the arid south side of Kauai up to the wet north side. The change in vegetation from sparse and dry to lush and wet was matched by the sky. At Jasper's the afternoon sun was intense in a blue sky. In Princeville the sky was overcast and a light drizzle called for wipers and turning on the headlights.

Thos's townhouse was on a beautiful stretch of grass and garden adjacent to one of the famous Princeville golf courses. An end unit with a view of fairways and mountains beyond, it had a lush elegance that, for many prospective owners, no doubt more than made up for the reduced sunshine of the north side of the island. We parked on an immaculate blacktop drive and Street let us in with the key.

The inside of Thos's home was excessively neat. "This place looks more like a show unit than a place where someone lived," I said.

"Cleaning service," Street said. "You can see the vacuum tracks on the carpet. I think they've come through since Thos was here. Even a fastidious guy isn't this clean."

We took a quick look through the downstairs. There was a large living room with black leather furniture and an entertainment system against one wall. Another wall was glass with a patio outside. The décor of the kitchen was modern, with stainless steel kitchen appliances. Upstairs were two bedrooms. The smaller back bedroom had a double bed, a dresser, and a bookcase made of polished black wood, dramatic against the off-white carpet.

To one side was a chair, upholstered in black leather. The larger front bedroom with a view of the golf course was Thos's office. A wrap-around desk, multiple filing cabinets, copier, fax, computer and color laser printer nearly filled the space.

"What can I do to help?" Street asked.

"I'm going to poke around in his computer and look for Thos's email friend. If he has a phone index, you might look for the friends that Jasper mentioned. Or look in the phone book."

"Donny Kyono, Tom Rypel and Caesar somebody, right?"

"Yeah. And Brian Malone, the manager of Pacific Blue Wines. Maybe look around through his desk drawers, too, and see if you find anything that hints of trouble or stress or bad financial decisions."

Street went to work, methodically searching Thos's office and, eventually, the rest of the townhouse, while I tried to make a methodical search of his computer. Next to the monitor was a stack of new Zip disks and I put one in to make copies of anything potentially useful.

I started with his email program. Fortunately, he'd set it up to remember his password so I had access.

There were 137 emails in his inbox. They dated from three days before his death, presumably the last time he left Kauai. I started at the beginning and opened them one by one.

The majority came from an online discussion group affiliated with a wine-making trade group. Scanning them quickly, I saw a wide breadth of issues and concerns relating to every aspect of growing and harvesting grapes as well as making wine, marketing and distributing it. But none of the emails revealed anything about his murder.

The next biggest category of emails was the kind of ads and promotions that get through junk mail filters. I perused them quickly. Chamber of Commerce updates, airline specials, surfing newsletters and many more.

A third category was business correspondence. I learned nothing from it except for the general impression that Thos was quite successful with his wine distributorship. And he was beginning to get inquiries about his own Pacific Blue line of wine.

The smallest group of emails was from friends, a total of seven. I read through them carefully.

From Jimbo at an AOL address:

"Hey, Thos, you were right about recommending that Merlot. Awesome. Yes, definitely try to pick up that account. Then can I get it cheap by the case through you? Just kidding. ;-) As for the surf on Miami Beach, let's just say I have more fun in my bathtub. Later."

From Tammy at a .com address:

"No thanks, hon. Last time was pretty trippy, but I don't think you can replicate it a second time again. A second time again is redundant, right? You're always so careful with words. Where is the backspace key? Love you."

From William Jones at a ca.us address:

"Dear Mr. Kahale, I received your email and am pleased to inform you that we do know of an antiques contact working in your subject area. He is in the Reno area. His name is Avery Ginsberry. Unfortunately, we don't show a phone number for the listing. But he teaches at the Sierra Nevada College in Incline Village, so you can find him easily enough. I'm glad I could be of service. And, yes, I do enjoy an occasional glass of wine."

From RogerThat at a local ISP address:

"You kill me, surf dude. 1st you're all campfires-on-the-beach-and-smoke-some-good-weed-laid-back. Then U grow up and become a killer biznessman. Good 4 U. Glad we bumped into each other again before we got ancient or something."

From an msn.com address:

"Hi Mr. Thos, Let me know your plans ASAP. I have a busy schedule and I need to figure out times. Looking forward to your arrival. Hermes."

From Donny at a local ISP address:

"Hey man, I think you are on the plane to CA, so here's a calendar note. First Saturday in Feb. I've got an Andrew Jackson per hole on a rematch. Good luck cuz you're gonna need it this time."

From Suz at a local ISP address:

"Yes to both. See you at 5:30. Suzy."

Appended below it was: "Original message: Hey, Suzy, just finished my paperwork, but it's too late to call (2:00 a.m.). So while you snooze, Suz, I'll make some reservations for Friday. I know I can count on you for the hop to Honolulu and dinner up above Waikiki. But would you like to hit some clubs afterward or take a quiet beach walk? (A clothes horse like me needs to know which shoes to wear.) Either way, plan to be ready by 5:30. Thos."

I saved all of the messages to the Zip disk.

Next, I opened Thos's draft folder. There were three letters in it, all business correspondence, nothing revealing.

All that remained was his address book. There were several dozen addresses. He'd put in a comment here and there after some of them. But only a few of them had names and phone numbers, and most appeared to be vendors and clients. There was nothing that would suggest a confidant. I made a copy of the addresses for further use.

Next I opened Internet Explorer. There were no bookmarks or history bar records. He obviously didn't use the browser. I tried Netscape and found lots of both. I made note of his bookmarks and the records of websites he visited most recently. None of them seemed revealing. The cache files from the previous months contained hundreds of images, too much to copy them all. I opened four different images at random and got a picture of a wine label, a map of a Napa Valley winery, an ad for his wine distributorship and a picture of a square-rigger sailing ship.

The old ship was the odd item, so I continued to sample his cache files for something else similar or equally odd, hoping to find anything that could provide a window into Thos's personal interests. But I found nothing other than more wine-related items.

I saved the image of the sailing ship and several other images at random from his cache files.

I opened Microsoft Word and looked at a couple dozen files. They consisted of typical business documents, letters and bids to his clients and vendors, notes to himself, ad copy ideas and other miscellany.

I was running out of ideas of where to look. There was a spreadsheet program and on it were his cash-flow charts and sales records. From what I could see he had a good business going. But nothing stood out as being worth investigating.

His checkbook program was as neat and orderly as his townhouse, same for his receivables and payables.

When I was done I had the clear sense that I'd come across nothing worth pursuing. There was nothing in Thos's computer that would help me conjure up suicide and murder and intrigue involving secret shrines. To all appearances, he was simply another hard-working small businessman.

When I was about to shut off the computer I had another thought about the emails. None of the emails in his inbox had been opened before I found them. Everything prior to that had been deleted. I understood deleting many or even most of the incoming emails. But all of them? It seemed unlikely that there were no emails Thos would want to save. Of course, it was possible that Thos printed out any important messages and saved the hard copies. There was only one other explanation I could think of.

After Thos made his last and final flight to California, a visitor like the Viking could have entered Thos's townhouse and gone through his email just as I had. If the Viking found anything useful he may have erased all of the emails so that no one else could learn the same information.

I was ruminating on that when Street walked in.

"I have a question," she said.

"Hmmm?"

"I've found nothing revealing of anything unless piling

surfing trophies in cardboard boxes in the back of a closet means something. I did get the phone numbers for the friends Jasper mentioned. Would you like me to call them? Or do you think it would be better if you do it?"

"Actually, your impression of them will be more accurate than mine, anyway. So yeah, that'd be great if you'd do the honors."

"Any particulars you want me to pursue?"

"I'd just touch on whether Thos had talked to them about the secret shrine or recent troubles. That sort of thing. And whether he was romantically involved with anyone. If one of them knows the more personal side of Thos then we'll be able to call him back when we have more specific questions."

"Got it. I'll do the calling downstairs."

I went back to the computer, deciding to take a blind shot and send an email to all the people in his address book hoping to flush out a confidant if in fact one existed.

In the subject line I wrote: "Regarding Thos's untimely death."

The body of the message was:

"Dear friends and associates of Thos Kahale,

My name is Owen McKenna. I am a private investigator working for Thos's family. You may be aware of Thos's recent murder in Lake Tahoe. My deepest sympathies to all of you.

I've been hired to find Thos's killer and am working in conjunction with the authorities in Tahoe and in Kauai.

We have reason to believe that Thos had a friend in whom he confided, and that this friend and he communicated by email. If one of you could be that friend, please email me as soon as possible.

Even if you believe you know nothing that will help with our investigation, if your contact with Thos was about anything other than routine business transactions, please contact me anyway. Thank you."

I concluded with my own email address and sent it out to everyone in his address book.

I turned off the computer, put the Zip disk in my pocket and went downstairs to find Street. She was just hanging up the phone.

"It was just as Jasper said," she said. "They all told me that they never spoke to Thos about anything personal. They golfed and fished and that was about it. One of them, Caesar, whose last name is Fernandez, said he tried to get to know Thos better, but that Thos was kind of a cold fish. His words."

I nodded and summarized what I'd found in his computer, which was basically nothing. "How long do you figure we have before our flight?"

Street looked at the time. "With car rental return, we should leave here in a little over an hour."

"Enough time for me to try Janeen again."

I dialed, but there was no answer and she hadn't turned on her machine.

We were about to leave when I went back upstairs and took another look in the smaller bedroom. I went in and eased myself down onto the chair.

Although it was now twilight, I could see out the window to a lush green mountain with two waterfalls cascading down through the jungle. Street came in and sat on the bed. I turned my gaze to the dresser. "Did you check in the drawers?"

"Yes. Underwear, some brand new shirts still in the wrappers, towels and more sweaters than you'd anticipate needing in the tropics, but they were probably for his trips to the mainland."

I looked at the bookcase. The top shelf had a few photos in frames. There were some of family members along with pictures of young men and women playing volleyball on the beach and sitting around a campfire. The middle and lower shelves were two-thirds filled with books, their spines neatly lined up with the edge of the shelves and held in place with bookends that were bronze sculptures of surfers riding a big wave.

I got up and went over to look at the titles. The books were mostly hard-bound and about wine: its history, its impact on civilization, its complex chemistry and its role in the economies of California and many countries around the world.

Aside from books on wine, there was a scattering of other reference and business books. The only fiction in the bookcase was a collector's edition of the complete works of Mark Twain. I pulled out one of the volumes. It was leather bound with gold embossed lettering and had gold leaf applied to the edges of the pages. I flipped through stories I'd read many years ago: The Celebrated Jumping Frog of Calaveras County, The Stolen White Elephant, The Mysterious Stranger.

"A sudden urge to read a tall tale?" Street said.

"I was just remembering something Jasper told me. He said that when his grandfather was a young boy he met Mark Twain. Twain supposedly gave Jasper's grandfather a handwritten manuscript in a leather notebook. It was a short story called The Amazing Island Boy And His Trick Wood." I explained to Street what Jasper had told me about Twain and the gift and the hurricane that swept it away.

"You think Twain really made the gift of a story?"

"I don't have any idea. But when I see this Twain Collection in Thos's bookcase it makes me wonder."

"Well," Street said, "for whatever it's worth, the title sounds like something Twain would write."

"I agree. Jasper said the story was about a kid who had a magical stick of Koa wood. The boy coaxed his gullible friends into paying him to put them under a spell with it."

"That also sounds like Twain. Maybe Jasper and the rest of the family read a lot of Twain. Could be his stories inspired them to create their own story about Twain."

"Yes, although Jasper said he's never read any Twain. He even knew that Twain earned his way to Hawaii by writing letters back to a California newspaper. Again, he said it was his granddad who told him that." I thought of Thos's emails. "There was an email to Thos from someone in the California school system, judging from the return address. Apparently, Thos had made an inquiry about an antiques expert in the Reno area and this person responded with the name of someone at the Sierra Nevada College in Incline Village."

"Which suggests," Street mused, "that Thos had an old and valuable item – a short story manuscript, maybe?"

"Maybe."

"Why an antiques expert in Reno? Why not San Francisco?"

"Twain spent some time in the Reno/Tahoe area and a few years nearby in Virginia City. It could be that something about the story or maybe the physical characteristics of the manuscript would draw Thos to the Tahoe area."

"Then again," Street said, "because Thos went to Tahoe to visit family, maybe he just wanted to find an expert close by so he wouldn't have to travel far."

"That makes more sense." I patted the computer disk in my pocket. "I copied the email so I can look the person up when we get back."

"Suppose that Twain's leather notebook did survive the hurricane," Street said. "Would it have been hidden in the shrine all these years?"

"According to Jasper, that would be unlikely. He made it sound like anything made of paper or leather would have quickly rotted away."

"Because rain gets in the shrine?"

"No, he said the cave is protected from rain. But not from small animals and humidity."

Street looked at me. "And insects. Bugs can chew their way into practically any container except a tight metal box."

"I'm assuming that you found no such thing when you went through the kitchen cabinets?"

Street shook her head. "If there is a metal box in this townhouse, it would have to be in a very good hiding place. Same for a leather notebook. I would have noticed either."

"How much time are we down to?"

"About forty minutes," Street said.

TWENTY-TWO

We made another search of Thos's townhouse, this time looking for a hiding place large enough to put a leather notebook or the insect-proof box it might be in. Having been a homicide cop prior to going private, I have a good idea of where people hide things.

There is a three-tiered hierarchy of places. The obvious places comprise the first tier, like putting the door key under the doormat. Clever places like inside jars in the freezer comprise the second tier. But they are still obvious because they seem like they would be good places to hide something. The third tier is made up of the places that people think aren't hiding places at all and hence are places where no one looks.

So Street and I concentrated our search on those places. We found some screwdrivers in a drawer and used them to look inside the toaster, the microwave, the bread machine, the giant-screen video, the stereo speakers. I got my hand behind the bathroom exhaust fan and into the vent hood above the stovetop and the air-conditioning vents throughout the townhouse. Street dismantled furniture, picture frames, lamps and electrical sockets. We looked for false panels in the cupboards, the kitchen drawers, the bathroom vanities and the closets. Street crawled around the perimeter of the floors in every room tugging at the carpet to see where it might lift up. I pulled out every file drawer in Thos's office, looked in the laser printer, the computer tower and even took apart the fax. Exhausted, I sat down in his desk chair to think.

It was possible, of course, that Thos had nothing to hide, metal box, leather notebook or otherwise. Or that he had left it in the secret shrine all along.

I caught a glimpse of my reflection in the dark computer monitor. I looked like hell. Every bit of skin that wasn't bandaged showed bruises so sickening that, had I been filming a horror movie, they would have sent me back to makeup for a more realistic treatment. In fact, I could see myself so clearly it was almost as if I were looking in a mirror.

Which led me to the answer.

I turned the computer monitor on its swivel base. It was a standard model, but old, with a 17-inch screen and about 20 inches deep. The depth was for the old-style cathode ray picture tube. The plastic housing narrowed toward the back in a cone shape that approximated the picture tube inside the housing. Turning the monitor back around to face me, I saw my reflection again. The reason my reflection looked so clear was that the front of the monitor was flat. Not the convex curve of older style monitor.

I looked more closely at the edge where the plastic housing met the glass. The plastic was curved and made a little gap on the flat glass. A thin bead of clear silicone filled the space.

Thos had taken the cathode ray tube out of the monitor housing and replaced it with one of the newer flat screen monitors and glued it in place. Some flat screen monitors are only a couple inches thick, so that meant the monitor housing was mostly empty inside.

"I found it, Street," I called out.

She came into the room as I was removing screws. "A hiding place?"

"Yes. A good one. And bigger than a bread box." I popped the thing apart and turned it to look inside.

It was empty. But there were some foam sheets wadded into place to keep any item hidden there from rattling around.

Street pointed at the desktop. "Look at the desk near the base of the monitor. The wood is scratched like what would happen if you moved the monitor around a few times to put something inside it or take it back out."

"So we found the hiding place," I said. "Now we just need the item that was kept there."

"My guess," Street said, "is that Thos got it out of the cliff before the Viking could, hid it here in the monitor, then took it to Tahoe. The Viking followed Thos to Tahoe, and tried to force the location of the box out of him. When he thought he'd gotten the information, he shot Thos to cover his tracks. But Thos tricked him and the box wasn't where Thos said it was. So the Viking thought that Thos left it in the cliff all along. The Viking came back to Hawaii and hiked back up to the shrine when we were going on the helicopter ride. Now the Viking is gone, possibly back to California, maybe even back to Tahoe. Why?"

"Because," I guessed, "he finally found the item and wants to sell it to the antiques person in Tahoe. Or else he didn't find the item and he thinks Thos must have hidden it in Tahoe after all."

"Or," Street said, a frown wrinkling her brow, "he found the box and is going back to Tahoe to cover his tracks."

"What do you mean?"

"Maybe," she said, "he learned of other witnesses he needs to silence."

TWENTY-THREE

When we landed in L.A. early the next morning, I tried Janeen again.

She answered on the third ring. "I'm glad you're coming back," she said after I identified myself. "I heard about my nephew John. That is so terrible. And we've had a scare here."

"What was that?" I said, alarmed.

"We weren't harmed directly. But our neighbor Jerry Roth was."

"What happened?"

"Jerry was attacked last night. He often has insomnia and he couldn't sleep last night. When he got up he looked out the window and saw someone coming up our mutual driveway. Jerry went outside to confront the man and that's when he was attacked."

"Is he all right?" I asked.

"He will be eventually. Jerry had grabbed a snow shovel and the man took it from him and hit him on the neck with it. The gash required several stitches. He's still at the hospital for observation. They are worried that he hit his head hard when he fell to the ground. But I just spoke to him, and he said he's coming home soon."

"Did he say what the attacker was doing?"

"No. Just that he accosted the man and, well, Jerry can be brusque."

"Was Jerry able to see what the man looked like?"

"Only a little. When Jerry fell to the ground, he managed to get his cellphone out and quickly dial nine-one-one. The man saw him do that and ran. Jerry didn't see his face well because the man had long blond hair and a big bushy beard."

"Janeen," I said calmly, "I'll be in Tahoe in a few hours. In the meantime, I'm wondering if there is anyone you can go and stay with?"

"Do you think we're in danger?" Her voice, shaky before, was worse now.

"Possibly. Is there a friend you can call?"

"Yes, I suppose. I'll call Lyla Purdue."

"Does she live nearby?"

"She's on Mountain View Court. It's just two blocks from here."

I wrote the number down as she gave it to me. "Do that and stay inside. Phillip, too. Keep the blinds closed and don't open the door to anyone you don't know."

"Okay. You'll be in town soon?"

"I'm in L.A. now and will be back in Tahoe in three or four hours."

We said goodbye.

"What's wrong?" Street asked.

"The Viking is in Tahoe and it appears he's stalking Janeen and Phillip. Their neighbor surprised him coming up the drive in the middle of the night and was attacked." I explained what happened as we headed to the gate where the plane to Reno departed.

I called Captain Mallory. They put me through to him in his cruiser. He knew of the incident with Jerry Roth. He said the county deputies had sent patrols out to check on Janeen and Phillip. He also said he'd tried to get surveillance on Brock Chambers, but the man was gone, out of town according to people at the Rubicon Lodge.

When we got back to Tahoe, we didn't stop at either Street's condo or my cabin and instead went straight to Lyla Purdue's house. The house numbers were large and easy to find. There were no cars in the drive. There was a large ice flow across the walk and driveway. I stepped over the ice and knocked on the door. After a minute I called out, but there was no response. We drove over to Janeen's house.

There was a dark blue Buick parked in the drive. When I knocked, Janeen looked out through the living room window before she opened the door.

"Mr. McKenna," she said after I'd introduced her to Street. "You look terrible. What happened?"

"Street and I were in the helicopter with your nephew John when it crashed. I'm sorry about John."

She put her hand to her mouth. "The police chief called me about John. He said two other people survived the crash, but I had no idea."

We were still standing outside.

"Come in," Janeen suddenly said. She ushered us inside. "Lyla's house had a broken pipe yesterday. Everything was flooded. The workmen can't get to it for another day, so she is staying here with us. That man who attacked Jerry hasn't been back." She turned to Street. "You were in the crash, too. I'm so sorry. All because I hired Owen. I didn't mean to start something that would cause more pain."

"Don't worry," Street said. "I wasn't hurt at all. I only wish John could have been so lucky."

Janeen asked about John and the crash and we filled her in, leaving out the worst details. She shook her head as we explained.

"The car out there belongs to your friend?"

"Yes. Lyla is in with Phillip. I'd ask her to come out, but Phillip is happy right now and, well," she gave me an embarrassed look, "with your bruises, maybe it would be better to wait a few days?"

"Of course. Janeen, the man who attacked Jerry was probably coming to your house. Whether he intended to see if you were home or something else, I don't know. My best guess is that he wants to search your house in case Thos hid something here. I'd like you to relocate for the time being. Maybe you could stay with your father down in the Carson Valley?"

Janeen immediately shook her head. "No. He has mellowed over the years, but no. He doesn't have room, anyway. He lives in a little camper. With Lyla here, we have safety in numbers. Lyla understands there is a possible threat. She is prepared."

"Isn't there someplace else you can stay?"

Janeen shook her head. "I'm sorry, I don't have friends like that. And besides, the disruption would be difficult for Phillip and his school schedule."

"What about Jerry?"

"His place is no better than mine. Now that he's laid up, about the only thing he can do is call the cops. I wouldn't feel comfortable over there. He's a good neighbor, but not a friend like that."

Short of staying on her floor, I couldn't think of a good solution. My only thought was to swing by whenever I got a chance.

Street and I said goodbye and left. Street backed down the drive and swung into a space near Jerry's garage. I wanted to see if he was back from the hospital. Street held my arm as I eased myself up Jerry's snow-covered steps.

"Come in," a voice called out after I pushed the doorbell.

Street and I walked into a dark interior that had a Craftsman design from the early 20ᵗʰ Century. Jerry was in a leather recliner that faced away from us, his legs up, his crutch leaning to the side. He lifted a remote and clicked off a huge video screen. He had a bandage on the side of his neck.

"Hi, Jerry," I said.

"Sorry, old boy, about not taking Janeen in," he said as he reached for his crutch, laboriously got up out of the chair and turned toward us. "But this bloody sod came up the drive and... Good lord, what happened to you? Here I am feeling sorry for myself because I've got some pesky stitches while you look like hell. What on earth happened?"

"We had an accident in Hawaii."

"I'm sorry to hear that. I've always said Hawaiian roads are the worst on the planet. Narrow little things, one-lane most places. It's a wonder they even paint a line down the center."

"No matter, I'll be all right in time. Jerry, I want you to meet Street Casey."

He hobbled over. His head was bent toward the dressing on his neck. "Pleased to meet you," he said, shaking her hand. "Sorry about my bandages. I'm actually a handsome bloke when I'm not grimacing in pain."

"Jerry," I said, "Janeen told us about the man who attacked you last night."

"It was the bugger you told me about when you called from Hawaii. Ole Johnson."

"Knudson," I said.

"Oh, right. Long hair, big beard, looks like some movie version of a Swede. I could tell he was up to no good. On his way up to Janeen's, he was."

"He was on foot?"

"Yes. I wondered about that. He must have parked out in the road so I couldn't see his license plate. And with these walls of snow, I couldn't even see his car. When he knocked me down, I got out my phone. Lucky for me I always carry it with me." He pulled the yellow phone out of his pocket and held it up. "That sod saw it and ran. I didn't even hear him start up his car, but then all this snow muffles sound."

"He hit you with your snow shovel?"

"Righto. Grabbed it from me and had a swing at my face. Luckily, I'm quick with the reflexes. I ducked and he got the base of my neck. Still, it took the doc a bit to close me up." Jerry tugged at the bandage to show us the edge of his wound. There was a vertical row of stitches ending at a horizontal row, making the shape of a T.

Street bent down and picked something up off of the carpet. She said, "Jerry, when you dialed nine-one-one, did the ambulance come and get you? How did you get home?"

"The call didn't go through. My injuries weren't that bad and Ole whatshisname was gone. So I drove myself to the emergency room. They were a little concerned I'd gotten smacked worse than I had – I suppose I carried on a bit too much. So they kept me there a couple hours after sewing me up. But I didn't start drooling on myself, so they let me go." He turned and spoke directly to Street. "Why do you ask about the ambulance?"

"I'm wondering if Ole Knudson came back and let himself into your house when you were at the hospital."

"I don't understand," Jerry said.

Street gestured with her hand, her thumb and forefinger held together. "I just found a dead insect on your carpet. A beetle that looks to be of a species that is not native to Tahoe."

"What of it?" Jerry said.

"This is a tropical beetle. If I'm not mistaken, it is found in ecosystems from Papua New Guinea to the islands of the Pacific. This bug may have come from Hawaii."

Jerry's face colored with anger. "Why, that son of a bitch!" Jerry spun around, leaning on his crutch, looking at his house in a new way. "When I went to the hospital I was in such a hurry I didn't stop to lock up. If that bugger has been through my house... goddammit!"

I said, "Jerry, did you know Thos Kahale?"

"Not really. We'd say, 'hello, how do you do,' when he was coming and going. But that's about it. Seemed like a nice enough chap."

"I'm wondering if he gave you anything to hold for safe-keeping."

Jerry shook his head.

"Could he have come in when you weren't here and hid something in your house?"

Jerry's eyes widened. "That would explain why Blondie was in here poking around, wouldn't it?" Jerry turned again and looked around. "Maybe I'll poke around a bit, myself. What would I be looking for?"

"An old leather notebook is one possibility. Or a metal box big enough to put a notebook in."

"I'll let you know if I find anything."

I asked Jerry if he'd keep a watch on Janeen and Phillip and he said he'd stay by the window.

I got Mallory on the phone as Street drove around to the east side of the lake. I explained the situation with Janeen and he said he would continue to send patrols by. Street pulled in at her condo. She had wanted to go solo before we went to Kauai. Now the moment of separation was back. "Call me tomorrow?" she said, giving me a peck on the lips.

"Sure," I said, loneliness suddenly poking into all my soft spots, making me swallow, making my breathing unsteady. "Say hi to your bugs."

She touched the bandage on my forehead and caressed my cheek.

I turned back to my Jeep before she saw my eyes get moist. Some tough guy you are, Owen. I eased myself into the driver's seat and headed home.

TWENTY-FOUR

I drove the short distance down the highway and headed up the mountain to my cabin.

The Douglas County Sheriff Department Explorer that Diamond Martinez drove was in my drive. I honked, my cabin door opened and Spot came running out. He understands the No Jump command, but I didn't use it, so he was all over me. I gritted my teeth against the pain as I shadow-boxed with him, gave him a bear hug and let him do the pretend chew on my forearm. He stood up on his hind legs and put his front paws on my shoulders. We danced two or three measures while he sniffed my facial bandages.

"Who is Rogers and who is Astaire?" said a voice from behind me.

Spot and I did a little pirouette so I could face Diamond.

"My dog's getting better," I said. "You been practicing with him while I've been gone?"

"Sure. Why not. Best way I can think of to spend my time. What happened to your face? You look like a squished eggplant."

"Helicopter crash," I said.

Diamond looked at me for a moment. "So the putative drama of the private investigator's lifestyle is really true, eh?"

"Putative?" I said. "That a Mex word?"

Diamond shook his head. "English. Means 'supposed.' Helicopter crash, huh? What happened?"

I filled Diamond in on everything from the time we met

Jasper and learned more details of the secret shrine, to the crash at the hand of the Viking.

"Why are you back in Tahoe so soon?"

"Because the Viking came back to Tahoe. He attacked Janeen's neighbor Jerry Roth last night. Looks like he's okay, though."

"Oh," Diamond said. "What is the Viking's name? Mallory told me, but it is one of the funnier white-boy names and it slips my mind."

"Ole Knudson was the name on the ID that he showed the airline ticket agents."

"Any idea what this guy is after?"

"Just that the Kahale family is connected to something that this guy wants. One possibility is a hand-written manuscript by Mark Twain."

"You're kidding."

"No. Twain met the family when he went to Kauai in the eighteen sixties. He supposedly gave them a story."

"The putative story?"

"Something like that," I said.

We went inside my cabin and I got a Sierra Nevada Pale Ale from the fridge. I offered one to Diamond and he declined. When I opened it, Spot walked over by the kitchen counter, sat down and gave me the look of expectation that means he's hungry.

I noticed his food bowl was empty. Diamond watched as I filled it up with dog food and refreshed his water bowl.

Spot continued to sit there. He glanced from me to the fridge and back to the counter where the microwave sits. Then he stood up, walked past his food bowl, turned a few circles on the rug by the woodstove and lay down.

"Spot looks with total boredom at his food," I said.

"That's funny. He's had a hearty appetite the whole time you've been gone," Diamond said. "Especially for breakfast. Every morning we ate together at the kitchen counter." Diamond saw me looking at him. "Don't worry. I wiped the counter clean."

"He ate his Science Diet on the kitchen counter?"

"No, no," Diamond said with a dismissive wave of his hand. "The dog food I put in his bowl."

"Then what did he eat for breakfast?"

Diamond acted like it was a silly question. "A Danish. Just like me."

"You gave him Danishes for breakfast?"

"He's a Great Dane, ain't he? Anyway, he loves 'em. You should see the look on his face when I take them out of the microwave."

I turned toward where Spot was lying on the rug. He lifted his head off the floor and looked again toward the microwave. Then he rolled over onto his side and sighed.

TWENTY-FIVE

It was late afternoon when Diamond left. My head was pounding worse than ever so I decided to call it a day. I found a T-Bone in the freezer and a Black Mountain Cab I'd picked up cheap at Trader Joe's in Reno. Although I often barbecue on winter nights, I didn't want to be on view in case the watcher was in the snowy clearing. Nor did I want to face the cold weather with how the wind had picked up outside. My body missed the tropics. So I turned on the broiler to warm up while the steak defrosted in the microwave. I knew a sensible dinner would include vegetables and salad, but I was too tired and this was my first night without Street in months. Making a full dinner just for myself would make me even lonelier.

Spot jumped up and trotted over when the microwave beeped. I pulled out the steak and transferred it to the broiler. Spot studied my every move, his ears focused, eyes intense, nostrils flexing. "I suppose you think, 'Danish for breakfast, ergo steak for dinner?' Don't you know you're a dog?"

Spot stared at me. "Sorry," I said, shaking my head. I walked over and pointed at his food bowl. "Science Diet. Yum! Yum!" Spot hung his head. He ambled over to the rug in front of the woodstove and lowered himself down with a groan. He lay in an S-curve with his rear legs facing to the right and his front legs and head to the left. He hooked a paw over his nose and pretended to sleep.

When I was through eating I took the scraps of fat and stirred them into his dog food. Spot jumped up and stood waiting for the okay, tail held high. By the look in his eyes you'd think an Omaha Steaks truck had just pulled up in the drive.

When I said, "Okay," he dove his head into the bowl. He didn't inhale the dog food Hoover-style as was his norm, but instead rooted out the scraps of fat. He pushed the bowl across the floor, hit the wall and proceeded toward the bedroom until he extracted every piece of fat leaving the dog food untouched. Then he lay back down and went to sleep, this time for real.

Leaving the indoor lights blazing, but the outdoor lights off, I pulled on a dark baseball cap and stepped out on the deck. There is a place next to the corner of my cabin that is out of sight from the clearing where the watcher had stood. When my eyes adjusted, I pulled the brim of my cap down low and peeked out.

In my former life as a cop, before the kid who robbed the bank, I had some practice on stakeouts. The most important skill for the job is patience.

I waited a long time without moving. My thoughts went to Street and the Calder mobile that she'd given me. It seemed that I was after something similar to what Calder wanted. Take the different parts of my life – Street, Spot, art, and detective work – and arrange them so they balanced. I'd made a kind of emotional mobile. Street was the biggest part, but often the farthest away. So I kept Spot and art and my work on the other side of the balance point, close by, always accessible, pulling my emotional core back toward center.

Twenty minutes later, nothing had moved in the clearing. Maybe the watcher had decided it wasn't a good place to hang out. Never know when McKenna comes flying down the mountain behind you, on the skinny boards, unpredictable, out of balance.

I went back inside, put on a Borodin String Quartet CD and sat in front of the fire, thinking of Street and her need for independence. Twice I glanced at the woman in Rodin's Eternal Spring. She arched up toward the man. Her desire for physical love was evident. But her passion for romantic love seemed even stronger. More than an idealized figure, she conveyed idealized emotion. But in the real world a perfect woman sometimes needs to go home and sleep alone.

Eventually, I followed suit and had dreams of helicopters crashing in tropical jungles.

The next morning I ate several aspirin with my coffee and took Spot with me in the Jeep. I headed south down the East Shore and turned up Kingsbury Grade to my office. Spot trotted up the stairs in front of me.

There was a pile of junk mail and bills inside the mail slot. I tossed it all on the desk and turned on the computer to check my email. Spot stood and looked out the window, his chin resting on the windowsill.

I had dozens of messages, mostly junk. I scrolled down, clicking briefly on each one that might have been a reply to the letter I sent to the names in Thos's address book.

I came to one with a subject line that said, Re: Your Question About Thos.

I clicked on it. It was from Tad at the .com address of a Napa Valley winery.

"Got your email. Didn't know about Thos. So sorry! I didn't know him well. We sold wine to his distribution company, so our relationship was mostly business. But we had lunch a couple times when he came to Napa. I can't think of anything he would have told me that would help, but you asked me to respond regardless. Call anytime and we can talk."

I hit reply, told Tad thanks and said I'd be in touch if I had any questions.

I scrolled down farther and came to several more messages that were similar from people who'd had social contact with Thos but offered nothing revealing.

Then came a message from Suz at a Hawaiian ISP address. I remembered that she was one of the people whose last message to Thos came after his death. In it, she'd said, yes, she would fly to Honolulu with Thos for a night on the town.

"Dear Mr. McKenna, My name is Suzy Moffett. I'm not sure what to say except that Thos was my boyfriend. We weren't necessarily a permanent thing, but the closest thing to it. I loved him and he maybe loved me. I know he liked me a lot. He confided in me to some extent, but about nothing that would get him killed. Why would someone kill him? If you find out, please let me know. It's just that...I guess I thought we might get married or something some day. If you want to ask me questions or whatever, write me back. I'll do my best to help. I'm praying that you find whoever did this, Mr. McKenna. All I've done is cry since I heard the news. Suzy"

I clicked on the next email and the next and the next. There were several more from people wanting to be helpful but probably not in possession of the kind of information I needed.

Then came another name I recognized from reading Thos's messages when we were at his townhouse. It was from Hermes at the msn.com address.

The subject said, "Re: What got Thos killed."

"Hello Owen McKenna. I'm a friend of Thos Kahale. Before Thos died he emailed me about something he used to have that was very valuable. He said it had caused the deaths of three people and that a fourth person was after it. So Thos destroyed it. He said the person who was after it would know that he destroyed it.

I can't believe that Thos had to die. But now the murderer must know the thing is gone and this will be over. Hermes"

I hit reply and typed,

"Hermes, Thank you for writing. Unfortunately, I think you may be in danger. Thos's killer won't believe Thos destroyed the item in question. Worse, the killer might assume that you know something of this item and may try to find you. Even if he finds you and is convinced you know nothing, you will still be in danger because then you will know who he is. Would you please identify yourself to the police or to me? In the meantime be on the watch for a man with long blond hair and a beard. His name is Ole Knudson and I believe he is Thos's killer. Please write immediately."

I hit send.

I knew that Microsoft owned msn.com. I assumed it would be extremely difficult to get them to turn over information about Hermes. Even if they did, email addresses can be obtained with fictitious names.

Nevertheless, it might be worth pursuing. I got Diamond on his cellphone and explained the situation. He said he'd contact the District Attorney and find out what was involved in trying to get a warrant to crack open the Microsoft archives.

I hung up and pondered the situation. I was confident that if the Viking could track down Hermes he'd get whatever information he could by any means. I had to find out Hermes's identity first.

I'd brought the Zip disk that I'd copied Thos's address book onto. I loaded it into my computer, then wrote another email.

"Hello, this is Detective Owen McKenna. I have learned that one of Thos's email friends is in grave danger from the same person who murdered Thos. This friend goes by the name Hermes. It is imperative I learn Hermes's identity as soon as possible. If you know or can even guess at Hermes's identity, email me immediately. His or her life is at stake. Thank you, Owen."

I sent it to everyone in Thos's address book except Hermes.

There was nothing else I could think of to do so I turned off the computer. I snapped my fingers. "C'mon, Spot. Let's get some breakfast and go for a drive."

We headed across town and stopped at the Red Hut. When I was done with my breakfast omelet, I brought out the requisite leftover morsels, a single one of which, to Spot, is like the Hope Diamond to a jeweler. Every time I lifted one to his snout I risked losing fingers.

I started the Jeep and drove around to the west side of the

lake.

It was blustery as I left town and went north on 89. Light snow filled the sky. I thought I'd check in again on Janeen and Phillip.

I turned in on Spring Creek Road, took a right on Cornice Road and pulled slowly up the white tunnel-like driveway. Jerry waved at me from his window.

Lyla Purdue's Buick was still there. Phillip was outside, standing in his snowshoes on a snow bank near the house. He didn't run away as I expected. Was school closed because of snow? Or was it the weekend? My head hurt as I thought about it and I wondered if my concussion had done permanent damage.

I pulled to a stop and got out carefully, trying to go easy on my throbbing head. I kept my face turned somewhat so Phillip wouldn't see the worst of my bruises and bandages. Spot's head was hanging out the window. I pet him as I called out to Phillip. "I brought Spot again, Phillip. You can pet him while I go talk to your grandmother. Or if you want, I can let him out to play."

I hesitated, giving Phillip time to respond. "He likes to play with kids." I kept petting Spot's head. He leaned into it, turning so I could better scratch his ears. "What do you say, Phillip?"

"I don't believe you," Phillip suddenly said, the first time I'd ever heard him speak beyond a whisper. His voice was tiny, but high and clear in the cold winter air.

"Believe what?"

"I don't believe he'll play. He'll just run away."

"Spot won't run away, Phillip. I promise."

"Adults don't keep promises."

"Sure, they do," I said, feeling bad as soon as I uttered the phrase. Obviously Phillip had a reason for his thoughts.

"No, they don't."

"Who doesn't?"

"Thos didn't. He said he was going to take me to Hawaii. Now he's dead."

"He probably was going to take you there. Dying isn't the

same as breaking a promise."

"My mom said she was going to bring me to L.A. to live with her. She said I could go to the beach. She promised. But she's just a druggie."

"I'm sure her intentions for you are good."

"I don't care about intentions. She broke her promise. Jerry did, too. He said he was going to take me out on his boat some day. He said we'd sail on the ocean."

I turned toward Phillip. I gestured toward my face. "Just bandages. I was in an accident."

Phillip didn't speak. But he didn't run, either. Owen, you devil, you are so smooth with kids.

"Phillip, you know the kids at your school. Some of them are careful about what they say. Others say anything that pops into their minds whether they mean it or not. Most are somewhere between. Well, adults are the same way. I'm sorry some of them have broken promises."

I smiled across the snow bank at Phillip. "Shall I let Spot out of the car while I go inside to talk to your grandmother?"

"No," Phillip said in a frightened voice. He turned and ran off into the snowy forest.

"Sorry, your largeness," I muttered. I gave him another pet and walked to Janeen's door. It opened before I knocked. "Hi, Janeen. I asked Phillip if he might want to play with Spot."

"I saw out the window. It was nice of you to try." She gave me a weak smile, then turned and looked toward the trees where Phillip had disappeared. "It's okay, isn't it, for Phillip to go into the woods?"

I glanced toward the forest, then down their drive.

Janeen continued, "I know Jerry was attacked, but Jerry probably took a swing at him first. Jerry can be very abrasive. Besides, I think it wasn't as bad as Jerry makes it sound. He's kind of a hypochondriac in my opinion. And I think he's going through some financial distress."

"Really? I thought he was wealthy."

"He is," Janeen said. "But even wealthy people can have setbacks, right? One day when I stopped by and knocked, he hollered for me to come in. I waited while he finished a phone call. He only said a few words that I heard, but you know how you sometimes get the drift of something? Well, it sounded like he owed money to somebody. And when he hung up, he muttered something about bill collectors.

"Anyway," she continued, "I think that kind of stress really brings out aches and pains in a hypochondriac, don't you? As for Phillip, I can't keep a little boy cooped up inside day and night. He'd go crazy. And the woods are really safe for a boy." She seemed to look at me for approval.

"I agree the woods are probably quite safe as far as bad people are concerned. I don't know about animals. Phillip is quite small."

"He knows the rules. If he sees a bear or mountain lion or coyotes, he's not to run but move away slowly, hands up to look bigger. He even carries pepper spray just in case. The only kids who've ever been hurt by wild animals were much smaller children bitten by coyotes."

I looked out at the snow, which was so deep no one could walk through it. With Phillip so agile on his snowshoes, the forest was probably the safest place in the world for him. "I'm sure it's fine, Janeen."

Lyla Purdue appeared from the kitchen and Janeen introduced us. Lyla kept her distance, glancing at my bandages. Janeen turned back to me. "Do you still think Phillip and I are in danger from the man who attacked Jerry?"

"Possibly," I said. "More likely, however, he is not after you but after whatever he thinks Thos had."

"Something he thinks was hidden in the shrine in Kauai?"

"Yes." I proceeded to give Janeen an account of our time in Hawaii, including our fruitless search for a possible manuscript by Mark Twain. Lyla retired to the kitchen while Janeen and I talked for a long time, but none of Janeen's thoughts gave me any new ideas.

"Can you think of any place in this house where Thos may have hidden a notebook? Or a small box?" I gestured with my hands to approximate the size.

Janeen shook her head. "No. Thos was never here alone that I can recall. It would have been difficult for him to hide anything without us knowing it."

"Would you mind if I have a look around?"

"No, of course not. Can I be of help?"

"Yes, please," I said. A search was better done alone without distractions, but I wanted Janeen to be comfortable.

We went through the little house in less than an hour. Everything was neat and clean and orderly, even Phillip's room. Having previously found Thos's computer monitor hiding place, I knew something of Thos's way of thinking. By that guideline, there were several very good places in Janeen's house that Thos might have used, but I found no manuscript or other treasure in them.

"Are you disappointed?" Janeen asked me when we were finished.

"No. I want the killer to find his loot elsewhere. Then you and Phillip will be safe. Do you have a computer?"

"No. I know I should get one for Phillip, but I haven't gotten around to it. Why do you ask?"

"I'm trying to contact anyone who communicated with Thos through email."

I thanked her, told her I'd check on them tomorrow, and left.

TWENTY-SIX

It was now almost 2:00 p.m. The winter sun was low in the southwest and was obscured by clouds on the mountains of the Sierra crest. There is a high overlook as you approach Emerald Bay, and you can see the entire lake. The wind patterns across the water were dramatic as the mountains made chaos of the prevailing wind. Huge, dark clouds rushed over the mountains and hurtled out across the lake toward Nevada.

I tuned the radio to a local AM station and got a forecast as I cruised past the rock slide at Emerald Bay. The DJ reported that the storm in the Gulf of Alaska was just starting to move south down the coast of Canada. It wasn't expected to hit Northern California for another couple days, yet already it was throwing tendrils of clouds down the coast and up into the mountains. They weren't predicting snowfall totals yet, but they said the storm had the potential to deliver a major punch to the Tahoe area. We should expect the possibility of road closures from north of Truckee south to Yosemite.

I turned in at Rubicon Lodge. From my memory of the argument I had witnessed between Brock Chambers and the Viking, I believed that Chambers knew who the Viking was. I also believed that I could get the information out of him.

There was a young man with short blond hair so light his scalp showed through, and a stern-looking middle-aged woman at the reception desk. They seemed to be having a disagreement as I walked up. The woman noticed me first and moved her head and eyes to try to signal my presence to the young man whose back was toward me. He didn't get it.

"No!" he said. "I don't believe a word he says. If you think you're going to get some severance out of this, forget it. Brock is a lying snake. There's only one person who is going to make out on this collapse and that's McCloud the hunter. You know she's tight with him. The rest of us are going to get screwed to the wall. Frankly, I'm surprised the jerk didn't try arson or something so he could stick the insurance companies with his financial..." he finally noticed the woman's frantic gestures.

He turned around. "Oh. Good afternoon, sir." If he was startled by the bruises on my face, he didn't show it. "May I help you?" His face was red.

"I had an appointment with Brock at three o'clock," I lied. "Name's Owen McKenna."

"I don't understand. I can't imagine that Brock had set up any appointments for today. He's..." the man stopped speaking, wary, finally on guard.

"Three o'clock. That's what we set up last week." I thought that as long as he'd handed me the financial problem concept, I may as well go with it. "If Brock's late, that's one thing. But if he dropped the ball on this deal, well let's just say that time's running out. If I'm going to cover his overdue payables and his cash-flow shortage for the next six months, then he's going to show me the respect of showing up for his appointments. There are a lot of other places I can invest four hundred K. Now, where is he?"

"I'm sorry, sir, we don't know where he is. Ever since he filed for protection with the court, he hasn't been in. We've called all his numbers and Jimmy even ran over to his house. But no one is there. All I can do is direct you to his attorney, Lynette McCloud."

"Is she handling his bankruptcy?"

"I don't think so. But she's his friend and gives him general advice."

I tried to stand even taller than my six-six and leaned in over the young man. "You just referred to her as McCloud the hunter. What does that mean?"

"Nothing," he stammered. "We just call her that because she goes hunting with Brock."

I jerked my head toward the trophy heads on the walls behind me. "You mean she shoots big game?"

The guy steeled himself to answer. "I believe, Mr. McKenna, that Lynette McCloud would shoot any damn thing she felt like shooting."

I kept my eyes severe and unmoving for another couple of seconds. "Tell Brock to call me at my office. If I don't hear from him in twenty-four hours, I'm out." I walked out.

Back in the Jeep, Spot sniffed me all over just as he had the last time I'd been in the Rubicon Lodge. Was it the dead animals on the walls? Or the people in the lodge?

I drove back out the lodge's drive and turned north on 89.

I'd looked earlier and found the address of Morella Meyer's Commercial Diving and Salvage Shop in Tahoe City.

Her shop was a block from the Truckee River and three blocks from the lake. It was in a small building that backed up to the forest. The building had once been a gas station. Now, a beauty salon occupied the left side where the cashier's area had been, and Morella's shop was behind the garage doors on the right side where mechanics had once worked on cars. Although the garage doors still looked functional, it was a cold January day. They were closed tight. The beauty salon was shut as well with all the lights off on that side of the building. I parked in front of a huge bank of snow left by the plow. There was a little sign on the corner of the building and I found a door there.

I heard the hum of machinery before I opened the door. "Morella?" I said when I'd pushed in the door. "Anybody home?"

Morella stepped out from behind a large rack of scuba tanks. "Oh," she said, startled. "The compressor makes so much noise I didn't hear you come in." She spoke loudly to be heard over the racket. "I remember you. You were at the Rubicon Lodge last week. Captain Mallory's friend." Her demeanor was pleasant but not friendly. Her wayward eyes seemed to look at me in sequence. First, the left eye zeroed in on me, then it wandered a bit to the side as the right eye took me on. I still couldn't remember which one was glass. And she still looked beautiful in spite of her wild eyes.

"Owen McKenna," I said.

"I remember," she said. "You had a bad fall?" she said as she reached out to shake hands. Her hand seemed small and soft for someone who worked with scuba tanks and other heavy equipment.

"I was in a helicopter crash in Hawaii."

"Oh, my God. That's terrible. Well, I'm glad you're okay. Mostly, anyway."

"I wanted to talk to you about your dive that day."

"The dive where I didn't find anything."

"You were going to dive again the next day, weren't you? Find anything different that day?"

She shook her head as she reached over and checked a silver tank that was sitting in a fiberglass container that looked like a short shower stall. A hose from the compressor was attached to a valve on the top of the tank. At the top of the shower stall was a shower head that sprayed a light stream of water over the tank to keep it cool while it was being filled with hot compressed air. "You told me not to just look for a bullet, right? I was to look for anything unusual or out of place. So I did."

"Any luck?"

"No. Same clear ice water, same smooth bottom. No bullet, no dead bodies, no skull-and-crossbone clues floating around waiting for a diver to find." The compressor clicked off and the old garage was suddenly silent. "Excuse me, I need to switch tanks."

Morella unhooked the stiff black hose from the top of the tank. She pulled the dripping tank out of the mini shower stall and lay it down on a carpet-covered work bench.

"How much air do you put in these tanks?"

"This type is high pressure steel, they hold eighty cubic feet."

"Lot of pressure when you squeeze that much air into about, what, a third of a cubic foot?"

"Yeah. Thirty-five hundred pounds per square inch." She set another tank into the stall, hooked it up, and started the compressor. She was turning on the cooling water when the phone rang.

"Meyer's Diving," she answered. "Who? Oh. Hello. Well, I've got a customer. I don't know how long. Actually, it's Owen McKenna. No. He's a detective. He's working with the police on the murder of the guy in the water. What? No, just asking me stuff about my dive."

There was a pause. Morella glanced at me and then casually angled away from me. "No," she said in a softer voice. "Well, I suppose twenty minutes." She hung up.

"Someone who knows me?"

She glared at me for a brief moment. Then her eyes softened. "No. I just used your name because some people know of you even if they don't know you personally. It didn't sound like... I don't think this person had ever heard of you."

"Morella, remember when I asked you about the note in your day planner?"

She glared at me.

"I need to ask again."

"That is my personal business."

"But it may have bearing on this case."

Morella shook her head. She took a towel off a rack and wiped down the wet tank she'd just filled.

"Let me explain," I said. "I was gone in Hawaii for a few days checking into Thos Kahale's background. He's the man who was shot in Lake Tahoe."

Morella appeared to ignore me. She put the tank in a rack.

To the side was a separate rack. She pulled an orange tank out of it, checked an air pressure gauge, then cranked open the valve a little. The shrill rush of escaping air filled the small shop like the whoosh of a jet. It was much louder than the compressor.

I kept talking, louder than before. "Three other men were killed in Hawaii. Thos's cousin, uncle and grandfather. So it is critical that we consider every bit of information that could possibly pertain to this killer."

Morella looked at me, then turned to a cabinet and pulled out a drawer. It contained several large chrome-plated valves of the type that go on the top of the tanks. She selected one and shut the drawer.

"Morella, you wrote 'call Strict ASAP after dive' in your day planner. If it has nothing to do with your dive or Thos's murder, then tell me about it and I'll leave you alone."

She continued about her business as if I weren't there.

"But if it has anything to do with Thos, I need to know."

She ignored me.

I kept talking, telling her about Thos's grandfather who was smothered and his uncle who was killed in a car accident that may not have been an accident. And his cousin John who died in the helicopter crash. And the young tough named Napoleon who was dropped at the hospital in Kauai with a fatal knife wound. When she understood the depth of this killer's activities, maybe she would overcome whatever personal embarrassment or financial incentive she had to keep quiet.

It didn't seem to make a difference. There were face masks and fins and snorkels to rinse out and wet suits to hang up and CO_2 cartridges to check in the buoyancy compensator jackets and valves to change on tanks and regulators to check.

I ran out of story about the time she glanced up through the rear windows for the second time. I turned to see what was catching her eye, but there was only snowy forest turning dark in the approaching twilight.

The compressor shut off. Morella shut off the shower head,

pulled the wet tank out of the stall and hefted it up onto the carpeted work bench. She took a towel and dried the tank off, rolling it over on the carpet.

"Morella, if you are afraid to talk, I can help. Together, we can deal with whatever is bothering you. This killer will strike again. What you tell me now may save a life."

Morella stopped drying the tank. "Okay," she said. She leaned against the counter, her hands resting on the tank, its smooth round end against her flat belly. "Strict is the name I..."

She was cut short by an explosion. Glass filled the air as a garage window shattered. At the same time the valve on the back end of the scuba tank she was holding blew off in a percussive blast.

With the valve gone, the exhaust opening had 3500 pounds per square inch of thrust and the tank became a rocket with instant acceleration.

The tank shot into Morella's abdomen and carried her across the garage. It slammed her with tremendous force into a workbench. Freed from Morella, the tank flew at an upward angle toward the ceiling. There was a crunching boom as it blew through the sheet rock.

A fraction of a second later I saw the tank shooting down outside. It hit the icy parking lot near where Spot watched from my Jeep. The tank bounced off the ground and shot skyward, accelerating like a missile until it arced out of sight.

TWENTY-SEVEN

I rushed over to Morella. She was slumped down next to the edge of the workbench, her face against the concrete floor. There was a severe injury to her head near her temple. Blood and brain tissue were on the sharp corner of the workbench vise. The metal had cut through her head from side to front. I could see from the injury that her eye was destroyed and it wasn't the one made of glass.

Morella was not breathing. The small pool of blood on the floor was not expanding. I felt the carotid artery in her neck. There was no pulse.

Powdered glass hung in the air near the exploded window. I ran over and looked out. There was no movement in the dark forest. I sprinted out the door and angled down the road toward where I thought he would have parked.

In the far distance an engine revved. Red taillights flashed in the dark and the vehicle roared off. It turned toward the highway and disappeared. I couldn't see the make and I knew that there was no point in giving chase. The highway in Tahoe City went three directions and there were many neighborhood roads to disappear into. He could be anywhere.

I went back inside and knelt next to Morella's body.

Twice before in my earlier police career I'd been faced with the decision of whether or not to start CPR.

There are conflicting statutes and court precedents that apply and many more opinions from medical ethicists. But they all fade into the background when a person is dying and you are the only one to breathe air into their lungs and artificially squeeze their heart.

I knew that even if I could perform a miracle and restart her heart, I would not be prolonging life for a vital young woman. I'd seen too many head injuries to have any illusions about the outcome. The brain damage was far too extreme. Instead, I would be prolonging existence for a blind, comatose body, dependent on feeding tubes and other machinery.

I didn't think I was playing God when I finally stood up and walked with slow, heavy steps to the telephone.

My 911 call brought a Placer County Sheriff's cruiser in less than one minute. I stepped outside to meet him. The deputy was in his late twenties, old enough to be professional. When he saw the damage to the building he immediately called for backup. When I showed him my license, he didn't get huffy as younger cops tend to do and instead recognized me as one of his brethren. But when he stepped into the garage and saw what had happened to Morella Meyer, he staggered.

"Jesus, sweet Jesus," he said, then leaned over and vomited. I steered him back out into the fresh winter air and kept him there until reinforcements arrived.

The paramedics were first. Two young men in a red truck. The cockier of the two thought he was a TV actor. "Well, holy goddamn!" he sang out in a sing-song voice when he saw the body. "We got us hamburger! Ain't no CPR can fix hamburger!"

I took most of the front of his jacket in my fist, lifted him up and slammed him back against the wall. "One more word," I hissed in his face. "Just one more word."

He went pale. I let go of his jacket and he fell to the floor. He got up and scrambled out to his truck.

In time many other deputies arrived, along with a fire truck. As twilight turned to night, the flashing red and blue lights cast an eerie flickering glow into the snowy forest.

I'd spent some time explaining the events to the Placer County deputies when Mallory strode into the shop. "Long way from where I belong," he said. "But this probably connects, so I thought I'd stop by." He turned and saw Morella's body. His eyes showed horror for a moment and I thought he was going to be sick, too. He turned away, swallowed and stared at the forest outside while he took several deep breaths. Finally, he scanned the room without looking back toward Morella's body. He saw me. "What the hell happened to your face?"

"The helicopter crash in Kauai."

Mallory studied me. "Oh," he said. "What do you figure happened here?" He kept his eyes on me.

"I think we had a shooter out in the woods. Took a shot through the window at the scuba tank valve right as Morella was leaning over the front end. The tank became a self-propelled artillery shell. It lifted her up and..."

"Wait, wait," Mallory was shaking his head and waving his hand in the air as if to wipe off a chalk board. "What do you mean an artillery shell?"

"The tank was full of air at thirty-five hundred pounds per square inch. The opening in the tank is maybe a square inch of area. So if you suddenly uncork it, you've got a rocket with thirty-five hundred pounds of thrust."

Mallory's eyes widened the tiniest bit. "Why do you think a shooter?"

"I couldn't swear to it, but I had a sense that the glass in that window exploded a split second before the tank took off." I gestured at the window. "I ran outside and saw a vehicle start up down the road, but it was too far away to give chase. Morella got a call about ten minutes before it happened. I'd guess it was the shooter who called."

Mallory frowned. "The Placer boys will know if your idea is right when they find the valve that came off the tank and examine it. There'll be marks if it was struck by a bullet." He turned and looked around the floor. The valve was not in sight. He rotated on his heel, scanning for the valve, and ended up facing Morella's body. He turned away from her, his breathing heavy.

"You remember when I asked you if you had a cop on the roster named Strict?" I said. "I'd been talking to Morella after she finished searching the bottom for you that day. I saw a note she wrote herself reminding her to call someone named Strict as soon as she was through with the dive you sent her on. When I asked her about it, she said it was about another dive. But I didn't believe her. I came up here to try to convince her to talk."

"Did she?"

"She was about to. But it may have been a ploy."

"Meaning?" Mallory said.

"She mentioned to the person on the phone that I was here asking questions about the search dive she'd made. The caller asked her some kind of question to which she'd answered, 'twenty minutes.' After that, she glanced out the window a couple of times. I assumed she was expecting someone. When she believed that person had arrived, she may have been going to start to talk so that I would believe she intended to cooperate. Then the person who arrived would come to the door and interrupt. Morella would get me off her back for a time and she could figure out what to do."

"But the shooter decided to take her out and eliminate any question about it."

"I think so," I said.

"Isn't the whole thing pretty far-fetched? I mean, hitting that valve would require an amazing shot. And even assuming one could hit it, how would you be sure the tank would kill Morella?"

"I agree it is a reach," I said. "But a bullet through the heart would be a clear case of first degree murder. Whereas, even a lousy lawyer could get someone off a death-by-scuba-tank charge."

"But what about the improbability of it?" Mallory said. "The chances of succeeding at what happened must be one in a thousand."

"True. So maybe the shooter wasn't trying to kill Morella, but just disrupt our conversation. Maybe the shooter decided he didn't want to show his face to me and thought this was a way to get her to stop talking to me."

Mallory was chewing on his cheek. "There is another possibility," he said. "The shooter may think you wouldn't guess there was a shot. Maybe you'd think it was just a freak accident. The valve comes off, something flies and breaks the window. Maybe Morella dies. Maybe she doesn't. But if it looks like an accident, then no one thinks about a shooter and no one looks for a slug. The shooter can even come back when things have quieted down, find the slug and pocket the evidence."

"You could be right," I said.

"So what more do you want to tell me before someone else dies?" There was acid in his voice.

"I didn't think Morella would die over a question about calling someone named Strict. I would have told you if I even dreamed it could come to that."

"Maybe you ought to start dreaming possibilities regarding other things you haven't told me."

"Okay," I said. "Brock Chambers may be losing his lodge to financial distress. Sounds like he is in receivership."

"We knew that," Mallory said.

"And being a hunter he is probably a crack shot with a rifle."

"Knew that, too."

"He has a lawyer friend named Lynette McCloud. According to a young man who works behind Brock's reception desk, she's also a hunter and is reputed to be willing to shoot anything she feels like."

Mallory nodded. "Didn't know McCloud was his lawyer. I did know McCloud was a hunter. We probably could figure she'd play fast and hard with her weapons based on what a hot dog she is. Drives a red Lexus sports car. Wears spike heels to court. Charges four times what the next highest guy charges. Likes male jurors because she can get them to do her bidding."

"She get results?"

Mallory looked disgusted. "She only just moved to South

Lake Tahoe from L.A. eighteen months ago, but she's never lost a case here. People around the courthouse think she's pretty ridiculous, but it all gets down to the juries."

"She specialize in criminal defense?"

"I'm not sure how much of a specialty it is. But she's had several of them since she moved here. Now she's got a sugar daddy, a music producer from San Francisco. We booked him on a concealed weapons charge after he and his two bodyguards pulled iron at a disturbance at one of the casinos and then drove across the state line into California. Lusty Lyn was on him like an ambulance chaser. Convinced him he needed local legal talent. He took a chance on her and she got him off."

"He fall for the legal talent or the spike heels?" I asked.

"Who knows. Next thing, she traded in the three million dollar view from her house up on Keller for the twenty million dollar view from the music dude's spread. So maybe she's going to retire. He's got his own little private mountaintop place up above the pass on Kingsbury Grade. Mile-long private drive with a gate house, a mansion at eight thousand feet, a couple three guest houses, views of the Carson Valley and the lake as well."

"Sounds like you've been studying the place," I said.

"We were up there after his arrest."

"The employee at the Rubicon Lodge told me I should contact McCloud if I wanted to talk to Brock. What do you think? Does Brock have a secret stash of cash to pay her with? Or is he connected to the music producer?"

"Don't know," Mallory said. "I've heard that one of the reasons so many celebrities stay at the Rubicon Lodge is Brock's personal service. Especially for the ladies. Could be Lynette was on the receiving end of some of that fine attention and has stuck around."

I thought about that. "What's the music producer's name?" I asked.

"Algernon Petticock," Mallory said.

"That's a name?"

"It is in San Francisco."

"What's he look like?"

Mallory chewed on his lip. "Like the type who would date Spike Heels. Six-one, smooth olive skin, black hair slicked back, perfect teeth. He wears Italian suits and his grin makes you think of a barracuda. He looks Sicilian. Like a Sicilian movie star."

"A Sicilian with the name Algernon Petticock?"

Mallory shrugged.

"One more thing you probably knew about the Thos Kahale murder," I said.

"What's that?"

"I saw Brock Chambers arguing with the Viking that day Morella made her first dive."

"You mean the Viking named Ole Knudson who caused the helicopter crash?"

"One and the same. He and Brock know each other."

"Didn't know that," Mallory said.

I eventually left Mallory and drove into the night through falling snow, trying to shake the image of Morella dying, wishing I'd asked her one more question. Was she Thos's email confidant? Someone who went by the name Hermes?

TWENTY-EIGHT

I called Street's various numbers as I drove back around the dark lake. I found her at her bug lab. "Are visiting hours over?" I asked.

"Not if you bring Spot with you," she said. "I could use a warm footrest, and his backbones are heaven on my poor feet after standing in one place all day."

"Does the laboratory contain any libation or should I stop at the store?" I asked.

"I recall a couple of Sierra Nevadas in the ice box right next to my jar of Chrysomya megacephala. "

"Something tells me that's not a snack even though I'm starving."

"Actually, they are high protein and low fat. Ants love them. You might, too."

"I get the picture. A new batch?"

"Yeah. I'm doing a consult for the Placerville police. They called this morning. I went down immediately and retrieved samples."

"A homicide?"

"They don't know. The body was found in a sauna out back of an old cabin down in the American River Canyon. I left a hygrothermograph in the sauna, but it may not do any good."

"Save the details. I'll be there in a few minutes," I said and hung up.

Spot and I drove up Kingsbury and turned off on the side street where Street's lab was tucked in among several warehouses only two blocks from my office. We walked in and I hugged Street. I was so glad to see her after Morella Meyer's murder that I didn't want to tell her about it yet. I just wanted to hold her.

Spot came and jammed his nose between us, wedging us apart with the subtlety of a log splitter. Street gave him a hug while I fetched a beer from her fridge.

I pointed to a jar full of what looked like short white noodles in a clear liquid. "These guys the ones you got from the body this morning?"

"No, that's another project. The ones from the body are in here, feeding on a piece of liver." She pointed to another case about the size of a bread box.

Although it had a glass front, I had no desire to look inside. "When they grow up and turn into flies, then you'll know what kind they are."

"Right. Once I know the species, then I look at the development of the maggots that I killed and preserved at the scene. That is the first step in determining time-of-death. The question is what the temperature has been while the body has decayed."

"The hygrothermograph tells you that, right?"

"Normally, yes. But the body was in a sauna. Who knows what temp the sauna was at and how long it stayed warm?"

"If it ever was warm," I said.

"The cops think it was. The body was naked, clothes on a bench. It looks like he was taking a sauna when he died."

"Heart attack from the heat?"

"Maybe. Hard to tell," she said.

"Were there tracks in the snow?"

"No snow. This was north of Placerville. About two thousand feet of elevation, so it is too warm for snow most of the year. There are vineyards nearby, so they probably never get snow to speak of."

"If the sauna was warm, that would throw off your results, wouldn't it?"

"Absolutely. I can't do any kind of rigorous analysis. The

sauna had a huge pile of river rock around the wood stove that fired it, and there was a lot of ash in the stove."

I nodded. "A long fire and rocks that would continue to give off heat long after that. The sauna could have stayed warm for days. Meaning the maggots would develop much faster on a warm body than a cold one."

"Exactly. There won't be much hard science on this one."

"Cops get any clues? A wallet ID?"

"Not that I know of," Street shook her head. "The pockets of the clothes had been emptied."

"You said the victim was male?"

"A guess based on size. The corpse wasn't desiccated yet, but it was quite decomposed and unrecognizable."

"Are flies that efficient at laying eggs that the maggot development can always tell you time of death, assuming of course you know temperature and such? Do flies always get to a body right after death?"

"Think of when you barbecue," Street said. "If you left your meat uncovered and untended before you put it over the coals, how long would it be before you saw a fly land on it?"

"If it's warm out, about ten seconds."

"Well, there's your answer."

"You are implying that when a fly lands on your meat they are there to immediately lay eggs on it."

"Many flies, much of the time, yes."

"I may never barbecue again," I said.

"I've heard of entomologists who don't," Street said.

I hung around Street's lab while she finished her work. She eventually pulled up a chair to where Spot was lying, sat down and opened a Sierra Nevada. She worked her stockinged feet over Spot's back bones as she sipped her beer. I told her about Morella's death, but left out the terrible details. Facing our second night of being separate, we both sensed it was better not to get too morose over the violence done to the poor woman.

It was late in the evening by the time Spot and I left Street.

The wind was fierce. As clouds raced across the moon it was like flipping a light switch. On. Off. On again.

I turned on the radio as we drove home up the East Shore. The Pacific system was intensifying. We were expected to get lots of snow in the coming days.

Once inside my cabin, I opened a Sterling Cab and pondered another dinner alone with just my dog.

"Spot," I said. I snapped my fingers and he trotted over. He looked up at me, his pointy ears quivering with excitement. I pointed at his dog bowl which was still full of food from the last night. "What's up with this? You on a fast?"

Spot looked over at the microwave, then back up at me. He wagged, his tail thumping the dishwasher.

I pointed at the microwave. "Human food," I said. I pointed at his dog bowl. "Dog food."

Spot looked back at the microwave.

"Suit yourself. Diamond's gone," I said, feeling the way Amish parents would feel if the baby-sitter had squirreled the kids off to Disneyland for the first time in their lives. "Sorry, pal, you're stuck with me again."

I usually keep some of those miniature pizzas in the freezer. Desperate measures for desperate times. I popped one in the microwave, then poured myself some wine and made a fire in the wood stove. Spot lay down on the rug and watched the microwave. When the microwave beeped signaling that my pizza was done, Spot jumped up. He looked at me and wagged and I decided I was going to let the air out of Diamond's tires at the first opportunity.

Despite the wine before I went to bed, I had trouble shaking the image of Morella's grisly death from my mind. I lay awake most of the night thinking I should have figured out that the visitor she was expecting was, in fact, coming to kill her. Had I been more alert I might have saved her life.

I finally nodded off around 5:00 a.m., exhausted from my self-recriminations.

TWENTY-NINE

I awoke and saw snowfall out the windows. The wind from the night before had subsided, and large, gentle flakes floated slowly to the ground. Although we'd already received six inches overnight, it didn't seem like anything serious. It certainly wasn't like the howling, blowing snow that typified the normal advance of a large storm.

While I drank coffee and Spot ran around outside investigating olfactory secrets hidden under the white stuff, I dialed the Sierra Nevada College in Incline Village. I asked for Avery Ginsberry, the antiques contact mentioned by one of Thos's email correspondents.

"Avery here," he answered shortly.

"Hello, Avery. My name is Owen McKenna. I'm a..."

"Oh, sure, I've heard of you. You're the one with the spotted dog. I read about you during last fall's forest fires. Terrible business, those fires."

"Yes. Avery, I'm trying to find out information about Mark Twain during the time he spent in Kauai. Somebody gave me your name. I was hoping you could give me some direction."

"Hmmm. Not really my area. Better to speak with Hillary Addison for all things Twain."

"She teach with you at the college?"

"No, no. Hillary is a Mark Twain archivist. Runs a Twain library of sorts, serves as a comprehensive Twain scholar."

"Where do I find her?"

"Her office is in Virginia City. Not too far from where the Territorial Enterprise was published."

"The newspaper Twain wrote for?"

"Yes."

Avery gave me Hillary's phone. I thanked him and dialed her number. I got a pager, punched in my number and hung up.

The return call came before I'd finished my third cup of coffee.

"Owen McKenna," I answered.

"Hillary Addison returning your call." She had a tiny voice that cracked like a broken Oboe reed. I visualized a thin, bespectacled woman with unkempt hair.

"Thank you," I said, then proceeded to introduce myself and explain my interest in Twain. "I'm trying to learn about his visit to Kauai. Avery Ginsberry at the Sierra Nevada College said you were a Twain expert. I was hoping you could give me some direction."

"I can try. Have you read the letters he wrote to the Sacramento Daily Union during his Sandwich Islands tour in eighteen sixty-six?" As she spoke, her voice wavered up an octave, then cracked and went back down. She sounded very much like the sweet woman who used to work counter duty at one of the San Francisco precincts I frequented when I was a homicide detective. She'd been confined to a wheelchair and I now pictured the same for Hillary.

"The Sandwich Islands are...?" I said.

"Hawaii. Captain James Cook named them for his patron, the earl of Sandwich, when he discovered them in seventeen seventy-eight. They weren't renamed Hawaii after what the locals called the big island until a hundred years later." Now she sounded winded and I visualized her trying to roll her way around her office.

"I've heard of Twain's letters, but I don't know anything about them."

"Well, that would be the place to start." Despite her tiny

voice, her disapproval was palpable over the phone.

"Perhaps I could visit and you could show me the appropriate passages."

"When did you have in mind?"

"Today?"

She took a long moment then finally agreed to meet me at eleven o'clock and gave me directions to her office.

Before I left I called Janeen to check in. She said all was well and not to worry.

I took Spot with me and left early so I could take it slow through the snowfall. I drove north on 50 and crawled up and over Spooner Summit. It was like leaving winter behind in Tahoe as we headed down into the Carson Valley. When we'd descended to the 6000-foot level the snow stopped falling. At the 5000-foot level we drove into sunshine. By the time we got to the valley floor it was warm enough that I rolled down the back window for Spot. He stuck his head out, his jowls lifting in the head wind.

I drove through Carson City and headed up into the mountains of Virginia City. We climbed nearly as high up as Tahoe, yet the sky remained clear, the sun hot. Across the valley, the mountains of Tahoe were completely obscured by a thick gray blanket of clouds.

The main street of Virginia City was crowded as always, tourists strolling up and down the boardwalks of the old west town, staring unabashed at the wild-west storefronts, the horse-drawn carriages, the signs advertising garish attractions like the Bucket o' Blood Saloon.

I found a place to park near the address I'd written down, left Spot in the Jeep and knocked on an old door. There was an elaborate leaded window in the door made in the shape of a river-boat. I saw movement through the blurry glass. The movement stopped, then came again. I imagined it was Hillary trying to negotiate the space in her wheel chair. The door opened.

A woman in her mid-thirties with red hair cut in short curls stood solidly on two feet and looked up at me from all of five-two or so. She was wearing shiny cobalt blue bicycle shorts and a matching top. A jump rope was draped over her shoulders.

"You must be Owen," she said, still breathing hard from exercise. Her eyes were an equally intense blue green with very bright whites. She radiated fitness.

"Yes. Good to meet you, Hillary. You will be wondering if I'm some kind of a brawler with these bruises, so I'll tell you up front that I was in an accident."

"Uh, yes, I suppose I was wondering. I hope you are okay."

"Yes, I am."

Behind her in one corner of the office was a stationary bicycle. Next to it was a rowing machine. In another corner was a weight bench and a rack that held stacks of free weights.

"You are obviously a serious athlete in addition to Twain scholar."

"Triathlete," she said

"Like the Ironman in Hawaii? I've heard it is an incredibly grueling race, but I don't know the details."

She grinned. "You swim two point four miles, ride a bike one hundred twelve miles, then run a marathon which is twenty-six point two miles. Last fall I finished in little under twelve hours. Which is a long way off the winning woman's time of nine hours and some minutes, but still not too bad."

"Wow," I said. "I can't imagine doing any one of the those, never mind all three."

"That's what everyone says, but it's no different than doing anything else you are good at. So why the interest in Twain?" She turned and walked through an office space crammed with bookshelves, filing cabinets and three computers sharing two desks. She sat down on the edge of one of the desks, her arm and leg muscles bulging.

I followed her into the large room. "I'm a detective working on a murder case that involves a family in Hawaii."

"The man who was shot in Lake Tahoe."

"Yes. Thos Kahale. Several other family members have been

killed. I've nothing to go on except some information passed down from the victim's great grandfather. He claimed that when he was a young boy in Kauai, Twain met his family. They provided Twain hospitality in the form of food and drink and guide service up the Waimea Canyon."

"What Twain called the Grand Canyon of the Pacific," Hillary said, nodding.

"Supposedly, Twain stayed with them for several nights. Big family dinners. Campfires on the beach. Before Twain left he presented them with a gift. A story in the same leather notebook that Twain had been writing his letters in."

"The letters to the Sacramento Daily Union?"

"I suppose," I said. "The man I spoke with is Jasper Kahale. He is the murder victim's father and the grandson of the recipient of Twain's gift. He said Twain told his grandfather that the notebook was what he wrote letters to the newspaper in. I asked Jasper if he had read about that and he said that he'd never heard of them from any other source except his grandfather."

Hillary's eyes were afire. I could see her skepticism wrestling with excitement. "And the story?" Her jaw muscles were flexing, relaxing, flexing.

"It was called The Amazing Island Boy And His Trick Wood." I proceeded to tell Hillary the gist of the story about a boy and his magic Koa wood. I also told her how the story was evidently lost to a hurricane.

Hillary was trying to stay calm, but she was practically bouncing on the edge of the desk. Finally, she got up and started pacing, the jump rope still hanging from her shoulder. "You think the story still exists?" She turned and looked at me, rotated on the ball of her foot, then paced back the opposite direction.

"I don't know. The whole story of Twain meeting the Kahale family and then giving them a manuscript for a gift sounds like one of Twain's tall tales. Further, Jasper Kahale also told me that a hundred years before Twain visited, his family met Captain Cook when he first landed in Hawaii on the island of Kauai. And Cook supposedly gave them some tableware, which they loved because Hawaiians didn't have metal and were fascinated by it."

Hillary gave me a wry grin. "Sounds like Jasper is as imaginative as Twain."

"I've thought that several times. Then again, several people have died, possibly over this item."

Hillary said, "The way they supposedly got the manuscript sounds just quirky enough to be true. Twain was no angel, but he was extremely generous at times."

"I'm wondering, Hillary, about the potential dollar value of items connected to Twain. If such a short story manuscript by Twain really existed, would it be extremely valuable?"

Hillary stopped pacing and faced me. "Oh, God, yes. An original Twain manuscript? Undiscovered until now? This wouldn't be like the Twain story the Atlantic Monthly sat on until recently. This would be unique, a surprise. It would probably draw millions at auction."

"How would that take place? Suppose someone finds such a manuscript. Where would they go? Who would they take it to?"

"First, it would have to be authenticated. If they were new to the game, they'd typically ask around at libraries or museums and eventually get directed to someone like me. I would study it and arrive at an opinion as to its probable authenticity. Then one or more of my colleagues would examine it and verify or dispute my opinion. Soon, it would likely end up at one of the big auction houses. Sotheby's or Christie's."

"So if someone has such a manuscript, I could possibly track him by waiting until it comes to auction?"

"Maybe," Hillary said. "But maybe not. Many collectors wouldn't take it anywhere. It's like great paintings. There are rich people who pay enormous sums just to have a priceless painting and they want their ownership to be secret. Furthermore, if this manuscript exists and was stolen, the thief would not be able to sell it through a legitimate auction house."

"But how would a collector obtain a manuscript from the thief who steals it, if not through auction?"

Hillary resumed pacing. "There is a black market in literary artifacts just as in other antiquities or in the visual arts. It's like drug dealers. Private brokers who operate in the shadows, dealing only with known thieves and trusted customers."

"Could you direct me to one of these black-market brokers? Preferably one who would know how to sell a manuscript by Twain?"

She smiled and shook her head. "I'm a Twain archivist. Take me out of my athletic clothes and I'm as nerdy as the next bookworm. I deal with librarians and conservators and museum curators. Not exactly the dark world where thieves hang out."

"But you must hear things. Innuendo. Rumors. Point me in a direction. I won't say where I got the information."

Hillary had a pattern to her pacing. I now understood that she followed the lines of the floor tiles, turning left and right at regular intervals, then turning and coming back. She took many steps, a little scowl on her face. Finally, she stopped and turned toward me. "Mind you, this is only a rumor. I can't stress that enough. And you didn't hear it from me, is that clear?" Her sudden stern demeanor was surprisingly forceful.

"Scout's honor," I said.

"You might look up a person I've heard about. I'm not saying this person is a black-market broker. But it is possible. And you didn't hear it from me. Agree?" I wasn't certain but I thought I saw fear on her face.

"You can count on me."

Hillary Addison took a single deep breath and let it out. "I've heard of a lawyer named McCloud."

THIRTY

Driving away from Hillary Addison's office, I thought about Lynette McCloud. Brock Chamber's lawyer and fellow hunter. An expert shot with a rifle. A flashy defense attorney. The new girlfriend of a rich music producer named Algernon Petticock.

Lynette was overdue for a visit from Spot and me.

After Spot and I climbed back up into the clouds and snow of Tahoe, the driving became much slower. We were ready for lunch, so we stopped at my cabin.

When we got out of the Jeep, I heard a tiny bark and looked up to see my neighbor's toy poodle streaking down the road toward us. Spot stretched his front legs out in front of him and arched his back. His butt stayed up in the air and his chest touched the ground. When the poodle got to him he sprung into the air as the poodle ran under him. Then the two of them raced around in the street. It was odd how a 6-pound dog and a 170-pound dog felt a kinship that house cats and mountain lions could never feel even though the size difference between the two dogs was greater.

"Treasure! Treasure!" a high, almost operatic, voice called out.

I looked up to see Mrs. Duchamp standing in her drive wearing a shimmering, metallic gold housecoat. Her rotund shape in the glittering gold fabric had a circus quality to it.

I waved.

She seemed to not see me. "Treasure! Be careful! Don't let

that big dog hurt you!"

Spot and the toy poodle were doing figure-eights in the road. A happier poodle I'd never seen. Then Treasure shot up the road and jumped up on Mrs. Duchamp's legs. Mrs. Duchamp shrieked, then bent down, picked up her dog and marched inside.

After I ate a quick sandwich, I looked in the book and called the phone number for Lynette McCloud.

"Good morning, McCloud Legal Service," a low-pitched female voice said.

"Good morning. Is Lyn around?" I said, assuming my only chance of getting through was to pose as someone familiar. It didn't work.

"Who's calling, sir?"

"Her brother Owen. She's expecting my call."

"Sir, Ms. McCloud is not taking appointments at this time. If you'd like to leave a message, I'll be happy to connect you to her voice mail and..."

I hung up. I dialed Mallory.

"The music producer McCloud got off weapons charges," I said when he answered.

"Algernon Petticock?"

"Yeah. Where did you say he lived?"

"You gonna go up there and cause some trouble?"

"Probably."

"Good. He's on the Nevada side where we have no jurisdiction. I told Diamond about him, but Diamond's too nice a guy to bust Algernon's chops. You know where North Benjamin turns off of Kingsbury Grade up by Daggett Pass?"

"Yeah."

Mallory proceeded to give me detailed instructions to the man's house.

"Sounds like you been studying the map," I said. "Lynette McCloud's heels that spikey?"

"See for yourself," he said and hung up.

"Your largeness," I said to Spot who was lying in front of the wood stove. "You wanna go for a ride and roust out a lawyer?"

Spot lifted his head and looked at me with interest. I'm sure it was the word lawyer that did it.

"C'mon, let's go," I said.

Spot got to his feet and walked over to my kitchen nook. He gazed at the microwave.

"No Danish," I said. "Maybe popcorn and beer tonight, but no Danish."

Spot hung his head as he followed me out to the Jeep. The storm let up a little as we drove, the heavy big flakes giving way to light flurries, which made it a little easier to see.

The turnoff to the music producer's spread had a gatehouse and a large wrought iron gate. The gate was shut.

I looked at the hinges, wondering if I could blast through with the Jeep. I decided it wasn't a good idea. Instead, Spot and I could climb the fence, hike around and sneak up. Except, I wasn't sure that climbing wrought iron fences with points on top was a Great Dane specialty.

I was still thinking about it five minutes later when a large panel van came down the drive. I didn't see it at first because the snow was eight feet high on either side of the drive. The lettering on the side said Robertson Linen Service. As it approached the entrance, the gate retracted sideways at a slow, dignified pace. The van pulled out and exited onto North Benjamin. As the gate began its stately glide back to a closed position I gunned the Jeep and scooted through with an inch of room to spare.

I drove up a long, twisting ribbon of fresh white snow that climbed around granite outcroppings and large red firs.

The manor was as advertised. Done in retro Medieval Castle, the place had a turret and a fakey looking drawbridge that stretched over a pond. The water wasn't frozen which meant power circulation and a concealed furnace. The stone walls had little windows from which a princess could escape if her golden hair was long enough to cut off and braid into a rope.

I pulled around a circular drive made of bricks laid in an

elaborate pattern. The falling snow instantly melted when it landed on the bricks. There must have been heating coils under the brick. I parked behind a red Lexus and adjacent to a black stretch limo. Both were polished to a deep shine. Water drops from the snow balled up on the waxed finish like glass beads.

Behind the limo, sitting in chairs carved of stone at the beginning of the drawbridge were two men who telegraphed bodyguard. The drawbridge had a roof which protected them from the falling snow. There was a boom box at their feet. Both men stood up as I wheeled the Jeep to a quick stop.

The small one was a white guy, maybe six-two, with spiked blond hair died purple at the tips and a ring in his nose. He probably weighed 215, same as me. His well-muscled torso was dressed in a white jumpsuit, like he'd just come back from tryouts for a Hollywood movie.

The large one, a black guy, had another four inches of height making him even with me, but he weighed a good 280 and looked like he had done time in the NFL. His hair was long and brown and wet with some kind of goo and looked like squished eels plastered down the back of his thick neck. There were no rings in his nose and, judging from the smooth lines of his tight, black shirt, there weren't any rings in his nipples or his navel either. Probably wanted them but was too chickenshit.

I jumped out of the Jeep and walked around to greet them. Rap music boomed out of the boom box.

"Good afternoon, gentlemen," I said. "I'm here to see Lynette McCloud, please."

"How'd you get through the gate?" the large one said. Unfriendly.

"I just spoke to her on my phone. Told her I was at the gate and she pushed the button."

"Bullshit, mummy face. Get out or we'll throw you out."

"Mummy face? Okay, we'll start again. Yo, dudes, I'm Owen, Lyn's big brother. The Big O, you've probably heard her call me. How's it hangin'?"

No response.

"She around? What say you buzz her on your secret decoder rings and let her know I'm here."

The small one looked up at the large one. "We got us a joker, Tommy. Does that mean we get to kick his ass before we throw him out?"

"Come on, guys," I said. "I'm just kidding you. Anyway, call Lyn and tell her I've arrived. Meanwhile, I need my toothbrush. I'm pretty sure I put it in the glove box."

They still didn't move.

"All right. Don't trouble yourselves. I can get it myself."

They were immobile.

"What if I say please?" I said. "If Lyn thinks you were stand-offish to me, well, hell, I don't know what she'd do. Whisper into your boss's ear, maybe. 'Algernon, honeypot, your boys weren't nice to my big brother.' What if she did that? Whisper into the big kahuna's ear? Next thing you know, you two will be turning some nice, clean Nevada landfill into a toxic waste dump."

Both guys had reddish faces all of a sudden. The smaller guy turned to the big guy. "I'm gonna kick his ass, Tommy. I'm gonna rip those bandages off his face and smash it in. You can join in if you want." He advanced on me, his nose ring sparkling in the winter sunlight.

"Okay," I said. "I won't waste your time any longer." I walked around to the side of my Jeep. They probably thought I was going to get in and drive away. I opened the back door instead and let Spot out.

Both men's eyes got squinty as I came back around with Spot.

I looked at the bodyguards. I figured I couldn't take the big one, so I pointed at him. "Spot. Watch him. If he moves, eat him."

"Yeah, right." the big guy said. The smaller guy was in suspended animation, looking at my dog.

Spot looked at me, questioning. I nodded. "Yes, I'm serious."

Spot turned and growled at the large guy. Just as I'd hoped, he did the slow-build thing where he growls low and soft, then lifts his lips exposing his fangs and ups the amplitude of his growl until it sounds somewhere between an earthquake and the Second Coming. Once the earth was shaking, Spot lowered his head, swung it a bit from side to side and advanced on the large bodyguard.

The man took a little step back, tripped on the edge of the stone chair and fell on his ass.

At that moment, the other bodyguard took a wild swing at my head. I ducked fast, my aching body screaming with pain from the sudden movement, then I reached and plucked out his nose ring. He stifled a scream and grabbed me around the neck.

I gritted my teeth against my throbbing headache and chopped down on the sides of his neck. His only response was to tighten his grip on my throat. His thumbs pressed into my Adam's apple. I hit him a quick one-two in the abdomen, but he just squeezed harder. I couldn't breathe. He was close to crushing my trachea. Desperate, I boxed his ears hard enough to rupture his eardrums. He let go of me and screamed.

I staggered back, rubbing my neck, trying to suck air.

He held his hands up to his ears. His eyes were wide and he was still screaming.

Spot was hanging his head over the prostrate form of the big guy, his growl melting the nearby snow. The big guy's eyes were twitching, but his body was as immobile as it had been before when he was standing up.

"Shut up," I said to the smaller guy. My voice was a whisper. I swallowed, pain shooting through my throat. "You'll be fine if you see a doctor."

He screamed louder. "You wrecked my ears! You wrecked my damn ears!" He held his palms over his ears.

"Shut up!" I said again, louder.

He kept screaming.

I was tempted to punch him in the throat to quiet him down. But I didn't want to kill him. So I did my best to take a decent breath and punched him in the gut instead. I put some effort into it, rotating my shoulders and visualizing carrying the blow all the way through his body like they teach you in karate class.

The shock to my own body felt as if I'd ripped all my muscles and broken several bones. But it was worth it because he stopped screaming. He doubled over and collapsed.

I caught him and pushed him back until he hit the wall that was the side of the drawbridge. I kept up the momentum and lifted him up and over into the pond below.

There was a big splash. Yellow and orange koi fled the scene as the man coughed and gagged and flailed at the water. His fancy purple-blond hair turned into a wimpy pink mat. I returned to where my dog stood above the big guy who was still lying on the stone walkway. Spot had lowered his growl to a whisper. The man's face glistened with a thousand tiny drops of sweat.

"Good boy, Spot," I wheezed.

"Get that dog off me," the big guy muttered.

"Sorry," I said. I turned to my dog and pet him. "You're pretty good." Spot wagged. Shook his head. Saliva flew, some of it hitting the big guy's face. The guy reached up to wipe it off.

"Uh unh," I said to the guy. I'd lost my patience when the other guy worked on my throat. I turned to Spot. "Spot, if this beefcake's Adam's apple even jiggles, rip his throat out." I pointed with my finger at the man's neck.

Spot looked at the man, lifted his lip and did a little growl.

The man slowly lowered his hand to the pavement.

As I walked up to the castle, I reminded myself to buy some Danishes on the way home.

THIRTY-ONE

The front door of the house was five feet wide and had a rounded top. In the middle of the door was one of those miniature doors so that Igor could check for Goths before he opened up the master's castle.

The whole door opened as I approached.

I expected Bela Lugosi with blood on his teeth.

I got a barefoot woman in a red leotard and black tights. She had straight black hair to go with the tights and a red ruby on her right index finger to go with the leotard.

"Lynette McCloud?"

"I saw that," she said, pointing out toward the drawbridge. She turned and walked away from me, her feet silent on the stone floor. She walked around a bronze sculpture on a white marble pedestal. A nude with a good shape. I wasn't sure, but it looked like a Picasso.

She spoke over her shoulder. "You embarrassed Algernon's boys. That can be dangerous."

I shut the door and followed her. "I wanted to talk to you. They weren't forthcoming. What could I do?"

"Not all my clients are so persistent." She went down a hall that had a rounded stone ceiling. She turned into a dance studio. Hardwood floor, dance bar, mirrored wall on one side, windows with a view of Lake Tahoe on the other side.

"I'm not a client," I said.

"You are..."

"Owen McKenna. I'm investigating the murder of Thos

Kahale. I want to talk to Brock Chambers about it. He seems to be missing. I was directed to you as his lawyer. I was also directed to you as an antiquities expert."

"What did you do to your face?"

"It's just makeup. I put it on to scare your boys out there."

No smile, not even a crinkling of the eyes.

"You don't mind, do you?" She gestured at the dance bar. "I was warming up when I heard the commotion outside."

"Of course," I said.

She put a bare foot up on the dance bar, slid forward into a stretch and held it.

"Is Algernon home?"

"No."

"I thought that was his limo."

"It is. But he prefers to come and go in his helicopter. There was a break in the weather so off he went."

I couldn't tell if she was kidding or not. "Where is Brock?" I asked.

"I don't know."

"Who is Ole Knudson?" I asked.

"I don't know."

"Morella Meyers?"

"I don't know."

"Did you know Thos Kahale?"

"I see no point in saying 'I don't know' to all your silly questions."

"What is your relationship with Brock?"

She didn't answer.

"Why did you move from L.A. to a town so small that people gossip about your spike heels?"

Lynette McCloud straightened and took her foot off the bar. She turned the other direction, away from me, put her other foot on the bar and slid down into another stretch.

"Is dabbling in antiques a way to spend sugar daddy's money or is it a serious business?"

No response.

"Who is going to buy the Mark Twain manuscript and how much are they paying you?"

I saw her eyes twitch, but nothing else. If she didn't want to answer, she wouldn't. Very cool.

The woman had good lines, like the sculpture out front. Picasso would have whipped out his charcoal and done a drawing. Or taken off his shirt and beat his chest. Or first done the drawing and then beat his chest.

McCloud rose up from her stretch and went into a series of dance positions.

I knew nothing of dance, but I recognized one of the positions from the title of a sculpture by Degas. "Fourth position front," I said. "On the left leg. Very good, but really, aren't your hands a little tense?"

That got her attention. She snapped her head toward me, glared for a fraction of a second, then regained her composure and went back to ignoring me.

"If you don't answer my questions, I could use one of your lawyer tricks, get the papers and the authorization, make you talk." Even as I said it, I thought it wasn't true.

Without releasing her arabesque, Lynette rotated her head and looked at me the way an eagle looks at a baby bunny rabbit.

"Mr. McKenna, you have no idea how far in over your head you are. I have let you into this house because you amuse me. If I want, I can put you away for a long time. Assault and battery. Assault with a deadly weapon. Trespass."

She rose out of her stretch, turned sideways to the mirrors and did some more moves, one arm up, one arm on the bar. Her feet and knees were turned out as she lowered down and then rose up. She was graceful and had obviously spent many hours dancing.

"I've heard that you are a lousy shot with a rifle," I said.

She stopped her movements and looked at me. "That's a lie. I could shoot your left nut off from a hundred yards."

"How 'bout the valve off a scuba tank?"

"That too." She turned and went back to her bar exercises. "We are through talking. If you have any survival instinct at all, you will not tangle with me. Others have tried and regretted it. Good day."

I understood that meant I was to leave.

Spot was lying down in the snow next to the bodyguard. He wasn't growling or even paying that much attention. He didn't seem that tough. I held my hand up and looked at it. Maybe my fist was the deadly weapon she referred to.

The man lying next to Spot followed me with his eyes. The man with the nose ring was nowhere to be seen. Maybe he was sleeping with the koi.

"Let's go, Spot."

He stood and trotted over to the Jeep. "You done good," I said.

As I drove off, I saw the big man rise to a sitting position and stay there.

THIRTY-TWO

The next morning, I thought I'd visit Thos's other grand-father. I got Janeen Kahale on the phone.

"I'd like to visit your father," I said when she answered. "I don't know his name."

"He goes by his Christian name of Francis Plummer."

"Can you give me his address?"

"Certainly." She rattled it off.

"Do you think he will be home?"

"Yes, if you're going now. He always stays in during the noon hour. In the summer he naps during the heat of the day. In the winter he watches TV. I'll call him and tell him to expect you."

Spot and I drove over Kingsbury Grade, crested Daggett Pass, then plunged down toward the southern end of the Carson Valley three thousand feet below. Just like the previous day, half-way down to the valley we drove out of the snow and clouds and into sunshine. The weather system dumping snow at Lake Tahoe was stuck in place as if the clouds had gotten snagged on the mountains.

At the base of Kingsbury Grade I drove east on a blacktop road, then found the turn-off that Janeen had described. I followed a narrow gravel road to the south for a mile. It zig-zagged left then right, then left once again. Janeen had said the next turn was nearly hidden in a stand of cottonwoods. When I saw the trees I slowed to a crawl, watching for an opening. I still missed it and had to back up. I found a space between two trees, barely large enough to drive through. The passage was more like a horse trail than a driveway. It was clear the branches would scrape the Jeep so I told Spot to pull his head in and hit the button to roll the window up.

The scraping was loud and harsh and I was grateful my Jeep was not a new model. The drive was straight, but bumped and jolted us for a quarter mile before we pulled up in front of a seafoam green camper. The little camper box was the type designed for the bed of a pickup. But there was no pickup or any other vehicle in sight. The camper sat directly on the dirt. The high portion that normally projected over a pickup's cab was propped up with two wooden fence posts.

I left Spot in the Jeep with two of the windows rolled down. It may have been winter in Tahoe, but the Carson Valley is 1600 feet below the surface of the lake and much warmer than Tahoe.

Mr. Plummer sat outside in a folding lawn chair. He wore a leather motorcycle jacket and faded jeans. On his feet were big athletic shoes. One hand held up a small book, angled to catch the sunlight. He appeared to continue reading as I pulled up, then lowered the book only after I'd gotten out and walked up toward him. The words on the cover said Emily Dickinson.

"Good afternoon, Mr. Plummer, my name is..."

"McKenna," he finished for me. He didn't move and didn't reach out his hand.

"Janeen said she'd call you." I glanced at the little camper and saw no phone wires, nor electrical wires for that matter.

"Yes, she called me," he said in a voice that had strong tones of Native American speech. His face was more weathered than the desert mountains, his dark skin creased into a complex network of deep folds and wrinkles.

At that moment, a phone rang. Francis Plummer reached into a pocket of his leather jacket, pulled out a cellphone and answered it.

"Hello." Francis shifted and the little volume of Emily Dickinson poetry slipped off his lap to the ground. "Yes, he's here. No, I'm just watching TV. Yes, it's fine. Say hi to Phillip.

Bye." He put the phone back in his pocket, reached down and picked up the poetry book.

"I hope you don't mind my visiting."

Mr. Plummer looked at me, his face blank. He had no reaction to my bandages or bruises. "My daughter said it was important."

"First, let me say how sorry I am about your grandson's death."

Francis gave a solemn nod. "Janeen told me Thos isn't the only one to die."

"No."

"I feel sorry for Jasper," Francis said. "He was a good son-in-law to me. I still think Janeen made a mistake leaving him."

"You probably know that she hired me to investigate Thos's death. I'd like to ask you a few questions if I may."

He nodded. "That your dog?" he said, looking over at Spot whose head was out the window.

"Yes. His name is Spot."

Spot perked up his ears and looked very interested. Probably wondering if Francis Plummer had a microwave.

"Did Thos contact you in the last couple of months?"

Francis didn't answer immediately. I had no doubt that he could remember. He was just making up his mind about whether to tell me. "Yes," he said finally. "A couple of days before he died."

"Was it a routine, get-in-touch-with-your-grandfather kind of contact? Or something else?"

Francis thought a bit. "Something else."

"Would you tell me about it? It may have bearing on my investigation."

Francis nodded again. "Yes, it may."

"Oh? I wish Janeen had told me."

"She didn't know."

I looked at him.

He could tell he was frustrating me. "Janeen didn't know

because she didn't ask. My father taught me years ago not to poke my nose into other people's business. He said that giving information where none is requested is vanity. But if you say the information is helpful, then I give it to you."

I didn't dwell on the old man's reasoning. "Why did Thos contact you?"

"He wanted to know about sacred Washoe land."

"What did you tell him?"

"I told him that all land is sacred. Then he asked me if there were certain places that were special. More sacred than others. Especially up in Tahoe. I told him about Cave Rock and all the other lands that have been sacred for the Washoe people."

I immediately thought of the cave in Cave Rock and wondered if Thos had moved a Twain manuscript from the sacred cave of his father's family to the sacred cave of his mother's.

Francis shifted, lifting one of his legs up, athletic shoe on the chair, his fingers laced around his knee. He was old, but he was agile. "My grandson said he didn't want to know what was sacred for the Washoe. Just for our family. Like a private church. So I explained that there was no earth that was a church just for us, that our family worshipped the same land and the gifts of nature as all the Washoe worship."

"Did that seem to answer his question?"

"You mean, did it satisfy my grandson?" Francis shook his head. "No. He wouldn't let the idea alone. Finally, he said forget about what was sacred."

"And..." I prompted.

"And tell him if there were any places in Tahoe that were special to our immediate family. Not sacred, just special."

"Were there?"

"Yes. I told him the stories my grandfather used to tell me about fishing. Every spring they would make the journey from this valley up to Lake Tahoe where they would set up camp. They would spend the summer hunting and fishing. Mostly fishing. Rainbow and cutthroat trout and kokanee salmon. They had feasts at the lake, big fires and dances all summer long." Francis looked with wistful eyes up at the mountains to the west. I followed his gaze. Monument Peak with Heavenly's ski runs and Job's Peak. Just on the other side lay Lake Tahoe.

"I also told him a story my father told me. About an ice grave," Francis said.

"Is this a real place?"

"I don't think so." Francis pushed his lips out and gave his head a little shake. "It always sounded like the other stories. Like the Indian boy who was being chased by the devil. The boy carried a branch from an aspen tree. As each leaf fell off it turned into a lake that the devil had to detour around. That's how all the lakes around Tahoe were formed."

Francis looked at me with dark, impassive eyes. "Just like your culture, Washoe culture has many creation stories."

"What is the story of the ice grave?"

Francis looked up at the mountains of Tahoe. Without turning toward me he spoke as if the mountains were listening. "It's part of a fountain-of-youth story. There is supposed to be a cave in one of the Tahoe mountains. It is very hard to find. Some say that if you go into it and drink its waters you will experience a renewal."

"Have you been there?"

"No. I don't know anybody who has."

"Does the cave have a spring?"

Francis shook his head. "Just ice. Melting ice."

"And the water has special powers."

"Yes." Francis paused. "I was told the cave gives off light."

"The water glows?"

"No. The ice glows," Francis said.

"What is the ice grave?"

"According to the story, the cave has a hole that goes to the center of the earth. The hole is coated with ice. If an evil person tries to drink the magic water, they will slip into the hole and fall to their death."

222 TODD BORG

"If this cave does exist, do you think Thos wanted to find it?"

"Yes. He asked about its location. But I could only tell him that it is supposed to have a small entrance high up on a cliff."

"I'm wondering why Thos was asking you this," I said. "Did he give you any reason why he had such a sudden interest in the places of your family's history?"

"He was always interested in Washoe history and cared about our tribe. He wanted to start a winery in the California foothills and provide employment for the young people in our tribe." Francis turned from the mountains and looked at me. His face looked as old as time. "I think he also had something he wanted to place on the land that nurtured our family."

"Do you mean place the way someone would place a marker or a plaque?"

Francis shook his head. "My grandson asked if my ancestors had ever had a memorial, a way to immortalize someone. Years ago I had heard from Janeen about Thos's Hawaiian ancestors having a family shrine where they put a person's special objects. I think Thos wondered if he could do the same thing on our side of his family."

"Francis, I think Thos had a valuable item that he wanted to put on your family land. Would that make sense to you?"

Francis made a single nod.

"Did your ancestors always make their summer camp in the same spot?" I asked.

"Yes. On the west shore of Lake Tahoe."

"Would you know where on the shore it was?"

Another single nod. "A place that is now called Rubicon Point."

THIRTY-THREE

I made good time getting back up Kingsbury Grade until I hit the snowstorm. The snowfall was heavier than before. Traffic moved slowly down toward the lake and even more slowly going through town. It was late in the afternoon when I pulled into the drive of the Rubicon Lodge.

The young blond man I'd spoken with two days earlier was pushing a rolling cart with a computer on it through the lobby when I walked in. "Oh, it's you," he said.

"Has Brock been in?" I said.

The man's jaw moved left, then right as he looked up at me. "You creditors are all alike. You never give any thought to how hard you squeeze people. Brock is hiding on instructions from his lawyer, that much is obvious. You won't get your money, you might as well accept that."

"I'm not here to get, I'm here to give," I said, "to invest and pay Brock's bills. Remember?"

"Oh, now I remember. Whatever. He's gone."

"Do you know where?"

"Away. God, you're as pushy as that dead wine guy."

"What do you mean?"

"The guy from Pacific Blue Wines who got shot."

"Thos Kahale knew Brock?" I asked.

"Of course, he knew Brock. He sold him enough wine."

"I thought Pacific Blue Wines only sold wine in Hawaii."

"I don't know about Hawaii, but he started calling on Brock a few months ago and put Brock onto some deals on Napa and

Sonoma wines and his own Pacific Blue wine. Brock ended up cutting back on almost all of his local wines as a result."

"What do you mean, 'local wines?'"

"The El Dorado winemakers in the foothills. Especially that one near Placerville that he owes so much money to. American River Vineyards and Winery. Brock used to buy a lot of wine from them until that Hawaiian came around."

"Where is American River Vineyards?"

"Their label says Placerville, but they're actually quite a ways north on the American River. Brock had all of us from the Rubicon Lodge go down there once for a tasting. Not bad stuff, even though they do an awful Pinot. They should leave them for the Oregon winemakers. At least they..."

I had stopped listening since he described the winery's location. It sounded like the place where the dead body was found in the sauna. I wondered if the body was Brock. "How long has it been since you've seen Brock?" I interrupted.

"I'm not sure. Four or five days. Maybe a week, now that you mention it. I don't miss him if that's what you're wondering. The guy's a jerk and if it gets me fired for saying it, I don't mind."

"Tell me,... I'm sorry, I didn't get your name."

"Mike."

"Tell me, Mike. Do you know how much Brock owed Thos Kahale?"

"No. A lot, I assume. Why else would the guy hassle Brock so much?"

"Any idea which creditors Brock owed the most to?"

"No. I'd guess the landlord, followed by a couple of the food wholesalers. But wait, if you're willing to invest in this operation, wouldn't you already know all this?"

"Just checking," I said. "Doesn't hurt to get information from more than one source, does it? What do you know of Brock's payables?"

"As if you don't know," Mike said. "I've heard he's out a hundred twenty days on a good half million." He walked off pushing the cart and disappeared through an office door.

I lingered in the lobby, gazing at the animal heads. A young couple was sitting together on a big leather couch in front of the crackling fire. I walked over to a rack of wooden rods with newspapers, pulled out the San Francisco Chronicle and sat down in an upholstered chair that felt sizable even to my outsized frame.

The newspaper was cover while I sat and pondered the significance of Rubicon Point.

I thought of Rodin. I believed that one of his themes was that passion is the strongest of emotions, a desire that was not necessarily good or bad, just powerful. I'd found plenty of passion, the crazed desire for a priceless, missing manuscript or something equally valuable. It was passion that killed so many people.

But if passion created my case, I felt that balance would solve it. To make his mobiles, Calder must have approached it like a puzzle. It was easy to collect all the disparate pieces. The problem was to assemble them so they made sense. To Calder, the answer was found by pursuing balance. When he was done, he'd transformed a pile of disconnected parts into a balanced whole. Once he'd performed his magic, one could step back and easily see how all the pieces joined together.

Could I do like Calder, arrange what I'd learned so that there was a kind of balance? Most of my pieces originated in Hawaii, the deaths of Thos's cousin, grandfather and uncle, the missing Twain manuscript, the death of the young tough named Napoleon, a wine company called Pacific Blue.

For a long time Thos's death in Tahoe seemed disconnected from everything else. But now his Washoe grandfather Francis Plummer had pointed me back to Rubicon Point as a place where his ancestors had summered for generations, a history that possibly went back as far as the Polynesian history in Hawaii.

Thos had recently begun selling Pacific Blue wine to the Rubicon Lodge. Brock owed him money. Thos got killed at Rubicon Point. Morella Meyers got killed not far away. How would Calder arrange it? What hidden information was needed to achieve balance?

Francis Plummer told me the story of the ice grave in a cave high up on a cliff. Could it be near Rubicon Point?

I stood up and walked over to the windows on the mountain side of the lodge. There was a row of 9000-foot mountains that stretched north from Emerald Bay. The northernmost one is named Rubicon Peak. The summit is a vertical point of granite hundreds of feet high. It was cloaked in ice and snow.

"Good day, sir. May I be of service?"

I turned at the voice and saw the woman who worked behind the lodge counter. She was a thin woman in her early forties. She was tall, but stood bent. She looked at my face as if to check that I'd washed. She seemed very disapproving of my bruises. "I remember you. You are the investor." She said the word investor with the same tone she would have used for the word rattlesnake.

"Yes. I was just admiring Rubicon Peak. Have you ever climbed it?"

"Oh, no. With all these insufferable outdoor types around here, they don't need one more hiker crowding the trails."

"Brock is a hiker?"

"Brock? No, he's more the type to drive up the mountains in his four-wheel-drive. It's people like Mike who think the end of the universe is hiking and camping and climbing."

"What about Rubicon Peak? Has Mike hiked up there?"

She laughed. "Only about once a week. He's into ice climbing. He goes up there with his brother all the time."

"Even now in the middle of winter?"

"Absolutely. He says there's some special area on the cliff that is all ice."

"I'd like to talk to him about that."

"Be my guest. He's in the office pretending he knows how to install reservations software." She gestured toward the room where Mike had pushed the cart.

I walked across the lobby and stuck my head in the open door. The cart with the computer on it was sitting in the middle of the small office. But Mike was not there.

I walked back out into the lobby. "Mike isn't in that office. Could you page him?"

At that moment, a red Toyota 4-Runner flashed by the window, out of the parking lot and up the drive toward the highway.

"That's Mike," she said. "What does he think he's doing? He can't just leave work like that."

For a moment, I thought of giving pursuit, but realized he'd be long gone before I even got to my Jeep. "Does he do this often, going AWOL?"

"No. Never before."

"Is Mike a hunter as well as a climber?"

"Oh, yes. He and his brother are like Brock. Their motto seems to be, 'If it moves, shoot it.'"

"Have you met Mike's brother?" I asked.

"No. I just hear about him all the time. Mike kind of worships him. But I think it is one of those love hate things."

"So you wouldn't know if he has long blond hair?"

She shook her head. "Looking at Mike, it would make sense his brother is blond, but, no, I've never met him."

"Any idea why Mike would suddenly leave? Was he acting sick earlier?"

"No. The only thing unusual around here today is you coming back. Come to think of it, Mike did seem stressed when he saw you walking up to the lodge."

"What is Mike's last name?"

"Packard."

"Do you know where he lives?"

"Near Tahoe City from what I've heard. Why?"

"I'd like to talk to him. Can you look up his address and phone for me?"

She suddenly became wary and took a half-step back from

me. "You know I'm not allowed to give that out."

"His job here," I said. "Does he mostly work the front counter?" I walked across the lobby to the registration desk and pushed through the swing doors.

"Hey, you can't go back there! That is private!"

"Call Brock and tell him you have an intruder. Maybe he'll finally talk to me."

"I can't... And you can't... Don't you dare!" she yelled at me as I began opening drawers in the back side of the front counter.

I rifled papers, looked through files, pulled clipboards off of hooks. The woman ran over and picked up the phone. I expected to hear her press the three digits of 911. Instead she dialed a seven-digit number. I kept looking for something, anything that might catch my eye.

"He's here," the woman said into the phone.

I turned and looked at her.

She was staring back at me, a touch of fire in her eyes. "Not yet," she said. "He's behind the counter, prying through our papers." There was a pause. "Yes, the sooner you get out here, the better." She hung up.

I kept searching. I found invoices, sales records, office supplies and a small DVD library. I found a petty cash box, the computerized cash drawer, credit card swiper and credit card printer. Over by the fax was a built-in cabinet with name tags on each drawer. Louise, Brian, Robin, Hazel, Mike.

I pulled open Mike's drawer. Inside was a disorganized pile of personal effects. I pushed the stuff around to see better. A leather glove, some spare change, a key ring with four keys and a plastic fob that said 'No Fear,' a deck of cards, several miscellaneous business cards, some pens, two triple A batteries, a floppy disk, a couple of climber's chocks, half a Mars Bar wrapped in a plastic sandwich bag. And a totem.

It was just like the one I found in Janeen's kitchen. It was painted glossy blue with two large, red, penetrating eyes, no arms, three legs. I slipped it into my pocket as I turned.

The woman was still watching me. She glanced at her watch, then outside at the parking lot.

"Thanks," I said to her. I pushed back through the half-doors and left.

As I drove away from the Rubicon Lodge, I called Mallory. "Do you know about the body the Placerville police found in the sauna?" I asked.

"I heard about it. Didn't they call Street down to take maggot samples?"

"Yeah. It may be Brock Chambers."

Mallory was silent for a moment. "That would explain why we couldn't find him. Maybe they've ordered a DNA test. I'll let you know what I find out," Mallory said. "Placer County Sheriff's Office got a look at the valve off that scuba tank. It has marks like it took a blow from some high-powered lead. Although they haven't found the slug."

"Any more news on that carved figurine you found near Thos's body?"

"No." Mallory sounded disappointed. "I just talked to Diamond about it. He's been showing it around the local gangs, asking the Mexican kids about the black wind and such. But he's got nothing to show for it. He said the kids all have stone faces. They pretend they've never seen the figurine before."

I proceeded to tell Mallory about the figurine I found in Mike's drawer at the Rubicon Lodge. I also told him that Mike, while having short blond hair, has a blond brother who likes to hunt and climb cliffs. Hair length unknown.

That got Mallory's attention. He said he'd call his colleagues on the north side of the lake and see if they could track down Mike and his brother for questioning.

I said goodbye and continued south through the snowfall.

They often close the highway at Emerald Bay due to avalanche danger and I worried that I'd be forced to turn and go all the way around the lake the other way. But I lucked out and went by the highway crew just as they were getting ready to shut the gates.

THIRTY-FOUR

I could paint two pictures of Brock and I discussed them with Street over dinner at Evan's Café on Emerald Bay Road. Outside, the snowfall was heavy and blowing, but the inside of the popular gourmet restaurant was warm and filled with the delicious scents of marvelous dishes.

"You think Brock bought the manuscript from Thos?" Street asked after we'd ordered appetizers and dinner.

"Could be he agreed to buy it, then killed Thos to avoid paying. Or maybe he hired the Viking to get it and the Viking killed Thos."

"Then why would the Viking still be looking for it after Thos's death?"

"Maybe Brock didn't pay for the actual manuscript, but for information about where the manuscript was hidden. He killed Thos, then sent the Viking off to Kauai to retrieve it."

Street was nodding, eating a shrimp in dainty bites, chewing thoughtfully. Who would have thought my hormones could respond to someone eating a shrimp.

"If Brock couldn't afford to pay his wine bill," she said, "then where would he get money for a manuscript? Maybe the Viking found it and sold it behind Brock's back."

"That's a possibility, although I don't think the Viking ever got it. My reading of Thos is that he's the one who took the manuscript from his computer monitor where he'd hid it for a time. I think he decided it would be better to hide it in Tahoe, away from the Viking and anyone else looking for it in Kauai.

He asked his maternal grandfather Francis Plummer about the Washoe side of the family and if they had special places like the Hawaiian side of the family."

"Do they?" Street asked.

"Sort of. Francis said he told Thos that Rubicon Point is where the family spent summers for generations."

"Where the Rubicon Lodge is."

"Right," I nodded. "He also told Thos about an ice grave."

"What is that?"

"I asked him and he said it may be a mythical place. But the story handed down is that there is a cave in a cliff, high up on a mountain. The cave is filled with ice, or maybe it is a cave inside of ice. Either way, the ice is supposed to glow."

"What's the grave?"

"An icy hole that goes to the center of the earth, into which evil people fall."

Street was squinting in the way that indicated excitement. "How would Morella Meyer be connected?"

"I don't know. But I think someone wanted to keep her from talking. My guess is that her killer wanted to learn if she found the slug that killed Thos."

"Earlier, you said that you had another interpretation of the events."

"Yes, almost an opposite version. It may be that the body you took the samples off of is Brock Chambers."

The waiter arrived with the wine, a Silver Rose merlot. I tasted it, nodded and he filled our glasses. When he left, I continued.

"Brock's been missing for several days. A guy I spoke to at the Rubicon Lodge says Brock is hiding from his creditors. One of those creditors is American River Winery. They recently lost their account with the Rubicon Lodge when Brock replaced their wines with Thos's Pacific Blue brand."

"Thos was expanding his business beyond Hawaii?"

"That's what Mike says. Further, the American River Winery is north of Placerville, near where the body was found in the sauna."

"The vineyards I saw," Street said.

I nodded. "Any idea yet on time of death?"

"No. I may never get an accurate estimate. But the police turned up a witness who saw smoke coming from the sauna chimney, so they have a time when they know there was a fire in the stove. Now they're doing a test to see how fast the sauna cools. I'll be getting temp and humidity data during that test. I might have an answer for you in another few days."

The waiter came back with our dinners, a filet mignon for Street and salmon for me. The entrees were accompanied by a perfect compliment of vegetables and other treats with fancy names, fancier aromas and flavors so tasty I had to restrain myself from eating as Spot would.

Street said, "If the body turns out to be Brock, what does that tell you?"

"Not much. We'd know it wasn't Brock who shot the valve off the scuba tank. So I'd be considering the Viking or Lynette McCloud, who is one of Brock's hunting companions. She is rumored to be a crack shot in addition to being a black market broker."

I explained how I'd learned about McCloud from the Mark Twain archivist and told Street about my subsequent visit to McCloud at her sugar daddy's retro castle up on the mountain.

Street was eating her steak at the same rate she drank her wine. She cut a tiny piece of meat off, switched her fork to her right hand, delicately pulled the beef off with her lips and chewed it with care. I watched her hands while she was cutting the steak. Then I watched her lips and jaw while she chewed. For a moment I considered grabbing her mid-bite and rushing her home to bed. But I decided I might seem more sophisticated if I waited until after dinner.

"McCloud," Street mumbled as she ate, "could have been the one to hire the Viking from the beginning. Maybe Brock never even knew about the manuscript."

"But I saw Brock arguing with the Viking. An argument suggests a relationship of some depth."

"If Brock hired the Viking to get the manuscript with the intention to resell it to McCloud, then maybe McCloud double-crossed Brock and went around his back to buy it directly from the Viking. McCloud could have killed Brock to keep him silent. And if and when the Viking gets the manuscript to McCloud, maybe she'll kill him, too."

We continued to discuss the victims and suspects while we finished dinner, and we decided I wasn't much closer to catching the killer than I was when Janeen first called me.

"Sounds like you're out of luck," Street said.

She sipped her wine. Her delicate throat was beautiful as she swallowed.

"Not if you allow me a conjugal visit before I go back to the prison of my empty cabin," I said.

Street sipped more wine, looking at me over the top of her glass. "Okay, maybe you're not out of luck," she said.

THIRTY-FIVE

I got up early and found another nine inches of snow on my deck. It was light and easy to shovel. When I was done it started snowing again. In Tahoe, the snow can come down so fast that even four-wheel-drives get stuck. If so, it is good to be prepared. So I fetched my cross-country ski gear and put it in the Jeep, just in case.

I headed across town to see Jerry about a better description of the Viking. But first, I thought I'd try again to see if Spot could break through the ice with Phillip. Inside the troubled and weary boy was a little kid in a kind of hibernation. If anyone or anything could wake up whatever innocence was left in Phillip, I thought it was Spot.

This time I decided to take the opposite approach from my earlier efforts.

I pulled into a foot of fresh snow in Janeen's driveway and parked. As before, I left the window down for Spot to stick his head out. Phillip was just outside of the kitchen door. He was adjusting a telescoping ski pole of the sort that snowshoers and hikers use for balance and support. I didn't call out to him, didn't even say hi, and gave no attention to my dog as I got out of the Jeep.

I walked up to the front door, knocked and was let in by Janeen.

"Hi, Janeen. I stopped by to see how you and Phillip are doing."

"We're fine. But things seem tense, somehow. Maybe it's the

snow that keeps falling. The weather man said to expect another three feet in the next two days. Which means we'll get five feet here under Mt. Tallac. We could be stranded for days."

"Do you have extra food and firewood?"

"Yes, but still it frightens me. Lyla thinks it's fun to get snowed in, but she hasn't lived here that long. The school was closed again today and they probably won't open 'til next week. So I can't go to my volunteer work."

"Have you had any more signs of the man with the long blond hair?"

Janeen shook her head. "No. Jerry must have scared him off. The man probably figures that Jerry is up at all hours watching out his window. Now if Jerry left for a few days, then I'd worry. But he says he's staying put at least until he feels better. Speaking of which, how are you feeling? Your bruises are looking more brown than blue, so I suppose you're healing."

"Yes. I..."

Janeen had stopped listening to me and was pointing out the window.

I turned to see Phillip climb off the snow berms and walk down the middle of the driveway toward Spot.

"Your dog is friendly to children, isn't he?" Janeen sounded worried. "He's awfully big."

"He's friendly."

Phillip slowed as he approached my Jeep. Spot's tongue was out, panting.

"Phillip may not know how to act," Janeen said. "What if he does something to startle your dog?"

I turned from the window and looked at Janeen. "You don't need to worry." I touched her on the shoulder. "Only his wagging tail could hurt Phillip, and his tail is in the Jeep." I looked back out the window.

Phillip took little steps, closer and closer, then reached his mittened hand up toward Spot. His body wasn't much bigger than Spot's head and neck.

Spot sniffed his hand, then nosed it sideways and Phillip jerked back. Eventually, he extended his hand again. Spot pushed it around, left and right, up and down. Phillip's arm was stiff, his body braced, as Spot bounced his hand around. Soon, Phillip understood that Spot wanted a pet. Phillip touched the top of Spot's head.

Spot nosed his hand sideways with such force that Phillip spun a quarter turn in the snow. Spot seized the opportunity to stretch his head out the window and lick Phillip on the side of the neck.

Phillip's grin was dramatic.

Phillip pulled away and raced on his snowshoes back up the snow bank and around to the kitchen door. When he was inside he called out in a whisper. "Nana? Nana!"

"What, dear?"

"Nana!" A shouted whisper. "Come here!" the boy said.

Janeen walked through the doorway. I heard more whispers. After a minute, Janeen returned. "Owen? Phillip wonders if your dog can come out of the car and play."

"Of course." I went outside and walked to the Jeep. Phillip kept well behind. Just because he liked my dog didn't mean he liked me.

I opened the car door and Spot bounded out. "Spot, sit." He took his time, fighting the impulse to run. "Sit," I said again. Spot did a partial squat, thinking that would appease me. "All the way," I said, pushing down on his hindquarters.

"Come on over, Phillip. I want you to meet Spot. Spot? Give our young friend a handshake."

Spot lifted a paw. Phillip stayed back. "It's okay, Phillip. This is how Spot meets people." Spot's paw moved up and down through the air. Phillip came slowly. I realized again that it wasn't Spot, but me, that he was wary of.

I backed away. Phillip came forward. Their heads were the same height. Phillip took Spot's paw with both of his mittened hands, held it a moment, then let go.

"Okay, Spot," I said. "You can run." Spot jumped up and ran around the plowed drive, inspecting what apparently was a fascinating collection of smells.

"Phillip," I said, "Spot is friendly and fun to play with, but I need to warn you about his tail. When he wags, it can hit you and it hurts. So when you see his tail coming, put your arms up like this so it hits your arms instead of your face." I demonstrated the position, forearms vertical, elbows down, hands up.

Phillip was busy watching Spot, but I think he got the idea. Then he turned to me. "Will Spot come with me in the woods?" he asked so softly it took me a moment to figure out his words.

"Yes." I turned and called out. "Spot. Come."

My dog ran over. Excited. He knew we were going to do stuff. Spot was a big fan of doing stuff. I pointed to Phillip. "Spot, go play with Phillip. Stay with him. Do as he says."

Phillip's eyes got wide. "Will he?"

"Sure. Try it. Tell him to do that thing where he gets his rear end down on the ground."

Phillip looked alarmed.

"It's okay," I said. "You don't have to."

"Sit," Phillip said in a tiny voice.

"Say it louder. Much louder. And use his name." I clicked my fingers to get Spot's attention and pointed toward Phillip.

"Spot, sit." Phillip called out, his voice only marginally louder.

Spot turned toward the little boy and sat. Phillip grinned. He turned and ran as fast as his snowshoes would allow. Spot loped after him. Phillip turned, saw and stopped abruptly, fear in his eyes.

"He won't hurt you. He just wants to play with you."

Spot made a loop around the kid followed by three trips up and down the drive. He stopped near Phillip, his panting breath making clouds in the winter air. Spot turned toward me, wagging. Phillip immediately put his arms up in front of his face, forearms vertical. My dog's tail smacked Phillip's arms. Phillip jerked from the impact, but otherwise didn't move.

"You two go play, Phillip, while I talk with Janeen."

Phillip ran to the end of the drive and clamored up the snow bank. Spot leaped up after him and the two of them went running out into the forest.

I rejoined Janeen in the cabin.

"It's amazing," she said. "I watched out the window. It's as if Phillip has been transformed."

"Dogs often do that for kids."

She continued to stare where Phillip and Spot had disappeared. "Will your dog run off? I worry that Phillip would try to find him and end up lost."

"No, Spot will stay with Phillip. He's been trained for it. As long as I tell him to stay with someone, he won't leave. He thinks of it like a duty."

"Like a guard dog?"

"Yes. He will stay with Phillip and protect him until I call him off."

"You mean if someone tried to hurt Phillip?"

"I'm sure that would never happen, but yes. If something threatened Phillip, even a bear, Spot would keep it away. Trained dogs are as enthusiastic about their duty as untrained dogs are about chasing cats."

Janeen turned from the window and sat down. She stared off into space. "Maybe I should get Phillip a dog."

"Maybe," I said. "While Spot and Phillip are out in the woods, I thought I'd go check in on Jerry. I'll be back in a bit, okay?"

"Yes, of course."

I let myself out and walked down the drive toward Jerry Roth's house.

I came around the corner formed by the huge snow banks on either side of their driveways and surprised Jerry. He was in his drive, crutch in one hand, snow shovel in the other.

"Oh!" he exclaimed, with a jerk. "You startled me bloody well, you did. These snow walls are so quiet, a bloke should wear a bell like a cow if you don't want to give someone a heart attack."

"Sorry, I didn't know you were there. Shouldn't you be inside letting your wounds mend? Most docs don't recommend shoveling snow for therapy."

"I know, but the snow has built up so much that the melt just dams up. I thought I could make a channel for it to run off." He jammed the snow shovel down into the ice where a large pool of water was backing up toward his garage. "You any closer to finding the sod that cut my neck with this shovel?"

"Possibly," I said. "Jerry, I wondered if you could give me a better description of him."

Jerry frowned. "Well now, like I told the police at the hospital, it was dark and things happened fast. I only had the outdoor lights to see him by." He pointed toward a fixture next to the door and another down by the garage. "I went out the front door and came down the steps. Of course, I couldn't exactly be speedy with my bloody foot, but I fairly hopped down the steps toward him. I think he was surprised, if I do say so myself. I barely had time to get a look at him when he grabbed this shovel and had a swing at my head." Jerry made a little ducking motion at the memory. "I like to think I'm good at faces, but with him trying to decapitate me, I must admit I didn't get a good look at his face."

Jerry paused, shut his eyes and angled his head up toward the sky, no doubt visualizing. "Of course, the main thing I remember was his hair. Lots of it and very long. It shined in the night, almost like he'd just brushed it. And he had a beard. Not blond like his hair, but darker. It was big, came out like this." Jerry gestured with his hands.

"As for his looks, well, I don't really remember. But his eyes were very blue. I could see them clearly in the night." Jerry narrowed his own blue eyes at the thought.

"Was there anything else unusual about him? A peculiar characteristic aside from his hair and beard that makes him stand out in your memory?"

Jerry thought about it. "The funny thing is, he didn't speak

Not even a grunt swinging the shovel. I guess that's what stands out. But then that's no bloody help at all, is it?"

THIRTY-SIX

I had Jerry go over the details of the attack once more, but he told me nothing new. Ole Knudson was a phantom, a striking figure that no one knew anything about.

"You think he's still lurking around here?"

"I don't know, Jerry. I think he's looking for something that Janeen doesn't have."

"What do you mean?"

"My best guess is that he thinks Janeen's son Thos had a valuable object. Knudson might think Thos hid it in Janeen's house. I made a thorough search and there's nothing there. But if the man thinks it's there, he may come back. I'd appreciate it if you'd keep an eye out."

"You can rely on it, mate. Only, next time I won't let him catch me off guard like that."

"Jerry, if you see him again, I think it would be best if you call the police."

"Oh, sure, I'll get the coppers, but I won't sit on my ass and let him bother Janeen and Phillip. This time I'll use something more persuasive than a snow shovel."

I looked at Jerry hard, trying to decide if there was anything I could say that would keep him from jumping the Viking and possibly getting himself killed. Nothing came to mind. "Thanks for keeping watch, Jerry," I said.

I walked back up to Janeen's.

"Phillip is still out with your dog," Janeen said after she let me into her house. "Do you want me to call him?"

"Yes, I should get going before the snow gets any worse. I have some driving to do before the day is out." I glanced out the window toward the forest where Phillip and Spot had run off.

Janeen opened the kitchen door, reached out and pulled on the bell rope. The deep gong of the bell shook the house.

Janeen and I sat at the kitchen table and waited. "I heard about the woman who died," she said. "The diver. Was her death connected to Thos?" Janeen's brow was furrowed.

"I can't say for certain, Janeen. Maybe."

"Will you tell me honestly if you think you're going to find the man who killed Thos? Mind you, I don't care about your fee. I just see that since I asked you to look into it, Jasper's nephew John died, the diver died, and you and Jerry Roth have been badly hurt. I wonder if I should have let Thos's death alone."

"No. You haven't made things worse. And yes, I think I will find Thos's murderer. The truth is I've had no great insights into the case that make me think I'm close to catching the killer. But I have more leads than before and I'm chasing them down."

"You are persistent."

I nodded just as noises came from outside the door.

Janeen opened it a crack and looked out.

Phillip was running toward the house at the same fast speed as when he left. Spot loped alongside. Phillip scooped up a ball of snow and threw it. Spot leaped and caught it.

When Janeen opened the door wide, Phillip exclaimed, "Nana! Nana! I told Spot to sit and run and he can catch snow-balls!" Phillip saw me and stopped talking.

"What do you say to Mr. McKenna, Phillip?" Janeen said.

Phillip looked from her to me.

"Phillip?" Janeen said.

"I like Spot," he said.

"I'm glad," I said. "I can tell that Spot likes you, too."

"Can he come again?"

"Yes, he will." I said goodbye to both Janeen and Phillip and left. I had to tug on Spot's collar to get him to come with me.

THIRTY-SEVEN

I drove through blowing and drifting snow back across the south end of the lake. Traffic was slowed to a crawl.

I turned up Kingsbury Grade to my office. I wanted to check email and see if there were any more messages from Hermes or someone who might know his identity.

Spot came inside with me and trotted up the stairs. There was a pile of mail inside the door. Spot sniffed it, moving envelopes with his nose, while I booted up the computer. Spot lay down on the carpet near the door, then flopped sideways onto the mail, no doubt getting it wet with the melting snow on his fur. Shows how much he respects bills.

I found several messages in my inbox. The third one was about my question. It was from someone named Zeus.

"Mr. McKenna, I met Thos Kahale at a business retreat in Napa. (I am also in the wine business.) I did not know Thos well. In fact, we met in a hot tub, traded email addresses, and never saw each other again.

I also do not know the identity of his friend Hermes. But I wonder if you have checked your Greek mythology. Did you know that Hermes was the god of thieves and liars? Perhaps this has nothing to do with your inquiries, but because Hermes is such an unusual name I thought it may have been chosen for a reason. I figured you would want to know just in case it has any bearing.

Good luck,

Zeus."

I spent the next half hour researching Hermes on the Internet. I learned that Hermes was the Greek equivalent of Mercury for the Romans. Hermes was the messenger god, the god of business and trade and was a great orator.

But as Zeus said, Hermes was also the god of thieves and a grand liar. Maybe the Greeks thought that to be very successful in business, one had to be a thief. Maybe they thought that to be a great orator, one had to be a liar.

I didn't know what it meant regarding Thos. Being a messenger would not have any significance that I could see, unless Hermes was an agent for Thos. But that seemed too much like secret agent stuff in spy novels. However, if Hermes chose his name because he is a liar, then I had no idea what that suggested about the emails he'd written. Probably, it was something he did for fun. Something no one would understand except fellow students of Greek mythology.

It was like art. I'd learned that many artists put certain references to other art in their works. One didn't need to understand them or even know of their existence to enjoy the work. But for artists, scholars and other insiders, the references informed the work. Sometimes the visual comments were simple and playful, sometimes they were serious signs of respect or disrespect, and sometimes they turned the work into a full-blown homage to another artist or work of art. When done, the work took on a new meaning, far from the initial, obvious subject.

I wondered if Hermes was an email artist, picking his pseudonym with great care for the subtle and not-so-subtle flavor it gave to his messages. Messenger god, liar and thief. A deeper meaning lurking behind the obvious.

My Calder and Rodin were home on my shelf, but I could visualize them clearly. They both had that quality of many layers of meaning. More is revealed each time you look at them. In the beginning, the Calder was about movement and play and the Rodin was about young love. Eventually, the Calder came to be about balance and the Rodin about passion, both in a metaphorical way that went beyond the materials and the shapes. But while the artists presented the obvious, it was up to the viewer to dive beneath the surface and find the rest. I assumed that I had yet to crack open the core of what Calder and Rodin were all about.

As I thought about the two sculptures, I remembered what Janeen's father Francis Plummer had said. He'd been taught not to volunteer information where it hadn't been requested. His daughter Janeen had talked at length. His son-in-law Jasper had told me everything that came to mind. But what else did Plummer know about this?

I stood up. "What did Newton say, your largeness?" Spot turned his eyes toward me, but not a muscle in his body twitched. "An object at rest tends to stay at rest?" I walked over and nudged his prostrate form with the toe of my shoe. "Let's see if we can turn you into an object in motion." I nudged harder. Spot groaned, but didn't move. I nudged again. "You were in motion playing with Phillip. C'mon, big guy, you can snooze in the Jeep."

I had to tug on his collar before he finally got up. We went down the stairs and out into a snow storm that was acting more serious than I'd seen in a long time.

I powered up Kingsbury Grade through thinning traffic. Although the day was still young, many people had quit work and gone home to wait out the storm. Even the tourists had given up trying to see the ski runs through their foggy goggles and headed back to the spas in their hotels and condos. The heavy traffic of South Lake Tahoe disappeared as I climbed higher up the mountain.

For a time I worried they would close Daggett Pass, but I got over without a problem and headed down to the Carson Valley.

The snow was now falling across the valley, but it was light and the driving was much better than up in the mountains. I got to Francis Plummer's camper without delay. He was inside the little box, and opened at my knock. He nodded recognition when he saw me and beckoned me to come in.

I ducked my head and squeezed through a doorway made for miniature people, then sat across from him at a little fold-out table that made me feel like I was a giant in Barbie-Doll land. Our knees touched and my head brushed the built-in cupboard above me.

We made no small talk.

"I had a few more questions," I said.

He nodded.

"Did Thos ever talk to you about his friends?" I asked.

The man shook his head.

"But Thos visited you from time to time?"

"He'd stop by every year or so."

"What did he talk about?"

"Nothing much," Plummer said. "Asked how I was doing. Things like that."

"There is a person I'm looking for," I said. "But I don't know who the person is. I only have an email name. He or she goes by Hermes. It's the name of one of Thos's email friends. Is there any chance Thos ever mentioned someone named Hermes?"

"Of course," Plummer said. "But I don't know that we ever used the name Hermes when we talked about him."

"I don't understand what you mean."

"I get email from Hermes, too. But Thos and I always use his real name. In fact, I think Thos was the one to give him the name Hermes. I don't know what it means."

I glanced at the little trailer with no sign of electricity. I'd never guess he had a computer. But he carried a cellphone in his pocket. Maybe he had a laptop as well. "Mr. Plummer, who is Hermes?"

"Phillip, of course."

I stopped. Mental gears shifted, reversed direction, shifted again. Hermes was the little kid who used an abacus and didn't own a computer. He was almost certainly going to be the target of the Viking if the Viking learned he was Hermes. I thanked Francis Plummer, turned and squeezed out through the little door. I was heading for the Jeep when I heard Plummer calling out. I stopped and ran back to where Francis Plummer stood.

"I'm sorry, what were you saying?" I was breathing fast.

"Just that it is strange that two different people ask about Phillip in the same day."

"Somebody else asked?"

"Yes. Phillip's teacher was here an hour ago. He was in the area and stopped by. He said Phillip often talks about me in class. I guess the boy is proud of his Washoe heritage. His teacher told me I'm a good role model, so he wanted to meet me."

"What did you and the teacher talk about?"

"Phillip, mostly. How he does in class. How good he is in math and how he can do almost anything with his abacus and on the school computer as well."

"What is his teacher's name?"

Plummer shook his head. "I don't know."

"Mr. Plummer, did you and the teacher talk about email?"

"Actually, we did. He wanted my email address so he could stay in touch with me."

"Did he want Phillip's, too?"

"Oh, I think he already had Phillip's."

"Are you certain? Did he say he had it?"

"Well, I suppose I'm not certain. But we talked about Phillip and his nickname Hermes, so I assume he must have Phillip's email address."

"Mr. Plummer, this is very important. Who used Phillip's email name first? Did his teacher say the name Hermes first, or did you?"

Francis Plummer thought a bit. "I don't know for sure, but it may have been that I said it first. Why does it matter?"

"What kind of car did he drive?"

"I don't know. One of those big four-wheel-drives."

"What did he look like?"

"Phillip's teacher? Not the way teachers used to, I can tell you that. Long blond hair, big beard..."

THIRTY-EIGHT

I didn't hear the rest of Francis Plummer's words as I sprinted for the Jeep.

I jumped in, key in hand, started it as I shifted into reverse and floored the accelerator. Snow and gravel shot out from under my tires as I flew down the trail.

The country lane had a thicker layer of snow than before and I fishtailed back and forth when I turned onto the road. Spot was thrown about in back.

I got on the cellphone as I raced across the valley floor, dialing Mallory first. The moment his voice mail answered, I hung up and dialed the dispatch number.

"Shirley? This is Owen McKenna. Can you patch me through to Mallory, please," I shouted.

"I'm sorry, Mr. McKenna, he's not available."

"Can you tell me where he is? He will want this call."

"A big rig jackknifed trying to turn onto Ski Run Boulevard from Highway Fifty. A dozen cars are involved, several injuries. Half the force is over there. The chief tried Captain Mallory a few minutes ago and couldn't raise him, either."

"Is the traffic moving through?"

"No, they're directing all traffic over to Pioneer."

I thanked her and hung up.

I thought about how to get roadblocks in place. For Kingsbury Grade I could call Diamond, but the Viking was an hour ahead of me. Even with the heavy snow, he'd probably be down off the grade and heading around the lake before Diamond could coordinate a roadblock on the Nevada side.

I dialed Mallory's voicemail again and left a message. "Mallory, I'm in the Carson Valley, headed up to Tahoe and Janeen Kahale's house. Ole Knudson, the Viking, is on his way there to find Phillip. He thinks Phillip knows where the Mark Twain manuscript is. You'll want to send a couple patrols out there immediately. Knudson has about an hour lead on me, so he is probably coming down into town as I speak. If you can alert your men directing traffic, tell them to look for any man with long blond hair and a big beard. I don't know the vehicle make, but it is probably a sport utility vehicle. Tell them to use any pretense to stop him." Then I tried Diamond. When he answered I gave him the same information. He said he'd get on it.

Next, I dialed Janeen's number. It rang and rang, but there was no answer.

I hung up, trying to calculate the driving time as I hit the bottom of Kingsbury Grade and started the 3000-foot climb into the storm clouds. I estimated the drive to Janeen's to be about two hours at the rate the snow was coming down. If I pushed it to the limit, I could make up some of the hour lead he had.

I pressed the accelerator to the floor. All four wheels dug into the snow and we shot up the mountain.

I pushed it to an extreme degree, engine roaring, four-wheel-drive churning. The snow got thicker and heavier as I gained altitude. I came upon a Lexus going my way. The car had chains on and was driving twenty-five miles per hour. I flicked on my high beams, moved into the oncoming lane and flew by at seventy. Snow and slush arced up from my wheels, covering the fancy car like a wet blanket.

An oncoming truck approached as I pulled back into my lane. The moment it went by I veered back out into his lane to pass more cars. Spot was hunkered down in the back seat, trying to resist being thrown back and forth.

A thousand feet up the grade, the snow grew denser on the highway. My steering became vague and I knew my tires were hydroplaning. I slowed to fifty to keep contact between tire and road.

Heavy snow blew sideways under a darkening sky. My wipers were on high and my defroster was on the warmest setting. But the snow was building up on the windshield too fast. The accumulation of frozen crud on the glass had me straining to see through the six-inch patch of glass where the wipers still made minimal contact.

I slowed down a bit, grabbed the scraper and hit the button to lower my window. It took concentration to scrape in time with the wiper blade, chasing it toward the center, then retreating quickly as it came back. I got most the left side of the windshield cleared and rolled my window back up.

I sped up as much as I dared, passing cars and trucks with abandon. Eventually I crested the pass and slowed as the road plunged down at a steep angle. I went easy on the brake, letting my speed build up. The wind whistled at the side window and the snow was moving horizontally.

It was an agonizing descent to the lake, slowed by the darkness of evening and the occasional car with chains. I pushed it hard enough that I spun out on one corner, hitting the snow bank at the shoulder before gunning it back onto the road.

Highway 50 was emptier than before. Every sensible person had long since gotten off the road. I weaved in and out of the few vehicles near the casinos and flashed across the state line under a yellow light that turned to red as I entered the intersection.

I took the turnoff to Pioneer Trail so I could avoid the accident at Ski Run. From Pioneer I followed back roads and shot back out onto Highway 50 a half mile after the accident.

At the far end of town, I turned right on Emerald Bay Road and raced out toward the Spring Creek neighborhood. When I got to Camp Richardson, I dialed her number again and listened to the ring over the roar of the wind outside the Jeep. Again, no one answered. I redialed just to be certain. Either Janeen had left home or she was dealing with the Viking. I hung up. I would be there in a few minutes.

The wind gusted so hard that my Jeep rocked sideways. The wipers and the defroster were on high. But the snow was again building up on the windshield. The dull gray twilight had given way to darkness and I could see almost nothing but the snow in my headlights.

I lowered the window and was working with the scraper once again when my phone rang. I hit the button to roll the window up and snatched the phone off the passenger seat. "Hello!" I shouted.

"Owen?" The single word was a tiny, plaintive keening. It took me a second before I realized it was Janeen.

"Janeen, what's wrong?"

She could barely speak. "The blond man..." Her breathing was audible over the phone. "I saw him through the window and kept the door locked. But he broke down the front door."

"Are you okay?"

"I think..." she stopped mid-sentence.

I took a curve too fast and the rear end fishtailed dangerously. "I'll be there in a few minutes. What about Phillip? Is he okay?"

"I don't know. He's gone." Her words had long spaces between them. "He went out the kitchen door. The man ran after Phillip."

"Any idea where Phillip went?"

"No. Into the storm. Before..." she stopped again and breathed. "Before the man came, Phillip walked out of his room and said he'd figured out who killed Thos. Then Phillip looked out the window like he'd heard a noise. He must have seen something because he ran into the kitchen, grabbed his jacket and snowshoes and went out the kitchen door. He said, 'don't worry, nana, I know where to go.'" Janeen stopped again. I pushed down on the accelerator and drove even faster.

Janeen continued, her words slower than before. "I don't have snowshoes..." she faded off for the second time.

"Janeen! Can you hear me?"

"I'm bleeding. I was chopping onions." Her words were soft and faint. "I tried to fight." She stopped. Her breathing had a sudden gurgle in it. "He stabbed me with my knife."

"Janeen, I'm going to hang up and call nine-one-one."

She mumbled something. I couldn't make it out.

"I didn't hear you, Janeen. What was it? Say it again."

There was no answer. I tapped the brakes, slid around a tight corner. "Janeen? Can you hear me?"

I heard her breath catch. She gave a weak cough. Her breathing sounded like she was sucking air through liquid.

THIRTY-NINE

I pressed the buttons for 911 as I skidded around a tight bend in the road.

Nothing happened.

I dialed again. "We're sorry," a synthetic voice said. "All circuits are busy. Please try your call later."

I disconnected and dialed Jerry Roth.

"Jerry here," he called out over a loud, roaring noise. The sound was like a giant fan blowing into his phone.

"Jerry, Owen McKenna calling," I shouted.

"Who? Oh, McKenna. Just a moment, let me turn the telly down." The roar got louder and then suddenly stopped. "Sorry 'bout that, old man. One of those disaster movies. Killer tornado and all that. What can I do for you?"

"Janeen Kahale just called me. Ole Knudson broke into their house."

"What!"

"Phillip has gone into the woods on his showshoes. Janeen said the man took off after Phillip. I was hoping the boy would double back to your place."

"Good God! Should I run over to Janeen's? But what if the boy comes over here? I should be here. Poor Phillip must be scared to death. What should I do?"

"Stay put in case Phillip shows up. I'm almost there. I'll go to Janeen's house and put Spot onto the tracks. Call nine-one-one. Janeen needs an ambulance in addition to the police. When they arrive, you should be outside to show them where the Kahale driveway is. Otherwise, they'll never find it with all the snow."

"Got it," Jerry said.

I hung up and concentrated on my driving. My headlights shined on a blinding curtain of snow whipping horizontally across the road. I focused on looking through it, watching the hints of previous tire tracks to see where the highway was. When I came to Spring Creek Road, I braked hard and cranked the wheel aiming more from memory than from what I could see in the dark.

Once I was into the turn I hit the gas to get through the deep snow, but my Jeep quickly came to a stop. My wheels spun, but I was high-centered. The buildup of snow was so thick under the Jeep that the wheels didn't even touch the pavement.

I put my cellphone in my pocket and jumped out into twenty inches of fresh snow that had fallen since I left Janeen's a few hours earlier. I opened the rear door for Spot, then the rear hatch. My cross-country skis were still jammed at an angle toward the front passenger seat, my boots and poles sitting in back. I pulled on my boots and gators and snapped my boots into the ski bindings. My gloves and ski poles were last. I shut the rear hatch and Spot and I were off.

Although my skis are the wide back-country design, the snow was far too deep to glide on. I had to break trail, lifting my skis with each step and pushing down until the deep snow compressed enough to support my weight. Breaking trail is hard work and I was streaming with sweat in a couple of minutes.

Spot loped alongside, his legs long enough that his feet could connect with the road below while his chest grazed the surface of the snow.

I ran like a high-stepping drum major, knees rising with each step to keep my ski tips from burying into the snow. My heart and lungs burned.

The falling snow suddenly stopped as the clouds parted. The moon shined like a spotlight through the snow-draped forest. I saw in the light the faint depressions of tire tracks under the snow.

Probably the Viking's vehicle, the last one to make it through before the snow got too deep. I tried to ski in one of the tracks where the new snow was shallow and I could make better time. Then, just as suddenly, the clouds came back across the moon and the heavy snowfall resumed.

In ten minutes I turned the corner and came into Jerry and Janeen's driveway. A Toyota Land Cruiser with knobby snow tires and high clearance was parked in Janeen's drive. It was covered in eight inches of snow.

There was one weak light on in Jerry's house as I approached. He hadn't thought to turn on the outside lights. Or Phillip had come and they were hiding from the Viking. I didn't dare take the time to stop and find out.

I skied through the dark drive, huffing like a steam engine.

When I got to Janeen's cabin, I clamored up the snow bank, pushing up the slope with my ski poles. I unsnapped my ski bindings and ran to the front door.

Light spilled out. The front door hung crookedly on one of its three hinges, banging back and forth in the wind.

I leaped past the broken door into the living room. Spot jumped after me. There was no sound save the roar of the storm and the loud staccato banging of the front door.

"Janeen?" I called out.

She didn't answer. Spot did the type of point that means he's smelling something very wrong. He tensed, lowered a few inches, flattened his tail, his back and neck, and pointed his nose toward the kitchen.

A deep rumble emanated from his chest.

"Spot, find the suspect! Take him down!" I said, knowing that if the perp was in the house, Spot would attack, oblivious to guns or baseball bats.

I didn't worry about whether Spot would know the guilty from the innocent. Dogs have an amazing ability to tell people who belong in a place from people who don't. But Spot didn't move.

"What is it, boy?"

Spot stopped growling. He glanced up at me for a second, then turned back toward the kitchen, sniffing. The tautness went out of his body and a small cry escaped from his throat.

It was a cry I'd heard before, and it meant the worst. I rushed to the kitchen. The metallic scent of blood was heavy in the air.

She sat on the floor in a corner, leaning against the cabinets, her head slumped sideways against the dishwasher. Her thick, beautiful braid cascaded down over her shoulder.

There was a widening pool of blood on the floor. Streaks of red on her clothes converged to a slash wound in her throat. I heard tiny gurgling breaths. The blood didn't pulse, but seeped. She was bleeding from a vein, possibly a nicked jugular.

I grabbed her phone, hoping the land line would get me through where my cellphone hadn't.

The 911 operator answered immediately. I told him where Janeen was and her condition. I stressed that the medics would need a helicopter or else snowmobiles and the type of toboggan that ski patrols use to carry people.

I pulled out drawers looking for some kind of tape and found nothing. You can't put a tourniquet around someone's neck, but Janeen needed compression on the wound until she could get a blood transfusion and emergency surgery. I ran back to Janeen's bedroom and jerked open the closet door. I pawed through hangers, pushed clothes around. Hanging loosely in the belt loops of a coat was a vinyl belt. I jerked it out and ran back to the kitchen where Spot stood, his brow furrowed as he cried softly.

There was a roll of paper towels above the sink. I wadded some up, pressed it against the wound where the blood was oozing. I used the belt to make a loop across the compress, around her back, then down and under the opposite arm. I tried to tie it off with enough tension to help slow the blood flow but not choke her to death.

Through it all, Janeen never moved or made a sound save for her gurgling breaths. I didn't have much hope that she'd make it even if the medics came by helicopter.

The kitchen door was standing open. It swung back and forth in the wind from the raging storm. One of the windowpanes had shattered in long shards. Snow made a crescent on the floor, melting into a puddle that had found a low spot. The water ran past the glass diamonds to meet the blood and mix in swirls of red.

Something flicked at my face. I turned to see what it was.

There was a split in the wooden doorjamb. Caught in the crack and waving like streamers in the ferocious wind were several long hairs so blond and shiny in the kitchen light they looked surreal.

I looked out at the trail of small, shallow snowshoe prints and much larger, deeper snowshoe tracks that were quickly being covered by the blowing snow. The tracks appeared to go deep into the woods and nowhere near Jerry's house.

Phillip had the advantage of light weight and terrain that he knew well. But he was a small boy. And I'd already seen the Viking's physical ability on the Na Pali cliffs.

The only weapon I had was Spot. I wondered if I should focus him on protecting Phillip or taking down the killer. If Phillip found a place to hide and I sent Spot as a protector, then Spot might draw attention to the boy and make him even more vulnerable. Spot had a good chance of finding the killer if I could find some article of the killer's to scent him on. But looking around revealed nothing that would give Spot a clear, strong odor of the killer to pursue. I had no choice.

I ran back to Phillip's bedroom and grabbed the pillow off the bed. Spot was at the doorway as I turned. I held the pillow out to him. "Smell this, Spot!" He stuck his nose into the fabric. I practically wrapped it around his snout. "This is Phillip! Remember Phillip? Do you have Phillip's scent? Okay, Spot!" I ran through the living room, into the kitchen and stopped at the open door. I stuck the pillow on Spot's nose once more. "Find Phillip!

Guard him! Do you understand, Spot?" I bent and grabbed Spot's head, hands on his jowls, my face directly in front of his. "Guard him!"

I pointed to the open door and gave Spot a pat on his hindquarters. "Go!" I shouted.

Spot leaped into the deep snow behind the cabin, sinking in to an alarming depth. He scrambled to find footing, but his legs floundered as his body was engulfed. He was a tall example of the tallest breed, but the snow was eight feet deep.

I watched as Spot floundered, leaping and jerking, trying to gain purchase. He jumped sideways to the left, then right. I saw his left front paw land in one of the Viking's tracks. Spot felt the difference and clawed himself in that direction. Another paw found invisible footing under the soft snow, then another.

Spot bounded ahead, following the snowshoe tracks more with his nose than with his eyes, and never looked back as he charged off into the dark storm.

FORTY

I had left my cross-country skis at the front of the cabin. I stepped over Janeen's slumped form, ran back through the cabin and jumped out over the broken front door. A violent gust of wind seemed to suck the air out of my lungs.

As I popped my boots into both bindings, I had a disturbing realization.

Janeen Kahale had been chopping onions and the intruder stabbed her with her own knife.

Nowhere had I seen a knife.

I pushed through deep snow around the side of Janeen's little house and came upon the tracks just behind the kitchen door. The blowing snow had nearly obliterated the old marks and was filling in Spot's fresh tracks. I could see their direction in the weak light coming from the house. I followed them into the forest, trying to make my strides as long and fast as possible, thrusting hard with my poles.

The wind blasted me as I came out from the cabin's wind shadow. Storm gusts blew down the mountain and through the forest as if to level everything that wasn't rock. Mature Jeffrey pines, 150 feet tall, bent and swayed like saplings.

The tracks I was following became nearly impossible to see in the dark forest. I couldn't make out the actual marks and had only a vague sense of where the snow had been disturbed. I concentrated on that, heading up at a steep angle through the woods.

After five minutes of the hardest skiing I'd ever done, I came to a clearing in the trees. The clouds thinned for a moment and the moon lit up the landscape.

Phillip's snowshoe prints were very faint but visible in the sudden moonlight. They were closely spaced. The Viking's prints were larger and deeper, yet despite the snow depth there was a good distance between his footprints as if he weren't struggling at all.

I continued on, hoping that on my skis I was faster than either Phillip or the Viking. Spot would be faster still.

But I realized that even if Spot got to Phillip first, the Viking could use Janeen's kitchen knife on him.

As I skied farther up the mountain, the clouds closed in as thick as before and the snow came down in heavy waves. I could see almost nothing.

I tried to ski faster, but I had to stop and bend down to find any tracks. The wind howled through the trees. A faint trail went up at an angle, through stands of pines. I became aware of a purpose to the direction Phillip had chosen. He was making a gradual ascent up toward the cliffs of Mt. Tallac, mostly staying in the trees to avoid the avalanche danger of the open slopes. I'd been below the area during the summer, on the hiking trail that went across the front of the mountain before making a big loop and arcing on up to the summit 3500 feet above.

After going up several hundred feet I was panting so hard it was difficult to think. The trail turned to the left and went up a short, dramatic rise into a grouping of Lodgepole pines. I planted my poles hard, turned my ski tips out in a wedge shape and struggled up the slope.

As I came over the crest I saw that the pines gave way to a large, open slope, steeper than before. The wind was stronger in the open and the tracks even more obscure. I stared through the dark, blowing snow, trying to see the tracks. The trail made a gradual curve upslope toward another stand of trees.

I skied fast across the open snow field. My vision was strained. As I stared it seemed the snow would get lighter, only to darken again. Suddenly, the barrage of snowflakes stopped and a bright shaft of moonlight cascaded through an opening in the clouds. The wash of light shot across the snow field. Low clouds raced through the sky, then closed together as fast as they'd opened. The moonlight disappeared and the landscape was plunged back into darkness.

During the brief flash of moonlight, I'd gotten a glimpse of Spot's tracks. I skied that way from memory now as my eyes readjusted to the darkness. The snow began again, blowing as hard as before.

When I entered another grouping of trees, I lost the trail. These trees were Red firs, thicker and denser than the previous pines. Spot's tracks went under some low branches. I ducked under to follow, got a clump of snow down my neck and found myself on virgin snow. I turned a full circle before I found the trail curving off to one side. I'd barely gotten out from under the branches when I followed the tracks under yet another group of trees with low branches. Phillip had made tracking him difficult. This time I skied around the side hoping to save time. But the snow on the other side was again untracked. It took precious seconds to find the trail in a small ravine that led sideways out of the trees.

The slope rose more steeply through scattered fir trees. Snow still blew, but it was lighter. The moon flashed through the clouds, disappeared, then flickered again. Although the mountain above me was still shrouded in clouds, the cloud blanket was beginning to break up. In another minute, the moonlight was constant enough that the marks in the snow were easy to read.

Phillip's snowshoe tracks were far apart relative to his size. Clearly, he was terrified and running at full speed.

The trail turned and led in a new direction, cutting up at a steep angle. At times the slope was open enough and steep enough to present a serious avalanche danger, but Phillip obviously had no other choice.

The path climbed dramatically higher, going around boulders

and the occasional stand of trees. Although I was nearly running on my cross-country skis, I felt like an ant as I inched my way up the mountain.

After another twenty minutes of climbing, I'd come up about 1000 feet. The trail went into another stand of trees and repeated the frustrating pattern of disappearing under thick, low branches. Again, Phillip had changed direction in the trees. When I rejoined the trail the Viking's footprints were more visible than before, despite the blowing snow. Was I getting that much closer? Or were the clouds thinning, allowing more moonlight through?

My question was answered by a muffled bark.

I pushed myself to ski faster. There was no other sound except the howling wind. I scanned the slope above me. It was steep enough to sustain a massive avalanche. Nothing moved except the clouds tumbling across the sky like a movie of bad weather on fast forward. The clouds were thinner and brighter than before with dark patches of open sky between them.

As I looked up, I sensed movement above me.

I stopped skiing and tried to steady myself against my panting so that I could figure out what I was seeing.

The slope I was on rose in a swath of white snow to a vertical face of rock. To one side of the rocky cliff was the famous cross of snow that made Mt. Tallac easy to spot from across the lake. On the other side of the cliff were scattered trees.

The first movement was a vague perception that I couldn't place. I continued to watch the mountain in the on and off darkness of racing clouds and bright moon. The second move-ment was completely obvious.

The Viking was suddenly exposed to the whole world, a small but brilliant figure on the moonlit cliff face. Even from my distance, his long blond hair glinted and flashed in the wind as he quickly made his way across the face of rock. Except for the ice and snow, the scene reminded me of when he was climbing across the Na Pali cliffs in Kauai. The biggest difference was a light flashing at his side.

I watched as it went dark, then blazed like a beacon as bright as the moon itself, and then went dark again. Then, as if in a magic act, the Viking suddenly disappeared.

Before I could figure out how he'd vanished, I suddenly understood what had been catching the moonlight and flashing at his side.

Janeen Kahale's chopping knife.

FORTY-ONE

Iwanted to call out to Spot and try to direct him to the Viking, but I didn't know where my dog was. And he wasn't that well trained. He wouldn't understand attack commands unless I was next to him. Any sound from me would only let the Viking know how close I was.

Directly above me were a few trees that would provide cover from the moonlight. If I could make it to them before the Viking saw me, I thought I'd be able to skirt around the side of the cliff and climb up after him unseen.

It was too steep to kick and glide. I turned my ski tips out and tails together in a wedge, drove my poles in hard and hustled up the incline.

The trees were more widely spaced than I thought. Moonlight shined through and I was exposed as I went from shadow to shadow. There was an open area between the base of the cliff and me. I hoped that the Viking was not looking down at that moment.

When I got to the base of the cliff, I still couldn't see where the Viking went. I scanned for any sign of Spot and Phillip. There was nothing, neither tracks nor movement. If I'd made a mistake leaving their tracks, it was too late now.

I continued across the base of the cliff to the trees at the side. Looking up at the wall of rock, I could see the place where the Viking had last been before he vanished from my vision. But he was not there.

I started up through the trees at the side of the cliff, setting my edges with each step and jamming in with my poles. My right ski slipped back. I recovered, and reset the ski, stomping it down into the snow. There was a layer of icy crust and my ski lost grip again. This time both skis slipped out from under me and I fell on my face.

I slid down the slope and rolled sideways. Both skis ended up above me. I could flip them over me, but I was now in a bright patch of moonlight. A rolling skier with windmilling skis is as obvious as a flapping flag.

I reached out, flipped up the binding catches and was free of the skis in a few seconds. The slope was windblown and crusted. Using my poles for support and balance, I jammed the toes of my boots into the stiff snow and charged up the mountain.

Most of the time the crust supported me. But every few steps, the crust gave way and I sunk up to my thigh. I used my poles to get back out, thrusting them down with both arms at once.

Soon, I saw how the Viking had vanished.

I'd just come out of a group of trees and could see a ledge stretching out across the rock face. There was a hole in the cliff. The tracks went out the ledge toward it.

The entire world seemed exposed before me. Beyond the cliff, Tallac's snow cross glowed brilliant white in the moonlight. Fallen Leaf Lake was a huge black finger of water 2000 feet below.

I looked away and started out onto the ledge.

The ledge was two feet wide and went up at an angle. I stabbed my ski poles down to stabilize myself on the icy surface. The ground dropped away below the cliff ledge so that after moving out only fifty feet, I was high enough that a fall would mean certain death. I inched along, aware that my ski boots were not designed for hiking on ice. My impulse was to rush, but I'd do Phillip no good if I slipped off.

As I stepped, my ski pole banged against the cellphone in my pocket. The clink of hard surfaces seemed to jar something in my brain, but I couldn't quite retrieve it. My foot slipped and I jammed my pole into the ice to catch myself, the pole shaft clicking again on my cellphone.

That was it. The cellphone was the object down in the mental cellar. It meant nothing by itself, but what it pointed to meant everything.

My heart sped as the Viking's passion came clear to me in the cold night air. I'd missed the obvious. He was much more devious than I'd thought. I could have caught him long ago. And my inability to understand him had put Phillip at much greater risk.

The ledge narrowed to 15 inches. I turned my shoulders and proceeded forward. My ski poles were the only thing I had that gripped the ice. I made certain they were firmly planted as I moved my feet. Both Phillip and the Viking must have had the type of snowshoes with metal cleats in them. I was glad I was over-due for trimming Spot's nails. He'd have needed them to make it this far.

A sudden, terrible thought intruded. Had Spot made it this far? Where had I last seen his tracks? Could he have slipped and fallen off, out of my sight down below? I didn't dare look down for fear of breaking my concentration and slipping. I continued forward to the opening.

It wasn't a hole so much as a fissure. The huge face of rock had a vertical split in it. The opening was three feet wide at the bottom, narrowing to one foot near my head. I took a step into it. From above came light. I looked up and saw that the fissure became a narrow crack that stretched up a hundred feet or more. As my eyes adjusted I saw that the the faint blue light from the moon filtered down.

I stepped forward, feeling my way, wondering if I was about to plunge into a chasm. How did Phillip know the way? He must have been here before during the day. Perhaps many times, so that he knew his way in the dim glow of night.

I took another step. And another. Water dripped on my head. I hit a wall of rock, slippery with ice. Water was running down inside the fissure and freezing on the walls. Something caught my peripheral vision on the right. I turned and saw more light.

The narrow passage went off at an angle, making a shallow S-curve through the rock. But if you moved your head just so, you could see through.

I was seeing a room of some kind, a hidden cavern. From where I stood, the cavity was about 20 feet down the passage. It looked sizable, and it had a remarkable feature.

The cave glowed.

I stepped forward, hit my head and stifled a grunt. I ducked and moved again, trying to be silent. Now I could see a portion of the room better. The walls gave off a shimmering blue light. They were coated with ice and the moonlight coming in from somewhere above seemed to flow through the ice. I was moving my foot softly forward when a cry filled the passage.

"NO! NO!" It was Phillip's voice, shaking with terror. I heard him clearly, but he sounded some distance away.

"TELL ME, YOU LITTLE SKUNK. TELL ME OR I'M GONNA CUT YOU LIKE I CUT YOUR OLD LADY." It was a man's voice with a southern accent.

"NO! I WON'T TELL YOU!" Phillip was crying, his voice a shriek between sobs.

Spot growled, the rumble echoing through the cave.

"TELL ME, DAMMIT! YOU'VE GOT THE COUNT OF THREE BEFORE I COME UP THERE AND SKIN YOU ALIVE!"

"NOOOO!" Phillip's cry hurt my ears, ripping through the air as if to tear it like fabric.

I concentrated on my foot placement as I hurried down the dark passage toward the glowing room. My left elbow rang against the rock, sending electric shocks up my arm.

When I came to the opening, the room was bright. The cave had a narrow opening to the sky. Moonlight flooded in, reflecting off the ice-coated walls and refracting within the ice. Somewhere above was a spring dripping water into the much colder cavern below, where it splashed and froze on every surface.

The room's glowing walls undulated with light and shadow, every glowing wall reflecting the blue of other glowing walls. I couldn't find the passage to Phillip.

I went to the right, scrambling over icy boulders. There didn't seem to be any place where the boy and the Viking could be. I slipped as I doubled back, going down on my butt onto water-wet ice. I stabbed my ski poles into the ice and clawed my way to my feet.

My circuit of the glowing room was nearly complete when I saw another passage. It was just wide enough for my body and went up at a sharp angle. I jammed my ski poles down, boosted myself up and got my boot hooked on a rocky projection. From there I climbed up eight feet and stuck my head into another glowing room.

The light here was less blue and even brighter than the other cavern. The room didn't have a floor to speak of. A narrow ledge of uneven rock led around the right side and came to a stop at a vertical wall. Spot stood at the base of the wall, facing sideways. Above Spot, crouched in a nook twelve feet up was Phillip. To the side of Spot the ground dropped away in a yawing crevasse of ice that disappeared down into darkness.

Above the crevasse, slowly working his way across the vertical wall of ice and rock was the Viking.

FORTY-TWO

Spot had forced the Viking to climb up the wall from some distance away. He was coming toward Phillip at a height that kept him out of Spot's reach.

Janeen's father must have told the Viking about the ice cave. He'd taken off his snowshoes and strapped crampons onto his boots, the spikes of which stabbed into the ice on the wall to hold him up. In his hand was a small ice ax. He swung the thin curved end toward the ice, sinking the tip deep while a star burst of ice chips flew through the air. When the ice ax was secure, he twisted one foot free, reached out sideways and kicked the crampon spikes back into the ice. The other foot was next, then he shifted the ice ax. If he fell, he would go into the crevasse to his death. But he moved with assurance, obviously experienced.

Phillip's dark nook had no ice and must have seemed like a good hiding place until the Viking found him. Next to the nook was a protruding rock large enough to stand on. When the Viking got to it he would be able to reach Phillip.

Below Phillip, Spot faced up at the Viking. He jumped his front paws up on the wall and growled. He knew the danger to Phillip. I did, too, as I saw the flash of light from Janeen's big chopping knife stuffed under the Viking's belt.

I scrambled up through the opening into the room and slid and slipped my way over toward Phillip and Spot. Spot heard me and turned his head, then quickly turned back toward the Viking. He bounced on his rear legs, his front legs scrabbling from side to side as the Viking drew near Phillip.

I ran over next to my dog and looked up at Phillip in the dark cavity. "Phillip, jump down. I'll catch you. Do it now!"

Phillip shook his head. I could see the whites of his eyes.

"Phillip! You must do as I say. The man will reach you in a couple of seconds if you don't jump."

Phillip strained to look out and up. When he saw the Viking he shrunk back in terror, pushing himself as far back into the nook as possible.

I wanted to climb up and rip the Viking from the wall and into the crevasse, but the walls were slick with ice. There was no way for me to grip. How Phillip got up there I had no idea. I reached up my ski pole to stab at the Viking, but he was too high.

"Phillip!" I shouted. I didn't want to frighten him further, but I needed to get him to respond immediately. "Phillip, it is only a few feet to my hands." I reached up with both arms. "Jump! Now!"

"Too late, you little skunk," the Viking said as he got to the rock projection next to Phillip's nook. He reached into the nook, grabbed Phillip and pulled him out while I stood below, helpless. The Viking held Phillip to his body with no apparent effort.

The Viking's bearded face was a dark shadow, but his long blond hair glistened in the moonlight and the spikes of his crampons sparkled. He leaned sideways against the ice wall. One arm was wrapped around Phillip. With his other hand he pulled the knife free from his belt and held it to the boy's throat.

I thought of running and leaping up to stab my ski pole at his foot, but I knew it was futile. His feet were twelve feet above me and enough to the side over the drop-off that I'd probably fall into the crevasse.

"Where is it, you little shit? Either you tell me or I drain your blood."

Phillip's breath came in choking gasps. The knife glistened against his throat.

"Count of three. One, two..."

"If you let the boy go," I said, "I'll let you out of here. I'll give you an hour to get down the mountain before we leave this cave."

"Not until he tells me where he hid it."

"I know where it is," I lied. I moved a step closer to the rock wall and the crevasse. "Let him go and I'll tell you."

"We both know that's bullshit," the man said.

"Thos told his mother Janeen where he put it," I said. "Janeen told me."

"Yeah, right," the Viking scoffed. "You want me to believe a story, you should have said it was Jasper's brother who told you. He was the one who flapped at the mouth after Jasper told him what was in the shrine."

"So John senior got you going on this?"

"I'd barely met him on a hunting trip three years ago when he drank too much and started talking about buried treasure."

"Well I know where it is now. We can split the money," I said. I shuffled forward another step until I was touching the wall. Next to me, Spot still stood on his hind legs, front paws on the icy rock, his eyes on Phillip and the man holding him. "After McCloud gets her cut," I said, "we'll split the rest, fifty-fifty."

"You lie like Brock Chambers. We had a deal. Next thing I know, he wasn't the end-buyer at all. He was just reselling it to McCloud for three times as much money. I should cut you like I cut him."

"Like you stabbed the kid named Napoleon in Kauai?" I said.

"All I did was hire Napoleon to learn where Thos's hiding place was. It was Thos who killed him."

"How do you know that?" I said.

The Viking laughed. "He admitted it. Thos realized Napoleon had been following him. When he challenged Napoleon, Napoleon attacked him, but ended up getting knifed himself."

"You killed Jasper's father and brother John," I said. "But why kill Thos? He was your source for what you wanted."

"He double-crossed me. Said he'd meet me at the lake that morning to sell me what I wanted. Then he swims out into the water, thinking he's fooling me. But I'm prepared. Screw with me and I'll take you down."

"Like Morella Meyers?" I said.

"The bitch tried to jack up her price. I just wanted a simple phone call to confirm what she'd found, that Thos was playing with me. Next thing, she's threatening to go to the cops. Says she won't if I pay her some real money. Well, she got paid what she deserved. But then, you know that, don't you?" He laughed with gusto.

The Viking's knife was pressing harder against Phillip's throat. If I could keep him talking, maybe I could think of how to get up to him.

"Why'd you go back to Kauai?" I said. "You'd already been there and tried to follow them up to the shrine."

"When Thos's mother hired you, the first thing you did was head to Kauai. It made sense to follow and see if you could learn what I couldn't."

The Viking was breathing heavily from the strain of holding Phillip. "So I booked the next flight to Kauai. I found out John junior was taking you out in the helicopter. I'd been across the cliff face twice before, but still couldn't find the shrine. I wanted to be across the cliff and hidden in the jungle when you arrived. The helicopter office gave me the wrong departure time for your flight. You got there too fast and saw me. But the stick put a stop to that." His laughter was sickening.

"I've been watching you, McKenna. You never realized how thorough I am." He laughed again. "It's all about misdirection, and you were always looking the wrong way. Then it turns out that this little shit had it all along." He shook Phillip and the boy screamed.

While he'd been talking, I was looking up at the rock below the nook where Phillip had been hiding. There were some small areas of rock that were bare of ice. Although the moonlight in the cave was bright, the rock was hard to see. I couldn't make out any knobs or holes that would make good handholds or footholds.

But looking up at the likely way Phillip climbed up, I assumed the holds were there. If I moved fast enough, maybe I could get to the nook. From there I could grab Phillip...

The Viking was talking as I took a running step to the side of Spot. In a fluid motion, I slammed my left ski pole down like a pole vault, reached my right hand up to a dark spot and found a nub of rock to grip on. I jammed my right boot toe into a notch, and pulled up. My center of gravity was off and I started to swing to the left. To the left above me was another dark spot, free of ice. I stretched, banking all on finding a handhold. It was above the crevasse. If I couldn't find a place to grip...

The tips of my fingers wrapped around a nub of rock at the base of the nook. I dug in, my fingernails biting hard rock. My hands were only a couple feet from the Viking's feet.

"You dumb asshole," the Viking hissed. "Time to cut this boy and toss him into the center of the earth."

I watched in horror as the Viking shifted and reached out with the knife so he could draw it back in a single sweep. I was about to leap, thinking I could pull Phillip free and throw him to safety as I fell into the earth. But Phillip moved first.

The boy twisted. His little fist swung up and struck the Viking in the face.

The Viking jerked and started to lose his balance. He struck the rock wall with the knife, stabbing its point into the ice to stabilize himself. It looked like he had regained his balance when his left foot slipped.

The crampon spikes scraped down the wall sending up little rooster tails of chipped ice. He rotated, tried to swing his foot and jam the crampon back in. Then his other foot slipped.

The Viking reached for the ice ax, firmly planted into the ice near his head. His hand slipped off it. The motion spun him around and, still clutching Phillip, the Viking fell with the little boy toward the gaping darkness below.

FORTY-THREE

I let go of the rock and dropped to the ground. I landed bent over, hands and feet striking icy rock. As I collapsed onto my belly, I shot my arms out over the edge of the crevasse and groped at the falling bodies.

The fingers of my right hand gripped fabric. I clenched my fist and dug my toes into the rock behind me, bracing for the impact.

The fabric I'd grabbed slammed my arm down into the rock of the crevasse. I reached down into the dark, gaping hole with my other hand and grabbed onto more fabric. I held on, holding 200 pounds or more. I heard a heavy grunt of man and whimpering of boy.

"Spot!" I yelled. "Spot, come!"

He came next to me, half squatting, trying to understand what I meant.

I was straining to see down into the dark, wondering whose jacket I held. I realized that I had both. My right hand gripped the shoulder of the Viking's jacket. My left fingers were wrapped around the back neckline of Phillip's jacket. The Viking still clutched Phillip to him with the knife at the boy's chest.

"You want to live," I said, "you'll let go of the boy. I can't pull you both up at once. Let go. Up he comes. Then you."

"If you let go of me," he said, "I'll grab the boy and we'll go down together. Understand?" The man slowly released Phillip, but kept his hand on the boy's arm. I pulled Phillip up with my left arm, a small muscle tearing in my shoulder, while I still held the Viking with my right hand.

I raised Phillip a foot when the boy's jacket caught on something. Phillip was stuck below the edge, the shoulder fabric of his jacket just rising out of the hole. I heard him crying softly.

"Spot. Grab Phillip." I jerked with my head as I raised Phillip as far as possible without dropping the Viking.

Spot nosed over by my hand and Phillip's head. "Grab on," I yelled. "Grab his jacket!" I jerked my hand. Phillip's head shook with my motion.

Spot got the idea. His teeth closed around my hand. I jerked again, pulling sideways so the fabric was in his mouth.

"Hold tight, Spot! Give a pull!" I jerked my hand again, Phillip's body shaking.

Spot bit down and gave a tug back.

"Hang on, Spot!" I knew that Spot didn't understand the words, but he got the meaning. He pulled back like he was playing tug-of-war. When I knew he wouldn't let go, I touched his snout. "Easy, Spot. Hold on."

My fingers holding the Viking felt like they were ripping out of their joints. I latched onto the Viking's jacket with my other hand to spread the tension. My teeth were on the dirty rock at the edge of the drop-off, my toes dug in behind me.

I had a strong impulse to drop the Viking, but I didn't doubt that he would do as he said and take Phillip down with him. We were at a stalemate. I knew that Spot wouldn't drop Phillip, so my only choice was to pull the Viking up, then get Phillip's jacket free.

"Drop the knife," I said. "Drop the knife, or I drop you."

I felt him move below me and I heard clattering down in the dark fissure below us. In a second there was silence and then more clattering as metal bounced off rock and ice hundreds of feet below us.

I lifted him up, holding his body so that he was facing out from me. I knew I couldn't bend him backward over the edge as

I pulled him up, so I turned him sideways, steering him by my grip on his shoulders.

I got him to a sitting position on the edge, facing away from me. "I'm going to let go." I said. "But don't move. You even twitch, I'll kick you in the back and you'll fall to your death."

I let go and he astonished me by snapping himself down onto his back. He rolled and his arm flashed out with the knife.

I leaped up and back, but my boots slipped on the ice and I went down. The Viking was up in a second. He jumped toward me and swung his leg out to kick me in the face. I saw the shiny spikes of the crampon arcing through the moonlight, heading for my eyes. I rolled my head back, striking a rock.

His crampon flashed by, half an inch away from my cheek. I caught his leg on the follow-through. My hands gripped hard ankle bone. The Viking went down. We both jumped to our feet.

I lunged and tackled him, my hand to the arm that held the knife. He maintained his grip on the knife as he went down. His body made a hard thud as he hit the ice. Something yellow flew out of a pocket, slid over the edge of the crevasse and down into the darkness.

The yellow cellphone.

The Viking thrashed with remarkable strength. He kicked me in the shin with the crampon. I yelled as a metal spike went through flesh into my bone. My grip loosened and he twisted free. He swung at me with the knife. I ducked and the knife stabbed into the ice. He spun around and did a high kick. This time his crampon spike scraped my chin, ripping flesh. Dazed, I tripped and fell. I rolled over twice to get away. I jerked myself to my feet, swaying with dizziness, instinctively stepping back.

He came at me with the knife held high. I slammed my forearm up against his wrist to block the knife and drove my other fist into his solar plexus. He fell back against a huge mound of ice built up on a rock wall near the crevasse. I wrapped my fingers around his wrist where he held the knife and hit him with my shoulder to his middle.

I swung up with my other arm and rammed my elbow into his face. He staggered against the giant mound of ice. I heard a dull rumble. I still gripped his knife hand. The noise grew into a loud, deep cracking sound that seemed to rip through the mountain. A line appeared in the bulging mound of ice above our heads. Slowly at first, and then gradually faster, the big ice buildup began to tilt away from the rock wall. I gave the Viking a sudden push and jumped back as a block of ice the size of a dump truck fell between us, just missing Phillip and Spot a few yards away.

The Viking was knocked down on the other side of the giant ice chunk. He scrambled to his hands and knees as the ice rolled sideways, pushing him toward the crevasse.

He stood up. There was another crack and a cut opened up just in front of his boots. The opening widened and the ice the Viking was standing on started to fall toward the crevasse. He fell back to his hands and knees.

I dropped to my belly and reached over the widening split. "Reach your hand out!" I shouted.

The ice block tipped farther. Its surface was too steep for him to crawl on. He tried to dig in with his hands. The spikes of his crampons clawed at the ice. He couldn't reach me. I flung myself another foot forward. My chest was bent over the ever-widening gap. I reached out to grab him. His hands were too far away. A gust of wind blew his long hair up. I gripped onto a good bit of it and once again dug the toes of my boots into the icy surface behind me, preparing for the worst. When his hair jerked tight, I flexed my feet to get the maximum purchase.

But the Viking didn't weigh anything.

His hair and beard came off in one piece. The giant ice chunk fell away and in the brilliant moonlight I saw pure terror on the face of Jerry Roth as he fell through space to his death.

FORTY-FOUR

Phillip was screaming.

I scrambled over to Spot. Reaching next to Spot's clenched teeth, I took hold of Phillip's jacket with both hands. I tugged, but Phillip was stuck.

"Okay, Spot, let go. I've got him."

I tried to lower Phillip, but he was holding on with both hands to a rock near his chest. I saw in the moonlight a wet darkness on the fingers of his funny hand. Blood.

"Phillip, you need to let go. I have to lower you a few inches to un-snag your jacket."

"NO!" he yelled, his terror reverberating through the cave.

"Yes, Phillip. You're stuck. I can't get you out of the hole unless you let go."

"NO!" He shook with fear.

I thought of reaching for his hands and forcing his fingers free. But I couldn't bring myself to do it. "Phillip, please listen to me."

"No! I won't!" His voice dissolved into sobs. "You have to get rid of it!"

"I don't understand."

"What that man wanted. What they all wanted." Phillip's body vibrated with spasms. His bloody fingers were like claws on the rock.

"Phillip," I said again, trying to sound calm. "If you let go, I can pull you up."

"Not unless you help me get rid of it!" He screamed the

words. He was hysterical and I didn't know what to say. His body jerked and he twisted in his jacket. His hands came off the rock and he started to slip out of the arms of the jacket.

As he was about to drop free, he caught one of the armpits of the jacket with his good hand. The sudden jerk on the fabric ripped the jacket and Phillip plunged three or four feet into the crevasse. He hung there, dangling in space, bouncing against the rock.

I gripped the torn jacket with one hand while I reached down into the hole with the other.

Phillip was too far below for me to reach him. But the jacket was now free of the rock it had been caught on. "Hang on, Phillip, I'm going to slowly pull the jacket up.

But Phillip had found a place to wedge his arm into the rock and he wouldn't come. If I pulled any harder, the jacket would rip the rest of the way and Phillip would fall into the crevasse. I felt the boy shaking through the taut fabric.

"Phillip, this is very important. You have to let go of the rock so I can pull you up." I tried to sound calm, although I was about to lose him.

"Not unless you help me!" he said again.

"Okay!" I said.

"Promise?"

The boy was going to die if the fabric started tearing again.

"Yes, I promise."

He let go of the rock.

I gently pulled him up, desperate not to make any sudden moves. When he was within my reach, I grabbed his arm and pulled him to safety.

EPILOGUE

Two days later we stopped at the hospital. Janeen was an unhealthy gray, but my friend Doc Lee said she was going to make it. She couldn't speak, but she opened her eyes at Phillip's voice and gave him a weak smile.

I had called Jennifer Salazar at Harvard and asked if we could borrow her boat. She'd agreed with enthusiasm and gave the caretaker at the Salazar mansion instructions.

He promptly answered the call button at the wrought iron gate and it swung aside to let us enter the long, stately drive. A few minutes later, he escorted us along the slate walkway that curved through the snow, around the mansion and down to the boathouse. He showed us where the life vests were and explained that the thirty-two foot powerboat was gassed up and ready to go.

When I started up the engine, its rumble in the boathouse brought back dark memories. The only other times I'd been in the boat were when I was trying to catch the murderer of Jennifer's twin sister. I shifted into reverse and backed out of the boathouse. Street watched the port side while I watched the starboard. The boat was nimble and powerful, and it was easy to back it out without scraping the dock.

Once we were away from the dock, I shifted into forward. I didn't know if there was a no-wake zone near the shore so I kept the throttle at low RPMs.

Phillip wore his over-sized life vest without complaint and sat in the left front seat. Spot sat next to him in the space between the seats. Phillip clutched his backpack as if it were the briefcase with the president's nuclear codes. When he carried it aboard I could tell it contained something the size of the metal box that Street and I had envisioned.

Phillip's baseball cap was on backward and pulled down tight. Spot leaned over and put his head on the seat next to Phillip.

The storm had passed. The high temperature was forecast to be 55 degrees, which, although warm for January, was not notable. Combined with a hot sun and calm conditions, it was comfortable out on the water.

The light bounced off the lake and lit up Phillip's eyes from underneath. He squinted against the sun. In his eyes was a weariness that didn't belong in a little kid.

"Are you sure you want to do this?" I said. "It obviously has tremendous value."

"I want to sink it," Phillip said. "I don't care about its value. It kills people. The world has done without it all this time. What difference would it make if the world keeps doing without it?"

At first I thought it was just a clever line from an exhausted kid. But I didn't have an answer.

"You've thought about this?" I said. "It isn't just a quick decision?"

"Ever since Thos emailed me about it. I was scared when I heard about it because I knew from the way Thos talked that people would fight over it. He said people had already died because of it. Then Thos died, and his cousin and my great grandfather and the scuba diver. And Mr. Roth."

And your grandfather's brother and the kid named Napoleon, I thought.

I considered the ways I would regret it. "Phillip, if this could be sold for a lot of money, you would be glad to have the money when you are older."

"Uncle Thos wanted to sink it. That was his original plan when he swam into the water. Now I want to sink it."

"Thos told you this?"

Phillip nodded. "He said Rubicon Point was the steepest drop-off in the lake bottom. He wanted to swim out and let it sink where the bottom is so deep that no one could get it back. Then no one would ever fight for it again."

We were silent as Street and I finally understood why Thos's suicide had turned to murder. Jerry Roth wanted to kill Thos before he could get to the drop-off. Then Jerry realized that Thos didn't have it.

"Yet Thos didn't sink it," I said. "Why not?"

"Just before he went to the lake, he sent me an email saying that he changed his mind and that he was going to fake sinking it. That way the murderer would think it was gone and I could sell it some day. He said the same thing as you. That I could get a lot of money for it."

"Don't you want that?"

"No. I want Thos back. If Thos had sunk it, the killing would have stopped."

I wondered what Phillip's response would be if I said that I'd decided not to help. But that was a kind of game, seeing if he would call my bluff. In a just world adults would always keep their promises.

"How long will it take to get to the center of the lake?" Street asked, more to change the subject, I thought, than for the information.

"Let's see, we're about nine miles from the center and I seem to recall that this speedboat does about fifty-five miles an hour. So what would that make it?"

I saw Phillip reach under the life vest and feel his way into his back pocket. He pulled out his abacus, held it with his left hand and worked the beads with his funny hand.

I kept talking. "Fifty-five miles an hour is close to sixty which would be a mile a minute. So I guess it'll take something like..."

"Nine minutes and forty-nine seconds," Phillip said. There was no smugness in his voice. He stuffed the abacus back into his pocket.

"Okay, start your watches," I said and punched the throttle. The boat surged up at a steep angle and then settled down on a level plane. The speedometer climbed up past fifty. A light chop rippled the surface of the water, but the deep-V hull sliced through the small waves and our ride across the lake was smooth. Street sat in one of the middle seats behind us. I glanced at Phillip. His face was stretched tight with a grimace.

While we raced across the water, I noticed that Phillip pulled something out of his pocket and was turning it over in his hands. It was bright blue, but I couldn't tell what it was.

After eight or ten minutes I cut the throttle and the boat slowed and coasted silently. "We're about there," I said. "Halfway across the lake."

Phillip turned to look around. His hands opened up and I realized he had one of the three-legged totems.

"Phillip, I'm curious about the little carved figure you're holding. Where did you get that?"

Phillip looked at me as if I'd just come out of hibernation. "This is uncle Thos's Polynesian logo. He puts a picture of this on every bottle of Pacific Blue wine. And he hands these wooden dolls out wherever he goes."

"Oh, of course," I said. I looked at Street.

She grinned.

"So..." I looked around at the lake. "Is this a good place?"

Phillip looked across at the distant shorelines. "How deep is it here?"

I took out the map of the bottom that I'd brought for just this purpose. "We're about here," I pointed. "The bottom is one thousand six hundred feet below us."

Phillip looked at the map. Then, clutching his backpack tightly to his chest, he leaned over the side of the boat and looked down into the deep, indigo water. He seemed satisfied. "I guess that's deep enough," he said. He swung his legs into the space between the two front seats and scooted forward a bit so that he was touching Spot. "I suppose you would like to see it before I dump it overboard."

Street said, "Yes, we'd like that."

Phillip unzipped the backpack. He reached in and pulled out a tarnished, dented, metal box about the size of a cigar box. Tooled designs decorated its edges like the fancy stitching on cowboy boots. There was a little catch on the front. Phillip flipped it up and raised the lid.

When I saw what was inside I felt a pain grow in the hollow beneath my sternum.

The inside of the box was lined with burgundy velvet, worn raw in places. Floating on a depression in the velvet was a dagger with a golden handle. The handle pattern was ornate and glistened so brightly that it could only be real gold.

I remembered the toy dagger that Morella Meyer had found on the bottom of the lake. I now realized it was a decoy that Thos had clenched in his teeth to convince Jerry Roth that he was going to sink the real dagger.

Phillip lifted the dagger out with his funny hand and handed it to me.

It was heavier than it looked. The dagger had a good balance with a seven-inch blade sharpened on both edges. The handle had two rubies set in the swirls of gold, one in the middle of each side. There was engraving at the top of the blade. I turned it in the sunlight to try to see the words, some in larger letters, more that were smaller. The words 'Captain Cook' were easy to read. The engraving below wasn't completely clear, partly because of the wear and tear of two hundred-plus years and partly because of the unusual spelling and syntax. But I could make out words of appreciation and something about the company that made the sails for Cook's ships, the Resolution and the Discovery.

I handed the dagger to Street. She carefully turned it over in both hands and then studied the writing. "It looks like a gift for Captain Cook from the company that made the sails."

"My thought, too," I said.

"It's gorgeous."

I nodded. "This is where the rumor about Cook's tableware came from."

"And it has been in the family shrine ever since," Street said.

Phillip suddenly spoke. "Then Mr. Roth found out about it and people started dying."

I tried to think of a way out of what we were about to do. The dagger was not only priceless, it would be of immeasurable value to scholars and students and museum curators, perhaps even more than a Twain short story.

Phillip watched as Street inspected the dagger. She took her time, perhaps to give me a chance to consider the enormity of what we'd gotten ourselves into. The boat gently rocked. The sun sparkled on the golden handle. Red flashes like lasers shot out of the rubies as she turned it in her hands. She handed it back to me, a questioning look in her eyes.

I turned it over in my hands. It looked like there was dried blood on the blade near the handle. I remembered that the Hawaiian kid named Napoleon had been killed by a long, narrow knife. The dagger was not just a historical treasure, but a murder weapon as well.

I considered taking the dagger from Phillip. Street and I could hold it for him until he was older or sell it on his behalf and give him the money. I was certain he would appreciate it some day. The choice was clear. It was worth breaking Phillip's wishes and my promise. A much larger principle was at stake. The rights of millions to see and learn from Captain Cook's dagger trumped the wishes of a young boy, stressed and saddened by so many deaths in his family.

I could still try to convince him to see it from this larger perspective. If I could change his mind, I wouldn't have to break my promise.

"Phillip," I said. "Now that I've seen this, I'd like to talk about this a minute. There is a larger perspective to consider."

Phillip started shaking his head. "No, I won't reconsider. You're going to tell me all about how this should be studied at a university or something. But I don't care. Think how many people died over it." He looked at me hard. There were no tears in his eyes.

I suddenly felt that the weight of justice was on my shoulders. Which principle was greater? The right of the world to the artifacts of one of the world's greatest explorers? Or the right of a child to the promise of an adult?

Phillip and I looked at each other for a long moment while I fought an internal wrestling match. Finally, I held the dagger out to him.

"I'm not very good at throwing," he said, taking it in his funny hand. He stood up, gripping the dagger awkwardly between his misshapen thumb and two fingers and gave it a hearty toss. The dagger traced a shallow arc over the water. There was a flash of gold and red and then it plunked into the water with barely a splash.

Spot lifted his head at the noise and saw nothing but the three of us staring at the water. He put his head back down on the seat.

"What about the box it came in?" I said. "Do you want to sink that as well?"

Phillip picked up the box and ran his fingers over the intricate designs. "No. This box is neat. I think I'll keep it."

I started the engine, shifted into forward and eased the throttle up.

"Now can I give it to him?" Phillip hollered over the roar of the engine.

I nodded.

Phillip reached into Street's canvas tote. He pulled out a paper bag, unfolded the top and gently removed a large Danish.

Spot went from casual awareness to Red Alert.

Phillip gave it a little toss and jerked his hand back to safety.

Spot caught the Danish in midair.

When we got back and had the boat stowed in the boathouse, Phillip and Spot bounded out onto the dock and ran up the snowy path toward the Salazar mansion.

Phillip had left his things on the boat seat. Street picked up his pack. I took Captain Cook's box. I opened the lid and touched the fabric. It was worn smooth where the dagger had rested. I gave the box a shake.

Street looked at me.

I pinched the fabric and lifted one corner. It was glued in place. Angling the box for better light, I saw several small drops of glue on the edge of the fabric, drops that did not look like they were 200 years old. My pocket knife sliced through them easily. I pried up the fabric and the thin wooden board it was attached to.

Underneath was a slender leather notebook. The letters MT were embossed on the cover. Street's intake of breath was audible. I pulled the notebook out and opened it up.

All but four sheets of paper had been torn out of the notebook. The handwriting was messy. The title on the top of the first page said, "The Amazing Island Boy And His Trick Wood."

The writing filled both sides of all four sheets. At the end it was signed Mark Twain.

We didn't have time to read it. I stuffed the notebook inside my shirt.

"We need some way to glue the fabric back down," I said.

"I have some nail hardener that will work," Street said. She dug in her canvas tote and pulled out a little bottle. She used the little brush to dab where the fabric met the edge of the box.

"Phillip doesn't know the notebook was in there, does he?" Street said as we walked up the path toward where Phillip and Spot were playing in the snow.

"I'm sure he has no idea."

"Are you going to tell him?"

"Certainly," I nodded. "When he grows up. About eighteen years from now."

About The Author

Todd Borg lives with his wife in Lake Tahoe where they write and paint.

To contact Todd or learn about the other Owen McKenna novels, please visit toddborg.com.

A message from the author:

Dear Reader,

If you enjoyed this novel, please consider posting a short review on Amazon. Reviews help authors a great deal, and that in turn allows us to write more stories for you.

Thank you very much for your interest and support!

Todd

Made in the USA
Columbia, SC
29 July 2020